THIS BOOK IS FOR
those like me who enjoy trashy reality TV.

F

LEABHARLANNA FHINE GALL
FINGAL LIBRARIES

Items should be returned on or before the given return date. Items may be renewed in branch libraries, by phone or online. You will need your PIN to renew online. Fines are charged on overdue items. Damage to, or loss of items, will be charged to the borrower.

fame

THE KEATYN CHRONICLES: BOOK 8

JILLIAN DODD

Jillian Dodd Inc.
N. Redington Beach, FL

ISBN: 978-1-940652-61-0

Books by Jillian Dodd

The Keatyn Chronicles

USA TODAY bestselling young adult contemporary romance set in an East
Coast boarding school.

Stalk Me

Kiss Me

Date Me

Love Me

Adore Me

Hate Me

Get Me

Fame

Power

Money

Sex

Love

Keatyn Unscripted

Aiden

That Boy Series

Small-town contemporary romance series about falling in love with the boy
next door.

That Boy

That Wedding

That Baby

That Divorce

The Love Series

Contemporary, standalone romances following the very sexy Crawford family.

Vegas Love

Broken Love

Fake Love

Spy Girl Series

Young adult romance series about a young spy who just might save the world.

The Prince

The Eagle

The Society

The Valiant

Jillian Dodd and Kenzie Harp

Young adult travel romance.

Girl off the Grid

TUESDAY, SEPTEMBER 23RD
MOVIE PREMIERE - PARIS

Riley

I ADJUST MY tie in the mirror, mute my cell phone, and check my watch again. "Are you almost ready, Sh—" Shit, what the fuck is her name? Shell—something. Shell—y, Mi—chelle, Ra—chelle? No. I'm pretty sure it's Shelly, but I decide to go with Shell, just to be safe. "—ell?"

"I just need a few more seconds! It's not my fault you kept me in bed for so long, daddy," her voice shrills.

Which is such a lie, it's totally her fault.

She was impressed with our beautiful Parisian hotel suite and decided to show her appreciation by sucking my dick then riding me like a cowgirl.

At the time, I didn't care if I was a little late but, now, as my arrival time looms, I'm getting irritated.

I'm Riley Johnson.

I've got it all.

Brand new jet. Exotic cars. Luxury penthouse. Black card. A different aspiring actress—or two—in my bed every night.

I run Captive Films.

Where we leave you begging for more.

Or, maybe that's just me.

My life is perfect.

No relationships. No distractions.

I'm all business.

Even with the girls I date.

And by date, I mean fuck.

Because that's all it is to me.

I've never been much of a rule follower, except for the one I made for myself a long time ago.

No love. Just sex.

And never more than forty-eight hours with the same girl.

With the flight from L.A. to Paris, I'm nearing sixteen hours with Shelly.

I wait another ten minutes before giving up. "If you don't come out now, I'm leaving without you."

She pops open the bathroom door and smiles at me. "Looking this good takes time."

And, I will admit, she looks damn good.

Her long, red silky dress, with the dangerously plunging neckline barely containing her double D's, is hugging all her curves. Yes, I made a good choice.

We met a couple days ago at one of the clubs I like to frequent when I mentioned to my friend, movie star Knox Daniels, that'd I'd be in Paris for *The Keatyn Chronicles Trilogy* movie premiere this week.

She slid her ample ass next to me on the couch and told me she would go with me.

I laughed at her, honestly.

I was planning to be here stag because after the premiere I'm attending a fashion show. One of Keatyn's little sisters, who at sixteen isn't so little anymore, will be walking the catwalk. And then it's to a party filled with some of my favorite kind of people.

Models.

"What do you think?" she asks, spinning in a circle that

causes a boob to pop out of her dress.

"Didn't you tape those things in?" I ask, horrified. "That can't happen on the red carpet."

Keatyn would kill me.

Shell-whatever looks down and goes, "Whoopsie!" She shoves the offending boob back in place while chomping on a piece of gum.

Okay, so maybe she wasn't the best choice.

"Spit out the gum," I say.

She slides up to me and cups the front of my pants with her hand. "Why? Is there something you'd rather I have in my mouth?"

"Maybe in the limo," I tell her and drag her out to the waiting car.

Once we're tucked into the backseat, she reminds me why I brought her.

With her very talented mouth.

WE SURVIVE THE red carpet walk and subsequent interviews without any nipple slips. After joining Keatyn and Aiden, her long time beau, we are seated in the ornate theater.

The Keatyn Chronicles movies are about Keatyn Douglas' real life, when at seventeen, the daughter of famous actress Abby Johnston, was almost kidnapped by a stalker and was sent to an East Coast boarding school—under an assumed name—for her safety. Since the boarding school is where Keatyn and I became friends, I get to see some of my own life unfolding on the screen before me. I watch the day we met. It was Eastbrooke's New Student Orientation. I was sitting next to Dallas McMahon, who is now Captive Films' Chief Legal Counsel and a partial owner. We were already checking her out before she marched in our direction. With her long blonde hair, tan skin, and killer body, it's safe to assume all the guys were doing the same. It shocked the hell out of us when she marched up the bleachers—wearing a dress and cowboy boots—and sat down between us.

I chuckle watching the three of us sneaking out of our dorms after curfew to smoke and talk.

Then I get lost in the rest of the movie.

Keatyn showing up at my dorm room in tears when my older brother, Dawson, dumped her for his ex-girlfriend.

The three of us shooting a naughty music video to get back at him.

And, then, the part I can't bear to watch.

If only I could turn off my ears, then I wouldn't have to relive how crazy I was about Ariela Ross.

In this scene, we're in my dorm room.

I keep telling Keatyn how pretty Ariela is. How I'm scared to text her after hanging out with her the night before. Keatyn telling me she thought she had a boyfriend at home, but I didn't care. I was here. He wasn't. And I was freaking Riley Johnson. She was so pretty. A cheerleader with dark brown hair, gorgeous eyes, and a perfect body.

I had no idea at the time that I would fall totally and completely in love with her.

Or that she would break my heart.

Thank god, that's not in the movie. It was bad enough that I included a photo at the end showing the real Keatyn and Aiden with the cast and crew of *A Day at the Lake 2*. Keatyn's stalker was obsessed with her mom's first movie, the cult classic, *A Day at the Lake*. Because of Keatyn's resemblance to her mother, he wanted to remake it with Keatyn. And while you'd have to watch the movie or read the books we just released to understand it all, Keatyn managed to pull off a hostile takeover of the stalker's movie production company. At seventeen, she was named Chairman of the Board of what would become Captive Films.

It's hard to believe that my career as a director, producer, and CEO started with a friendship and a music video. The naughty video we did to make my brother mad turned out so well that when Keatyn's childhood friend, Damian Moran, needed a music video made in a few days, she suggested me. I didn't really have a clue what I was doing, but went with my gut. That video, and the fact that Keatyn looked damn hot in it, took his band, Twisted Dreams, to the top of the charts and I went on to produce many more videos. The summer before our senior year, Keatyn and I teamed up to make our first movie, the remake of *A Day at the Lake* that Captive Films owned the rights to. With Keatyn's connections, her acting ability, and my direction, we had our company's first hit.

In the eleven years since then, Keatyn's become one of today's hottest actresses and together we've built Captive Films into what it is now. A multi-billion dollar company.

Keatyn is sitting in front of me with Aiden. Her head is on his shoulder and, knowing her, she's crying as she relives their love story.

Little does she know, he's going to ask her to marry him tonight.

MOVIE PREMIERE - PARIS

Keatyn

AIDEN PUTS HIS hand on my knee and whispers to me as *The End* rolls across the movie screen in front of us. "It's really hard to believe we've been together for over ten years."

I give him a kiss thinking how crazy it is that a silly wish I made on the moon led me to the love of my life. It's even crazier to think we just watched the story of that love on the big screen with other people portraying us.

The audience is clapping and cheering for their favorite

Aiden escorting me to the Academy Awards.

The two of us dancing cheek-to-cheek at the lavish rock star wedding of Damian, and Aiden's sister, Peyton.

Then there are numerous travel photos of us. We started a trend with the hashtag #SunsetSelfies and are working toward watching a million sunsets together.

"WHAT'D YA THINK?" Riley asks as I stand up.

I turn around and hug him, ignoring the blonde attached to his side.

"I know I fought you on adding the parts from your and Aiden's point of view. But, you were right. The car chase scene where you and Aiden crashed into the stalker's van after he kidnapped me and Dallas was amazing." I hug him again as my eyes tear up. "I'll never be able to repay either of you for rescuing us."

"Baby, I need to pee," the blonde says, at a totally inappropriate time.

"So, go," Riley says, shrugging her off. "It should have been amazing. We used a lot of my actual footage from that day—digitally enhanced, of course."

"And, more importantly," Aiden adds, teasingly, "I didn't have to sacrifice another Maserati. So, Boots, I hate to break up the trip down memory lane, but we need to head out."

I swoon when he calls me Boots. It's what he called me before he knew my name.

I glance at his watch. "We have plenty of time before the fashion show. Speaking of memory lane," I say to Riley. "I was surprised to see you added a photo with Ariela in it. Maybe you should call her sometime. See how she's doing. It'd be nice to see you with the same girl more than once. I swear you must have a stable of blondes hidden behind your penthouse."

"No fucking way," he replies. "I'm perfectly happy with Shelly."

I bite my lip, holding back a smile.

"What?" he asks.

"Her name is *Shelby*."

He rolls his eyes. "Whatever. Close enough."

The actors who played Keatyn and Aiden join us. We all congratulate them on another success, and I give them huge hugs.

I watch Riley pat Aiden on the back and say something discreetly to him.

"All right," Aiden says to me, "we have to get going."

I take his hand. "You and Riley looked sneaky. What's going on?"

"Nothing," he says, dragging me toward the exit.

"I heard him say something about luck."

"Oh, he just said with any luck, he'd *accidentally* lose Shelby somewhere between the premiere and the party so he could hang with all the models."

"Are there any models left that he hasn't already dated? Or any aspiring actresses? I wish he'd aim a little higher, age-wise. Maybe find someone who's already successful. Maybe I should set him up with—"

"Riley doesn't want strings. Ariela broke his heart when she wouldn't come to California with him after graduation."

"Did you talk to him about it? I was shocked he added that photo of the cast party. They looked so in love."

"I tried to talk to him, but he just turned it around and gave me shit."

"About what?"

"Us. He said I couldn't give relationship advice until I'd put a ring on it."

"You did put a ring on it," I say, holding out the vintage diamond and emerald four-leaf clover ring he gave me years ago. "That's all we've ever needed."

I realize I've been silly. We don't need a piece of paper to tell us we're in love. We can have a baby and not be married. Our love is all that matters. It's all that's ever mattered.

The corners of Aiden's beautiful mouth turn down for a second. I'm about to ask him why, but am interrupted by him telling my bodyguard that we're going straight to the car and not stopping for autographs.

Which is weird, because he's always so supportive.

As he drags me toward the car, I'm trying to at least wave to all the fans yelling my name.

"Stop rushing me, Aiden. You're starting to piss me off."

When the limo door shuts behind us, he gives me a hard kiss, which manages to both cool down my temper and heat up my insides at the same time. He still gets me as worked up as he did the day I met him. It was my first day at boarding school, when I decided to stop scripting out my life and do something crazy. I ran down a hill wearing a dress and cowboy boots, interrupting a shirts vs skins boys' soccer game, stole the ball, dribbled it down the field, and kicked it past the goalie's head. A goalie so beautiful I immediately nicknamed him the God of All Hotties.

And have been in love with him ever since.

He looks so handsome tonight. His dark blonde hair, those gorgeous green eyes, the sexy freckle on his cheek, a dark suit perfectly tailored to highlight his tall, lean body.

I move my hands to the front of his pants, forgetting I'm mad and thinking about the hotness behind his zipper, when his phone rings.

He checks the display and hands it to me. "It's Dallas. I'm sure he wants to talk to you."

"Hey, Dallas," I say.

"Riley's predicting box office success."

"He always does."

"What do you think?"

"I think I agree with him. Releasing the full three-movie

"Not yet," he says, kissing my neck. "I'm not done with memory lane. Remember when you tutored me in French—back when you were still trying to resist my charm—and I told you I was going to ask you to marry me here someday? And, later, how I asked you to go to Winter Formal with me by having the guys in the dorm build that lame Eiffel Tower replica?"

"It wasn't lame. It was so romantic. I'll remember the way you looked that day for the rest of my life. It was one of those *take my breath away* moments."

He whispers in my ear. "I hope this is another one of those moments."

"What do you mean?"

I glance over my shoulder, not seeing him.

I turn around.

And.

Ohmigawd!

He's. Down. On. One. Knee.

He takes my hand.

I hold my breath, trying to capture every feeling, every single thing about this moment. The smells of Paris, the sunset, Aiden's sexy voice, the way my hand still feels like it belongs in his forever. He makes me feel like anything and everything is possible.

"You and I are like a promise," he says. "A wish. Proof that fate and luck bring people together. Proof of love at first sight. Proof that true love will survive. I promise you a life that's better than anything you've ever scripted. So, what do you say, Boots? Wanna get hitched?"

"Hitched?"

"Yeah. Get it: boots, hitched?"

I laugh. "You're silly."

"And you're beautiful. Seriously, will you marry me?"

"Yes, I will."

When he stands up, I throw my arms around his neck and

kiss him.

"That was easier than I thought," he says, an adorable smile playing on his face. "Dallas said I'd need the ring to get you to commit to planning a wedding."

"Is there a ring?"

"Is there a ring? Of course, there's a ring. Wanna see it?"

"Hell yeah."

He pulls a velvet box out of his jacket pocket and opens the lid.

The ring is ablaze with color.

A large round canary diamond set into a thick band, baguette stones ringing the band in rows, starting with clear brilliant diamonds then moving across the band in graduating shades of light yellows and pinks.

"It looks like a sunset!" I gasp.

"That's by design." He slides the vintage four-leaf clover ring off my finger and replaces it with the engagement ring.

I admire it for a moment.

"Turn your hand over and look at the back."

I flip my hand around. The back is also ringed with stones, graduating to brighter shades of oranges, hot pinks, and reds.

And one single emerald. I know exactly what the emerald means. When we were in St. Croix over Thanksgiving break of my junior year, we saw the green flash together. I had thought I'd seen the flash at sunset before, but I was wrong. And I didn't know I hadn't seen it until I saw the real thing.

It was like our love. I thought I had been in love with other boys, but I didn't know it wasn't real until I had experienced the real thing. When my ordeal with the stalker was over, I told Aiden he was my green flash. My true love.

"You're my green flash too," he says, giving me another kiss. "Always. Only. Ever yours."

"Um . . ." I say.

"Um?"

"Yeah, we might need a rewrite on that part."

"*What* part?"

"The *only* part."

"You don't want *only* me?"

"It's not going to be just us anymore."

"What do you mean?"

"I'm pregnant, Aiden."

"How?"

I laugh at him. "Um, I think you know *how*."

He lowers his voice. "But you're on the pill."

"Remember about six months ago when you said I should go off it and see what happens?"

"You did?"

"Yeah, I didn't say anything because I didn't want the pressure of trying. I was hoping it would just happen. Honestly, I was starting to worry that I couldn't get pregnant."

"You shouldn't have worried," he says, holding up my palm, reminding me of what a palm reader predicted so long ago. "You know we're having four kids. It's fate."

"Maybe sorta like fate," I add with a laugh, mimicking what he said years ago. I'll never forget tutoring him in the library. After he told me he would ask me to marry him at the top of the Eiffel Tower at sunset, I laughed and said, *Why would I marry you? I don't even like you.* Then he asked me what the French word for fate was. When I told him it was *sort*, he gave me that cocky grin of his and said, *Exactly, we're sorta like fate.* That line was used in the theme song for the movie. Damian wrote the song 'Sorta Like Fate' and his band, Twisted Dreams, recorded it. It might just be my favorite song ever.

Aiden holds my hands tightly and looks into my soul. "Are you really pregnant?"

"Only a few weeks, but, yes, I took a test this morning and it was positive."

He has the same shocked look as he did when I kicked the

soccer ball past him.

Then a smile starts to form, the corners of his mouth turning upward.

Which turns into the full-wattage powerful god-like smile that still makes me swoon.

"Come on, beautiful. Let's get going so we can tell everyone the good news."

As we drive to the fashion show, the moon slides into view.

I make another wish on it.

That our baby gets their daddy's smile.

THURSDAY, SEPTEMBER 25TH
MOVIE PREMIERE - LOS ANGELES

Riley

I'M BORED AND sitting on a little cream chaise waiting for Shelby to try on yet another designer dress. Granted, I should have planned this better, but I had no idea I'd be taking her to all three *Keatyn Chronicles* premieres: Paris, New York, and now L.A. But I'm too busy and too tired to care. I just have to get through this last one and then I'll cut her loose.

Maybe.

The girl is freaking crazy in bed. Wild ass shit that I've never done and will probably never do again but that's fun to try.

Once.

"I like the backless black one," I tell her. "We need to get going. The hair and makeup team will be at our suite in an hour."

She comes out in a red dress with a big bow on the shoulder, looking like a present. Not that I wouldn't mind unwrapping her, but it's a pretty ugly dress.

"But I think I luuuvvvee this one," she pouts.

I push her back in the dressing room. "If you choose the black one, we'll have about an hour to kill before hair and makeup arrive."

"Oh," she smiles. "That's what you want, huh, daddy?"

I cringe when she calls me daddy. What is it with young girls and that term?

"Yes, that's what I want."

"But what about jewels? Keatyn always gets to wear *real* jewels."

"Real jewels that are on loan. You have to earn that privilege."

"Well, whose dick do I have to suck to get them? I mean, this is my *third* red carpet appearance!"

I cringe again as I hear the stylist chuckle. "That's not how it works. You have to be a movie star."

"Or with someone rich. You could just buy me some jewels. Then I wouldn't have to borrow them. That's what I don't get. Keatyn has to be loaded. Can't she buy her own freaking diamonds and let people like me who can't afford them be the ones to borrow them?"

I ignore her comment and tell the stylist which dress we'd like.

ONCE WE'RE CHECKED into our hotel suite right across from where the premiere is being held, I pull a couple scarves out of my overnight bag.

"Oh, daddy wants to be naughty."

"Yes, I do. You've been a very bad girl. I'm going to have to tie you up and spank you."

She giggles, strips, and lies on the bed.

I wrap the first scarf around her wrist and tie it to the bedpost, then the other.

Once she's secure, I get naked and thrust my cock in her mouth, just like she likes it.

As soon as she gets me nice and hard, I pull out and turn her over, spank her ass, and get ready to fuck her.

"Oh, daddy!" she calls out, causing me to instantly go limp.

"Stop fucking calling me that!" I yell at her while stomping into the bathroom and locking myself inside.

I take a shower, trying to erase her words out of my head.

I know my thirtieth birthday is quickly approaching, but I'm certainly not even close to being old enough to be her daddy.

She knocks on the door. Apparently, I didn't tie her up tight enough.

"I'm sorry, Riley. Let me in. I'll make it up to you."

"Nope, hair and makeup will be here any minute. Get yourself in a robe and answer the door when they get here."

"Fine," she says, "but I'm ordering champagne!"

I punch the shower wall with my fist. This is why I never date a girl more than once.

"WOW," KEATYN SAYS at the after party. "You should've asked me to be your date instead of breaking your rule."

Keatyn knows my rule. I rarely take the same girl out more than once, and definitely never to three premieres in a row.

"She loved the one in Paris and asked if she could come to New York. Of course, she had my dick in her mouth at the time. What was I supposed to say? That was a difficult predicament to be in. I mean, what if I said no and she bit it off or something?"

Keatyn gives me a huge eye roll. "She's trouble, Riley. And she has no class. You'd be better off going stag or with a cast member."

"I know." I sigh.

"At least she's showing a little less skin tonight," Keatyn says, trying to make me feel better.

"That's because I picked out the dress."

"Well, thank goodness for that."

"Speaking of that, why isn't Aiden here? Why did you come with Knox?"

"Because Knox and I were filming today and Aiden has a

fundraiser in Miami. I feel bad for not being there with him."

"Rumors are going to start flying about you and Knox again."

"Rumors are always flying about us. Especially now that he and Becki broke up."

"You're not wearing your engagement ring."

"We're not ready for the public to know yet. As soon as they do, they'll start hounding me about a wedding."

"Or put you on baby bump watch."

"I've been on baby bump watch ever since Knox and I started working together. We slept together in a movie, certainly that would *have* to transfer over to our personal life."

Riley laughs as Knox sets three glasses of champagne in front of us.

"I better not have any," Keatyn laughs. "Since I'm on baby bump watch."

"Our love child?" Knox says with a knowing smile. "If only we weren't such good friends, I'd totally knock you up."

"Wait until I get pregnant in the movie. That will really start the rumors flying."

"You get pregnant in the next *Trinity* movie?" I ask, shocked.

Keatyn covers her mouth. "Shit. No one is supposed to know that. Thank god, I didn't accidentally say it in front of Miss TieMeUp."

"Shut up. I told you that in confidence."

"Told her what in confidence?" Knox asks.

He looks over at Shelby, who is complaining to a waiter because he doesn't have the right kind of champagne.

"Is she arguing with the waiter about not having cheap champagne?" Keatyn asks, looking perplexed.

"I may have bought something cheap in New York followed by the words, *Nothing but the best for you.*"

Knox punches my shoulder. "You dog. What about Miss

TieMeUp? She likes that kinky shit, huh?"

"I don't think there's anything she won't do. Quite honestly, it scares me a little. But, today, I tied her up with a couple silk scarves. When I was about to start doing her, she called me daddy."

"What's with young girls calling us old guys daddy?"

"Speak for yourself. You're in your thirties, you *could* be her daddy."

"It made him go limp," Keatyn says, grinning.

"Oh, wow, that sucks. Can't say I've ever suffered from that problem," Knox confides. "Unless I was too drunk. And if that was the case, I didn't really care much."

"I'm going to go rescue her from making a fool out of herself," I say, heading toward the bar.

"Let's just have whatever they're serving, Shelby. I'm sure it will be to your liking."

She pouts but then says, "Fine."

Once she has a champagne flute in her hand, she quickly chugs it, then leads me back to the coat closet, where she gets on her knees and tells me just how sorry she is about this afternoon.

With her lips.

And, damn, if I don't enjoy it.

FRIDAY, SEPTEMBER 26TH
COLLIN & ARIELA'S RESIDENCE - CONNECTICUT

Ariela

"WE HAVE DRINKS with the Pattersons at five. Don't be late this time," my husband tells me before he leaves for work.

"Collin, I have an appointment with a new client at three-thirty. I'll do my best."

He grabs my arm as I walk past him. "Quit. You don't need to work."

"I like my job."

"Do you know how embarrassing it is to have a wife who works? It makes me look like I'm not successful enough. You should be having lunch, volunteering, and taking care of our kids."

"We don't have kids," I reply with a sigh. This is not the first time we've had this conversation.

"Kind of hard to have kids when your wife is frigid."

"Kind of hard to be attracted to your husband when he's sleeping with his secretary," I say under my breath.

"What did you say?"

"You heard me. I know. About *all* of them."

He pushes me against the wall and pins my arms, his face

23

turning red with anger.

"Don't you fucking say that. I love you," he says, forcing his lips against mine.

I want to throw up.

I push him away. "Stop it."

"You better get your shit together, Ariela. Your dad wants us at their country house next weekend with a bunch of clients. *And* their wives."

"You're going to be late for work," I say, changing the subject and knowing that will get him out of the house. If Collin is nothing else, he is punctual.

"You better be on time," he threatens. "You don't want to piss me off."

"I will be," I say softly. He's right. I don't want to piss him off. It's easier to do what he wants. Go through the motions.

He smiles, kisses my cheek sweetly, grabs his briefcase, and walks out the door.

As soon as I hear the garage door shut, I slide to the floor and cry.

How did my life come to this?

The sad thing is, I know the answer.

Because I let it.

I STOP CRYING and pull myself together, getting up and taking a quick peek in the hall mirror to check my makeup. The girl staring back at me is almost a stranger.

My eyes have lost their zest for life. My hair is pulled back into a bun because Collin says it makes me look more proper. My shoulder bones are sticking out because I don't care if I eat.

Food has lost its taste.

No, life has lost its taste.

I GRAB MY handbag off the counter. Today's choice is a classic Chanel bag. Collin bought it for me. I was excited when I unwrapped it, thinking how sweet it was that he bought it for no reason. But, later, I overheard him telling my dad he got it because someone else's wife had one.

He'd already bought himself a Mercedes, an expensive watch, and a summer home in Palm Beach. This bag was just another way to show his status.

And, to Collin, a perfect wife who doesn't work is just another status symbol.

I SET THE alarm, get in my Range Rover, and head to my first appointment with a woman who doesn't like to be kept waiting.

I roll into the flower shop with two minutes to spare.

"You're late," my mother says, kissing me on the cheek.

"Nice to see you too, Mom."

She waves her hand at me and gives me a hug. "I love you even when you make me wait."

"Maybe you shouldn't tell someone to meet you at nine when you really want them to meet you earlier."

"You look thin," she says, ignoring my comment, her brows furrowing. "Are you feeling okay?"

"I'm fine, Mom," I say, putting on a smile. "Let's find you the perfect flowers for the event."

She pulls me aside. "You also look like you've been crying. Your eyes are puffy."

"Collin and I got into a stupid argument this morning."

"What about?"

"Same as usual. He wants me to quit work."

"Me too. I need some grandchildren. You've been married for six years. Don't you think it's time?"

"I'm not sure I want to stay married to Collin," I say, shocking myself for finally admitting the truth.

"But you and Collin are the perfect couple. He treats you so well, lavishing you with gifts. Your father is about to make him a partner."

"I'm pretty sure he's cheating on me, Mom."

My mother rolls her eyes and leads me to a bench outside.

"Darling, powerful men like to have an occasional liaison. It doesn't mean they don't love you. Don't let that affect your beautiful marriage."

I can't contain my shock. "You sound like you're speaking from experience, Mom."

She takes my hand and pats it. "A man like Collin is never going to be faithful, but that doesn't mean he can't be a good husband and provider." She laughs. "Why do you think all the tennis pros at the club are so good-looking? Why do you think I had a personal trainer for years?"

"You have *liaisons* too?"

"Well, of course, dear. It's only fair."

My head feels like it's going to explode. I didn't sign up for this when I said I do. Actually, I wouldn't have said I do if my dad hadn't practically dragged me down the aisle.

"We better not keep Diane waiting too long, if we want the best flowers," I tell her. I can't deal with this right now. And I know my mom, she won't stand for my questioning her about it.

I take my mother back into the floral shop and expertly guide her into making the right floral choices for the political fundraiser she's hosting in a few weeks. I've had everything else planned for months.

AFTER I WALK her to her car, she says, "You are such a talented event planner. There are so many worthy charities that could use your help."

"I love my job, Mom."

"I know you do. I just meant . . ."

"I know, and thank you."

As she pulls away, I walk across the street to a coffee shop, wishing it were a bar.

Everything I thought about my parents' relationship was

26

wrong.

I married Collin because my dad told me I'd have a good life, like he and mom had.

I shut my eyes tightly, realizing that's exactly what I got.

A husband who has liaisons.

I know everyone has to choose what kind of a relationship works for them and I can't deny it seems to work for my parents, but I know this.

It won't work for me.

I order a cup of coffee and jokingly ask the cute barista if he could throw in a shot of rum.

He laughs, takes my money, and hands my cup off.

I plop down on a couch, trying to wrap my head around my mother's confession. My eyes blur as I stare at the coffee table in front of me, not really seeing the newspapers and magazines piled on it.

Until something catches my eye.

A cover.

A photo.

A headline.

Captive Films: Exclusive interview with Keatyn Douglas and Riley Johnson.

It's not unusual to see Keatyn on a magazine cover. She graced six in our senior year alone.

But, to my knowledge, Riley has never been on one with her.

I gently touch his handsome face then quickly flip the pages to find the interview.

Exclusive Interview:
Captive Films' Keatyn Douglas and Riley Johnson

"Keatyn, tell us how Captive Films got its start."
"Our first project was a remake of A Day at the Lake,

starring Luke Sander as Vince, myself as Lacy, and Jake Worth as my boyfriend, Matt."

"That movie was a box office hit. And you were both how old at the time?"

"Almost eighteen," Riley says. "We filmed it over our summer break."

"How did you come up with the name Captive Films?"

Sexy Riley rubs the scruff on his face and says, "It was a nod to both holding our audiences captive and how we met."

"How you met?"

They share an inside joke, then Keatyn says, "You'll just have to see the movie."

So there it is, folks. Go see the trilogy that's taking box offices around the world by storm.

I look at the other photos of them. Riley looks good.

There were a lot of good-looking boys at Eastbrooke, but Riley was just so much more.

And I was madly in love with him.

Maybe it's not all Collin's fault that our relationship sucks. I've never given him my whole heart.

I'm scouring the captions when there's a tap on my shoulder.

I look up to see the guy who took my order with a cup in his hand.

"We called your name like four times." He sets the cup down and gives me a boyish grin. "Mind if I join you?" As he's sitting down, he extends his hand. "My name's Riley."

"What!?"

"I said my name's Kyle. Are you okay?"

I smile, trying to pretend that I'm not rattled. "I'm, um, having a rough morning. Haven't had my coffee yet." I grab my cup and take a drink.

"It's almost lunchtime," he says. "You free?"

"For lunch?"

"Yeah, at my place."

"Are you hitting on me?"

He grins. It's a naughty grin and reminds me of the one Riley used to give me before he'd lead me to the furry rug at Stocktons, our secret hangout at boarding school.

"Just how old are you?" I ask.

"Nineteen. Age doesn't matter. I think you're hot."

I blush.

And it feels good.

"I'm married," I reply, looking down at the clearly visible four carat diamond on my hand.

"I don't want to marry you." He leans closer, causing an irresistible smell of coffee and musk to invade my senses. "I just want to fuck you. Over and over," he adds for good measure, sliding his hand across my knee.

I look into his big brown eyes, full of desire.

I haven't felt desired in a long time. Sex with Collin has become perfunctory.

I swallow hard and take another sip of coffee, actually considering it.

I need to feel wanted, lusted after.

"First thing I'm gonna do is undo that bun. I bet you have gorgeous hair. May I?"

"Uh huh," I say as he reaches around me, his mouth so close that his lips brush mine.

I'm looking at Kyle but, instead, I'm seeing Riley in front of me, shirtless, telling me he couldn't wait to undo the bun I had been wearing for parents' weekend.

I feel my hair cascade down my shoulders. It's freeing.

"Oh, Riley," I say out loud.

"My name is Kyle, but you can call me whatever you want. Finish your coffee and let's go."

I smile at Kyle, grab his cheeks, and kiss him straight on the lips. "Thank you."

"Uh, for what?"

"For making me remember what it feels like to be desired."

I grab the magazine and my bag and stand up. Kyle gets up too and follows me to my car.

"He's still single," I tell him.

"Who?"

I hold up the magazine. "Riley. I have to go."

"Wait. Are we hooking up?"

"No, I have to go see the movie."

"By yourself?"

"Yeah."

"What are you seeing?"

"The Keatyn Chronicles Trilogy."

"Want some company?"

"Do you have six hours to spare?"

"Yeah, why not." He grabs the magazine and sees Riley's name on the cover. "You know *this* guy?"

"Yeah. That's why I need to see the movie."

Kyle takes my hand. "There's a movie theater around the block. I'll warn you. I'm not a cheap date. You have to buy me popcorn."

I laugh. "I can do that."

IN THE MOVIE theater, Kyle happily munches on popcorn and nachos.

I send a text to my boss, telling her I need to cancel my appointment and asking her to reschedule it.

As the movie starts, I whisper to Kyle, "My name is Ariela."

PART WAY INTO the movie, actor Riley is in his dorm room telling Keatyn and Dallas how pretty I am. I get to see him talk to Keatyn about how much he likes me. How nervous he is to even text me. I laugh when Keatyn takes his phone and does it

30

for him.

And I start crying, later, when he throws me a football with rhinestones that spell out *Homecoming?*.

Kyle leans over. "Are you *that* Ariela?"

"Yeah, I am."

I remember getting a document from Captive, allowing them to use my name and likeness in the movie. I quickly signed and returned it, hoping no one would call me about it.

I cry during parts of the movie, but some six hours later when they show photos of the real Keatyn and Aiden, including one from the cast party from *A Day at The Lake 2*, I start bawling.

Kyle pats me on the back. "Tell me about all this."

I spill my guts to this relative stranger who has held my hand through the entire movie.

I WIPE MY tears and say, "And that's it. I walked away and never looked back."

"Your marriage isn't happy, is it?"

"No. I'm miserable."

"Then you need to go get Riley."

"Go to L.A.?"

"Yeah. You started ugly crying when you saw that picture with you in it. Maybe he hoped you'd see it. Maybe it's a sign."

"But . . ." My brain is thinking of a million reasons why I shouldn't go, but my heart can't think of any.

"But what? You want to live the rest of your life unhappy? Is he married?"

"The article said he's single."

"Then you definitely have to go."

"I do have a couple sorority sisters who live out there. They always want me to come visit."

"Call them."

I take my phone out of my bag and see numerous texts from

Collin. It's nearly seven, and I'm over two hours late for drinks.

"Shit. I was supposed to meet my husband and his clients for drinks at five. Not that I even wanted to go."

"Go home and pack your bags while he's gone."

"I don't have anywhere to stay."

"You can crash at my place."

"Are you still trying to get me into bed?"

"I know you think I'm young, but I'm smart enough to know true love when I see it. You chose the wrong path back then, you need to fix it or your world will never be in balance."

"How'd you get so smart?"

He grins at me. "I'm taking Philosophy of Life this semester. Getting an A."

His youth and enthusiasm feed my soul. I know he's right. I shake my head, loving the way my long hair feels as it slides across my shoulders. "Why are you helping me?"

He laughs. "I'm still kinda hoping to get laid."

"It's not gonna happen."

"Fine, tell you what. When you reconnect with Riley, maybe you can help me get a summer internship at Captive Films. That would be killer."

I shake his hand. "You have a deal."

He takes my phone and puts his number in, naming himself *Coffee Kyle*.

He walks me to my car and gives me a kiss on the cheek. "Good luck," he says. "Go do it now, before you chicken out. And, if you start to chicken out, call me."

I nod, thank him again, and drive home.

I pull into the driveway of our beautiful home. The house I thought would make us feel like a family. Instead, it seems cold and full of empty promises.

I pack a suitcase and an overnight bag. Then I go to the back of my closet and pull out an old shoebox. The shoebox filled with memories of a boy I could never forget but didn't have the guts to fight for.

I see a text from Collin flash on my phone saying he's heading home.

I scrawl a quick note for him, leave it on the kitchen island, and head for the airport.

ONCE I'M ON the plane and the people around me are asleep, I pull the box out of my tote bag. I cry as the memories flood back. Memories I've tried so hard to keep buried.

Pressed flowers, prom tickets, photos, sweet love notes.

As I pull out a stack of photos, something falls into my lap.

I move the box, dig between my legs, and find it.

The jeweled Hello Kitty ring he put on my finger when he asked me to be his girlfriend.

I take off my jewelry from Collin and toss it into my handbag, replacing the emerald on my right hand with the ring that tells me I can do this.

That I have to do this.

MONDAY, SEPTEMBER 29TH
CAPTIVE FILMS - SANTA MONICA

Riley

I COME OUT of my office after an early morning overseas call to find Keatyn sitting at the conference table, papers spread out in front of her, and my assistant, Tyler, looking over her shoulder.

"Casting sent these," she says to me. "If we're moving into television production, we have to do it just right. I need just the right actress for it."

"I think we should bring them all in for screen tests," Tyler suggests. That's always his suggestion. Spend more money.

"We'll bring *two* in for screen tests."

"Then help me decide, Riley," Keatyn says. "This role is so different. She's got to be able to play both the preacher's virgin daughter and the wild hellcat equally well."

I walk behind her and look at the faces staring back at me.

"No, no, and no." I immediately pull three casting sheets off the table and hand them to Tyler. Then I study a fourth. I can't remember her name, but I do remember that she had her nipples pierced. "And, no."

"Jeez, Riley, don't tell me you've slept with four out of our six choices. At this rate, we'll run out of actresses to choose from

35

in the next year."

"What are you saying?"

"I'm saying stop fucking twenty year olds. Most of our films are about young people. Move up a decade or something. And, speaking of that, stop taking Knox out and getting him drunk. He was still hung over on set yesterday at three in the afternoon!"

"Why the hell were you filming on a Sunday?" I shrug. "Besides, it's not my fault he can't handle his liquor."

"He can't handle any of it. He's not dealing with it very well."

"She was cheating on him with the personal trainer he bought for her!"

"I know. I'm not saying it was right, I'm just saying he probably can't keep up with you. Go a little easy on him. Take him bowling or golfing. Not to a club every night."

"Fine, I'll try to."

"Did you see this mockup from the marketing department?" She slides a board out from underneath a bunch of papers. "It's brilliant, very sexy."

"We gonna have to sell this one to a cable network?" I ask, looking at the sexy ad with the words *Daddy's Angel* across the top of a very scantily clad girl tossing her halo away.

"This one," I say, picking up the face of the girl who looks like she could handle the role of hellcat.

"But I think this one," she disagrees, going for the girl who looks more like a repressed daughter of a small town minister.

"Remind me of the storyline again." I haven't really been involved in this project much. It's one of Keatyn's babies.

"Basically the girl is screwing her way through her daddy's congregation, while he's online trying to find someone to come court her."

"Court her?"

"Yeah, the old fashioned way. No sex before marriage. Hell, they can't hold hands until they are engaged."

"Seriously? People do that?"

"I guess so."

"What's gonna happen when Daddy finds out she's not a virgin?"

"The script is hilarious and sexy. And he doesn't. But the crazy thing is she actually falls in love with one of the suitors."

"Really?"

"Yeah. And what's funny is he isn't the good guy Daddy thinks he is."

"Bring them both in, then, and we'll see," I decide, handing Tyler the sheets. "And book me dinner tonight, somewhere kinda swanky."

"How many, boss?"

"How many do you think?"

"Uh, two? But . . ."

"Shelby, again?" Keatyn interrupts, rolling her eyes.

"If I wasn't fucking her, she could play this role. She's a freak in bed."

"I doubt she'd be very convincing as an angel," Keatyn mutters as Dallas strides in and asks, "Who's a freak in bed?"

"Shelby." I glance at my watch. "Wow, seven o'clock. That's really early for you, Dallas."

"Shit," Keatyn says. "I have to be on set soon. And, Tyler can't book you reservations. You're having dinner at my house, remember? With Dallas and RiAnne. We're celebrating."

"Shit, I forgot."

"Is it bad if I ask you not to bring Shelby?"

Riley rolls his eyes. "Jeez, you think I'm stupid? I couldn't bring her to your house. She'd think we're serious."

"Riley, trust me, she already thinks you're serious."

"No, she doesn't."

"Yeah, she does," Dallas interjects. "You can't take a girl to three premieres in three different cities and not have her think it's serious."

"Whatever. She knows it's just for fun. I've been very clear about that. But you're probably right. I shouldn't see her again. So, Dallas, you wanna go grab some breakfast?"

"Can't. I have an audit committee meeting I have to prepare for."

Tyler shakes his head at me. "You don't have time for breakfast either, boss. You have a meeting with the release team. They're dying to impress you with the opening box office numbers."

"I'm having Vanessa's company do the publicity for *Daddy's Angel*," Keatyn interjects.

Tyler pulls a magazine out of a stack of papers in his hand. "She sure did a brilliant job with this."

I glance at the popular women's magazine and see one of the photos from the cover shoot Keatyn and I did together. Hell, they even talked me into being shirtless in a couple of the pictures.

"I look damn good, don't I, Tyler?"

"Yeah, you do, boss. Must be all the sex, because you haven't worked out for five days straight."

"I've been traveling for the premieres. Give me a fucking break."

Tyler walks off. "I'm just saying."

Keatyn and Dallas are both snickering as they walk away.

SHOPPING – SANTA MONICA
Ariela

I'VE ONLY BEEN in Santa Monica for three days but I already love it.

Being back on the beach reminds me of when I was last here. It was the summer before our senior year. I had talked my parents into letting me spend the summer with Keatyn. I didn't really mention anything about the movie or the fact that I'd be spending most of my time with Riley.

During filming, I got to see all that goes into making a movie.

Really, it was like planning a large event. Lots of details and making sure everything is just right.

I spent my first day here catching up with my two college friends, the one I'm staying with and the other, who is pregnant and is expecting her first child in a few months.

Today, they both had to work, so I've been wandering around town, getting myself reacquainted with it. Because yesterday, when the three of us were relaxing on the beach, I made a decision.

I'm not going home.

I mean, I'll have to go back, pack up my things, get a divorce, and all that, but I'm going to live here from now on.

Whether I ever see Riley again or not.

Coming here was as much my dream as it was his.

And it's about time I start living my life doing what I want.

Not what my dad wants.

Not what Collin wants.

What *I* want.

I even called my boss today and quit my job. I know it's a bit irresponsible, and I have important events that I've committed to, but my capable assistant can handle them.

My friend said I could sleep on her couch for as long as I need to, but I don't want to impose. I want to find an apartment and a job before I even think about trying to contact Riley.

I stroll by a cute baby boutique and decide to look for a gift for my pregnant friend's upcoming baby shower. The shop is adorable and full of teeny pink and blue outfits, colorful cribs, and strollers that cost as much as a car.

I'm holding up a pink velour onesie with an appliquéd giraffe and trying to decide between it and a frilly lace dress when I hear, "Ariela, is that you?"

I turn around and am face to face with Keatyn.

I stand still, my lips frozen together, and nod.

"Ohmigawd, it's been forever!" She wraps me in a tight hug. "What are you doing here?"

"I, um, I'm visiting a friend, needed a shower gift."

"Were you going to call me?"

"I don't have your number."

"It's the same one I've had since high school."

Keatyn looks at the clothes in my hands. "I like the giraffe," she says. "Do you have kids?"

"Me, um, no."

"Married? Single?"

"Uh, married. But getting a divorce."

I know a divorce is what I want, but this is the first time I've said it out loud. It feels really good to finally say it.

"Oh, I'm sorry. How long have you been married?"

"It's okay. We've been married for six years. Together for about ten. My dad loves him."

"But you don't?"

Tears start to prickle my eyes. "Uh . . ."

"Oh, I'm sorry. I didn't mean to pry."

"You wouldn't happen to know a good attorney, would you?"

"Of course. Dallas."

"Dallas? Really? It's hard to believe the weed smoking, joke cracking boy I knew in high school would end up a lawyer."

"Yep, one of the best. He's Captive Films' chief legal counsel. You had to assume he'd go to law school with his dad being a senator and all. Never could get him into politics, though."

"Is he married?"

"Very. He and RiAnne are still together. And she's pregnant with their fifth! That's who I'm shopping for today. Hey, do you have any plans for tonight? We're all having dinner at my house in Malibu. I'd love for you to come."

A dinner with Keatyn, Aiden, Dallas, and RiAnne? That would be okay. Maybe I could ask them about Riley and find out if he's seeing anyone. Or if he'd ever want to see me again.

"Dinner would be great, if I'm not intruding."

"Don't be silly. We miss you."

"Thank you. I miss you all too." I don't say Riley's name but it's probably obvious that I miss him the most.

"So, I have to get going, but do you remember where the house is?"

"Yeah, I do."

"Awesome. I'll leave your name at the gate and see you around seven."

"Okay," I reply shakily. While I'm excited, I'm also scared to death. I mean, it wasn't just Riley's life I walked out of. It was all my friends. What if they hate me for it?

Keatyn takes her purchases to the counter where the ladies ooh and ahhh over her.

I put the lace dress back on the rack, deciding the baby needs something soft and comfortable. Actually, I think that's what I'm craving: a life that's comfortable, a life with friends, a life with someone who loves just me.

When I set the onesie on the counter, the ladies ask me how I know *the* Keatyn Douglas.

"We went to boarding school together. I haven't seen her in years, though." We complete our transaction. "Thanks ladies."

As I'm walking out the door, Collin calls me.

I've ignored all his calls so far, but decide to take this one.

The note I left on the kitchen counter led him to believe I came here last minute to help a friend in crisis. What I didn't tell him is that *I'm* the one in crisis.

"How're things going there?" he asks.

"Getting better," I reply, thinking how lucky it is that I ran into Keatyn. And how lucky I am that she doesn't appear to hate me for what I did.

"You'll be back in time for this weekend, right? Old man Foster needs to see that I'm a stable married man if he's going to trust me with his millions."

"I won't be back, Collin. You'll have to give him my regrets."

"Dammit, Ariela. I need you there. This is way more important than some bad breakup."

"Honestly, Collin, I've decided not to come back. I want a divorce."

"You *what?* What the fuck? Did you tell your parents?"

"No, I'm telling you."

"But we're a team."

"We stopped being a team when you started messing around. I deserve better."

"I've given you everything you could ever want."

"I don't want a husband who cheats on me."

"I'm sorry. It was a one-time thing, I swear. I love you. Please come back."

"It wasn't a one-time thing. I won't be back this weekend, Collin. I'll let my parents know."

"Don't say anything to them about a divorce. Not until I get a chance to make it up to you. Seriously, you're the only girl I've ever loved."

What he says makes me cry. That's all I've ever wanted. To be treated like I'm the only girl a boy loves. "I wish that were true. Goodbye, Collin."

I hang up, knowing that once upon a time, there was a boy who treated me that way.

I glance at my watch. Two hours until dinner.

What if Riley is going to be there?

Wouldn't Keatyn have mentioned him, if he was?

Either way, I need to look good, and all the clothes I brought with me are pretty East Coast professional. I need something cute and casual to wear.

Time to go shopping.

KEATYN & AIDEN'S BEACH HOUSE – MALIBU

"RILEY, LOOK WHO I ran into today!" Keatyn says excitedly, the second I step through the front door.

A mane of brunette hair moves through the air as she turns around, and I come face to face with the only girl who broke my heart. The girl I waited fifty-four excruciatingly long days to sleep with. The girl who is the reason I will never fall in love again.

Ariela.

I grab Keatyn by the arm and drag her into the kitchen. "What the fuck? What the hell is *she* doing here?"

"Riley, shush. I ran into her today at the baby store."

"Is she pregnant? Oh my god. That's even worse." I walk straight to the built-in bar and rummage to the back where I know Aiden keeps the good stuff, grab a bottle of 25-year-old scotch, and take a slug straight out of the bottle. "Is she married? A girl as beautiful as her would have to be married. Does that mean her husband is here too?"

"Riley, calm down. She's getting a divorce and she doesn't have any kids. I knew you and Dallas were coming for dinner, so I invited her." Keatyn looks sincere and I feel bad for yelling at her. "Since you're between blondes and all."

Okay, maybe I don't feel that bad.

"Thanks," I say sarcastically.

"Look. I'm sorry to just spring it on you both like that. I should have told you but, in my mind, I scripted it just like it happened. She turns around. Smiles at you. But then you were supposed to rush into each other's arms. Long lost love reunited."

"You and your damn scripts."

"My damn scripts have made us both a lot of money, Mr. I Just Bought A Jet."

I furrow my brow. "I needed that for business. It's a write off."

"Uh huh."

"Shut up. Fine, I wanted it." I shove my hands through my hair and hold my head. I can't fucking believe Ariela is here. I peek past the bar and see her standing by the window, the ocean spread out behind her, looking more beautiful than ever with her long eyelashes, luscious full lips and hips that always fit perfectly into my hands. "And that's beside the point. I have no desire to see her ever again."

I remember our last time. Her rising on top of me, hair flipped back.

"Riley, people change," Keatyn says, still not giving up. "I'm sure she's not the same girl who listened when her dad told her not to follow her boyfriend to California because he was going to make music videos."

"She killed me."

"I know she did, but she's here now. It's fate I ran into her today. We'd lost touch. She never went back for Homecoming."

"Neither did I."

"I know."

I take another swig. Trying to calm both my nerves and my dick, which is a fucking traitor. The second I saw her, he sprung to attention in a way no other girl has ever accomplished.

I hear Aiden, Dallas, and RiAnne making small talk with her. Asking about where she's living.

"Riley, I'll have her come talk to you. Maybe you can at least be friends again. You were always best friends."

I hide behind the bar while Keatyn goes to get her.

Juvenile, I know.

Aiden's probably going to pull my man card.

But I'm not hiding. I'm drinking.

Besides, I'm not the one who left. She owes me an explanation.

"Hey," Ariela says, a shy smile on her face. She smiled like that right before I kissed her for the first time. "I'm sorry, Riley. I didn't know you'd be here."

"Why *wouldn't* I be here?" I say coldly. "These are *my* friends."

"I wanted to see you. I was just surprised to see you tonight."

"Why are you here?"

"To find out how you are."

"That's why you came to California?"

"It's complicated, Riley. Do you think I could have a drink?"

"I'll give you something else." I grab her and push her up against the bar. "This means nothing," I say, forcing my lips onto hers.

I thought she would be repulsed. Hate me. Run away.

I want to disgust her and make her leave.

But she grabs the back of my neck with equal force and shoves her tongue in my mouth.

Heat rushes through my body, blood screaming, fire pushing through my veins.

Straight to my pants.

I lean toward the sexy skirt she's wearing, pushing it up, and shoving my massive hard on against her leg. I don't even care if she knows she's making me hard. The thought crosses my mind that I should rip her panties off and do her right here.

45

For old time's sake.

Especially when she hooks her leg around me, pulling me closer.

Slam. The refrigerator adjacent to us slams shut and Keatyn's chef, Marvel, says, "Oh! Excusez-moi."

But the fucker doesn't leave.

He places a bunch of vegetables on the island and starts chopping them.

Ariela slowly extricates herself from our embrace.

"I know," she says sadly. "It meant nothing."

She walks away from me, stopping by the patio door to grab a beer from an ice bucket.

She doesn't even turn to look back.

Just like the last time.

I should leave.

But I'll be damned if I will. These are my friends.

I try to pull myself together with another long swig of scotch.

Aiden slaps my back, sneaking up from behind me and causing me to choke. "How we doing?"

"I'm fine. I mean, I knew, eventually, I'd probably see her again someday. I was cordial."

"I guess kissing her like that would be considered cordial." He smirks. "That why you're downing my good scotch?"

"It didn't mean anything," I say, trying to convince myself. "Fuck." I hand him the bottle. "I mean, What. The. Ever. Loving. Fuck?"

"Maybe it's sorta like fate." He smirks again as he pours two fingers of scotch into a short glass.

Bastard thinks this is funny.

"Don't give me that bullshit. It might have worked on Keatyn, but it won't work on me."

He hands me the glass then pours one for himself. Damn, if he isn't a good friend.

"I forgot to tell you, but congrats on the engagement. It sounds like it went off without a hitch." Yes, I'm changing the subject. I have to.

"Mostly," Aiden says with another grin.

"Mostly?"

He glances out the patio door, where Keatyn is happily chatting with Ariela, Dallas, and RiAnne.

"Doesn't she look more beautiful than ever?" he asks.

I look at Ariela and say, "Yes," before I realize he was referring to Keatyn. I cover by saying, "She always looks pretty. RiAnne, though, gosh, she looks like she's ready to explode."

"Better not let her hear you say that."

"I don't have a death wish. What did you mean by mostly?"

"The engagement went well. She just always seems to surprise me."

"I woulda been surprised if she said no. You were so worried."

"It's not that we didn't want to get married. We just never had the time."

"Never *took* the time, you mean."

"And now, we are. Come on, let's go out there. Be nice and talk to Ariela. You'll regret it if you don't."

"I could care less about Ariela," I lie. "And I'm sure as shit not going to try to impress her."

"Okay," Aiden says, "then just be *cordial.*"

"Smart ass," I mutter.

As I follow him to the deck, I remind myself that I'm here to hang out with my friends. That we'll have a delicious dinner, some great wine, and enjoy the sunset.

And as soon as we're done, I'm leaving.

I'll go home, scroll through my phone, and choose a girl at random from the list.

Then I'll fuck her and forget all about Ariela.

WHEN I APPROACH the table, I do what I'm supposed to do. I pat RiAnne's tummy, tell her she looks great, and give Dallas my scotch.

With four kids under seven and another one on the way, he probably needs it more than I do.

I can handle this.

Although, I'm thankful when Marvel brings out the first course and Keatyn tells everyone where to sit.

I figured she'd keep trying to play matchmaker and seat me by Ariela.

But she doesn't.

Instead, I'm seated right across from Ariela.

So I have to see her face.

Watch her blink and flirt with Dallas, who even though he is happily-ever-after married to RiAnne, is fucking flirting with my girl.

My girl.

Where the fuck did that come from?

THE NIGHT GOES from bad to worse with one innocent question.

"So, what have you been doing since Eastbrooke?" Dallas asks Ariela.

She sets her wine glass down, absentmindedly pushing a few strands of hair behind her ear.

That simple gesture takes me back in time.

To her leaping into my arms and telling me she got accepted to USC. I had gotten my letter eleven excruciatingly long days before she did. We were both so happy. Our dreams were coming true.

Until later that night when she came to my room in tears.

Riley, I don't know what I'm going to do. My dad says I can't go to California with you.

Fuck your dad. You're eighteen. You can do what you want.

I have to be able to afford it, Riley.

We're in love, kitty. That's all we need.

Pushing her hair behind her ear, she sniffled and said, You're right, love is all that matters.

Except she lied.

"Well, I went to college at Princeton."

"Just like Daddy wanted," I snap, unable to bite my tongue.

She looks at me, her eyes sad. "Yes," is all she says before turning back toward Dallas. "I graduated with a degree in Art, did an internship with an event planner and fell in love."

Her words *fell in love* cut me deep.

How many times had we said *I love you* in the two years we were together? And how many times had we made love? We had a chart that hung on the inside of my dorm room closet. Every time we had sex, we added another to the tally. By the time we graduated, the whole back of the door was filled with marks.

"Event planning sounds like so much fun," RiAnne says, bubbling with excitement and probably thrilled to be talking to adults.

"It is. Demanding, but fun."

"What's your favorite kind of event to plan?" Keatyn asks.

I'm pouring myself more wine when she replies, "Weddings."

My body shuts down. The wine bottle drops from my hand, hits the glass, and shatters it, sending wine and glass in all directions.

I push my chair away from the table, as does everyone.

"Sorry," I say, quickly setting the bottle upright.

But the damage is already done.

She shattered my life like I shattered the glass and it can't be fixed.

"I'm sorry," I say to everyone. "I have to go."

I GET INTO my car and put the key in the ignition, flashing back to another time when I'm about to drive off, pissed at Ariela.

I'm sorry, Riley. You don't understand.

No, I don't understand. How could you do it? All this time? Leading me on. Telling me you were coming with me when all the while you planned to go to Princeton.

I kept hoping my dad would change his mind.

A knock on my window startles me and brings me back to the present.

"Riley," Keatyn says.

I roll down the window. "I'm sorry about the wine."

"I sorry I didn't tell you I invited her," she says, swaying slightly. She puts her palm on my car, closes her eyes, and sways again, her knees giving out.

I jump out of the car and grab her. "Keatyn!"

She quickly opens her eyes. "Oh, gosh, that was weird. I got hot and nauseous all of a sudden."

"You fainted."

"Oh, wow. Weird."

"How much did you drink?"

"I didn't drink anything."

"Shit," I say, knowing I can't just leave her. "Come on, let's get you inside. Has this ever happened before?"

"Um, no." She shakes her head. "I think I'm just hungry."

"Hungry and nauseated?" I put my arm around her and lead her back into the house. Aiden, who seems to have a sixth sense where she's concerned, is rushing toward us.

"What's wrong?" he asks, his face whiter than hers.

"I'm fine," she says, but I disagree.

"She fainted."

"I didn't faint. I felt a little woozy for a minute. I think I'm just hungry."

Aiden gently leads her to the couch, sitting down with her and rubbing her hand. "Are you sure, baby?"

When he calls her baby, my ears perk up. Usually, he calls

her Boots.

I watch the two of them. The way they care. The way they love.

I say I don't want that in my life. That I'm happy single.

That I don't want complications. Just sex.

But once upon a time, it's all I wanted.

I look out the window at Ariela.

The one I wanted to have it with.

"If you're okay, I need to go. Will you be in the office tomorrow?"

"No," Aiden says as she smiles at me and mouths, "Yes."

This time, I jump back in my car and tear out of the driveway.

KEATYN & AIDEN'S BEACH HOUSE - MALIBU

Ariela

KEATYN AND AIDEN sit back down as their chef serves the main course.

"I owe you an apology, Ariela," Keatyn says sincerely. "I should have told you Riley would be here. I didn't think it all through. It's been a long time."

"It has been. I'm sorry I didn't keep in touch, but it was just too hard."

"You were married," Dallas states, pointing at my finger. I took off my wedding ring, but I couldn't take off the tan line.

"I still am married. Keatyn tells me you might be able to help me file for a divorce?"

"What's your state of residence?"

"Connecticut."

"I know just the person who can help you with that. In fact, you know her. Well, used to know her."

"Who?"

"Annie," Keatyn says, scooping up another portion of mashed potatoes. I can't help but wonder how in the world she stays so thin.

"Annie is a divorce attorney?"

"Yeah," she replies, but then she hesitates. "Oh . . ."

"Oh, what?"

"Um, well, Dallas, you know, that might not be the best idea," she says to him.

"Oh," RiAnne says, covering her mouth.

"Why not?" I ask.

"She's married to Riley's brother, Camden."

"Really? Wow. First, Jake, then sexy Cam. That's awesome. Good for her."

"Yeah, they have a fun story. She was sort of forced to help him graduate."

"Only took him like seven years," Dallas says. "I was already starting law school by then."

"I'd love to get in touch with her," I tell them. "I expect my husband will want to fight the divorce. But enough about me, catch me up on your lives."

Dallas leans into his pregnant wife and says, "I had hot sex with my secretary today."

My face goes white. "What?"

RiAnne playfully punches him. "He's teasing. One time he heard a joke about a man who had an affair with his secretary and fell asleep at her house. Instead of freaking out, he told her to take his shoes outside and put grass and dirt on them.

Aiden laughs along with them, but I'm horrified. "Yeah, and when the guy walked in the house, his wife demanded to know where he'd been."

RiAnne rolls her eyes at them. "He tells her that he couldn't lie to her. He was having an affair with his secretary. The woman looked at his shoes, called him a liar, and accused him of playing golf."

"So, now, whenever he plays golf, he says he's with his secretary," Keatyn laughs too.

"I wish my husband liked golf more than his secretary," I mutter, taking a big gulp of wine.

RiAnne's eyes get huge. "It's funny to us because I used to be his secretary. Uh, but, now, it doesn't seem so funny. I'm sorry. Is that why you're getting a divorce?"

"Collin's been having an affair with his secretary. But that's just an excuse. I never should have married him in the first place."

"I couldn't help but notice you're wearing the Hello Kitty ring Riley gave you when he asked you to be his girlfriend," Keatyn says.

I look down and study it, tears filling my eyes. "Yeah, it's what gave me the strength to come here."

CLUB RAZOR – HOLLYWOOD
Riley

I WAS GOING to make a booty call but, instead, I call Knox.

"I am in serious need of a drink. Meet me at Razor in ten," I tell him. "I'll call and let them know we're coming so our section is ready."

A few minutes later, I'm handing my keys to the valet and being escorted to our VIP section.

The music is loud. The lights are flashing. The beat thumps in my chest.

And there are already girls lined up to see us.

This is more like it.

Knox strides in a few minutes after I do. We sit on the leather couch, toast to a good night, and down a few shots of tequila.

Make that four.

Or five.

Whatever. Thank god, I'm finally feeling buzzed.

And maybe a little drunk.

I have to pee, so I head to the bathroom while Knox starts grinding on two of the girls who were let into our section. Ron, our usual VIP bouncer, knows by now which ones to let in and which ones to turn away. Hot blondes with smoking bodies for me. Big tits for Knox.

I push the door to the bathroom open, remembering just a few months ago when a girl followed me in. I'd never seen her before, but she was hot and horny, so I leaned her over the sink and fucked her. I remember watching her titties bouncing in the mirror with every thrust. As I was coming, she said *ohmigawd* and proceeded to puke into the sink. I disposed of my condom and got the hell out of there as fast as I could. At least she waited to puke until I was done.

So she had that going for her.

Maybe tonight I'll do the same, just find a girl who's not as drunk.

I'M MAKING MY way to the dance floor, hoping to find my next bathroom fuck, when the DJ blasts the words no man in a club wants to hear: *If you want it, you gotta put a ring on it.*

I hate when they play this fucking song. All the girls put their hands up in the air and think they have the power.

Tonight, though, the song brings back a memory.

One I've tried for years to forget.

I'm back on the Eastbrooke campus, standing outside her dorm just before curfew.

What if we got married? Then your dad couldn't say anything.

He'd still cut me off.

So? My parents are paying for my college. What's mine is yours. I've got money coming from the movie and three more music videos lined up to produce. We'll get by.

She grabs ahold of my face and looks deeply into my eyes. You'd really marry me, Riley?

Right this second if I could. I don't have a ring, but I'll get down on one knee and ask you right now.

I drop to my knee, take her hand in mine, and say, Ariela, will you marry me, go to California with me, and love me forever?

She smiles at me, tears in her eyes, and says yes.

I shake my head, willing away the memory.

Clearly, I'm in need of another shot.

Bouncer Ron fist bumps me, smiles, and gestures to the women he's allowed in. He's proud of his choices. I'm not sure if I'm just drunk and horny tonight, but I'd have to agree.

In fact, I might skip fucking a drunk girl in the bathroom and take a couple of girls home instead.

A nice threesome.

That will help me forget.

I down another shot and slide between two of the prettiest. They sandwich me in, both grinding against me. I close my eyes and enjoy it.

When I open my eyes, I see Ariela out on the dance floor.

I blink my eyes, thinking I'm hallucinating. How many shots have I had?

But, no, it's her, looking hot in a skimpy little black dress. And some guy has his hands all over her ass.

I lose it.

Jump over the VIP railing and onto the dance floor, push the guy off her, and pull her into my arms.

"Are you following me?" I yell at her.

"No!" she yells back.

"Good," I say, as the guy comes back looking for a fight. I raise my finger into the air, letting Bouncer Ron know there's going to be trouble. He bounds over the railing and, with the help of two other bouncers, drags Mr. Hands off the dance floor.

What I'm about to do is so against my better judgement but, what the fuck?

Tonight Ariela is going to be just another sexy piece of ass.

I'll dance with her, get her drunk, hot, and horny, then I'll take her home, fuck the shit out of her, and forget about her for once and for all.

Just like all the others.

To all the girls I've fucked before.

That can be my theme song.

FRIEND'S HOME - SANTA MONICA

Ariela

WHEN I GET back from Malibu, my friend is waiting for me in her kitchen.

"So, the kids are in bed and my husband is home. Let's go to a club."

"A club?" A club is the last place I want to go. I'm mentally exhausted from seeing Riley.

From being near him.

From kissing him.

"I have a dress you can wear, in case you didn't bring one. Come on, I haven't been to a club in ages. And you need to get out there. Speaking of which, how was dinner with your old friends?"

"He was there," I say quietly, still barely believing it myself.

"Oooh, tell me all the details. I'll grab a bottle of wine."

"Uh, no, let's do the club," I say. On second thought, clubs are loud and talking is nearly impossible. The last thing I want to do is talk about my night. Drinking sounds like a better idea.

Drinking, dancing, and not thinking.

I SHIMMY INTO a spandex dress, throw on a pair of heels, and pretty soon we're waiting in line.

"I can't believe we have to wait in line on a Monday night. We look good, right? Like good enough to get in? What do you think of this shirt with this skirt? I picked this shirt since it's flowy on the bottom and hides my belly. I got my body back right away after my first two, but this third one is killing me."

"You look great," I tell her.

"So, tell me about tonight."

"He was there."

"Yeah, you said that already. How did he look?"

"He looked good."

"But you already knew he would, based on the magazine, right?"

"Yeah, but he looked better in person. He's matured. Filled out in all the right places. And that jawline of scruff. Holy shit."

"Did you talk?"

"It was kind of a disaster. He walked in, saw me, said *What the fuck?* to Keatyn, and hid in the kitchen."

"Oh, that's not the kind of reaction you want."

"No, not at all. Keatyn went to talk to him. Then she came out and told *me* to go talk to him."

"Awkward, much?"

"Yeah. But we didn't talk."

"What did you do?"

"We made out."

"You, what? How? Why?"

"I don't know. He said it didn't mean anything but it did. It

57

was the hottest kiss of my life. He pushed me up against the wet bar, slid his hands up my skirt. I would have done him right then and there."

"But you're married."

"Yeah, I'm married."

"You going to fix that?"

"Yes. I want a divorce."

"Based on what you told me about Collin, I would agree with you. And that's saying a lot. I loved the two of you together in college. I even stood up for you at your wedding."

"I know."

"You're lucky you don't have kids with him."

"I didn't want to get pregnant. He kept pushing for it. He's been pushing for it since we got married. I mean, sex with him was one thing. A baby, well that's a lot bigger commitment. I couldn't risk tying myself to him for the rest of my life in that way."

"So, you've known for a while?"

"I knew at my wedding, Sarah."

"What?!"

"It's true. I told my dad I didn't want to marry Collin. Well, that's not right. I told him I didn't love Collin the way I loved Riley."

"What did he say?"

"That I was being ridiculous. That it was just cold feet. That we'd been together for so long. That the family loved him. All very logical things."

"I was your maid of honor. You should have told me."

"I know. It's really not Collin's fault our marriage is failing. It's mostly mine. I never loved him the way I should have."

AN HOUR LATER, we're finally in the packed club. We immediately head to the bar and order a round of shots.

"Tonight we forget about our lives for a few hours and just

dance," Sarah says, clinking her shot glass into mine. "Let's get out there!"

We work our way out to the crowded dance floor and it's not long before a cute guy is dancing with me.

His hands are touching my ass and I don't care.

It's just dancing.

It's fun.

The place is full of energy and I feel alive.

The guy yells into my ear, "Can I buy you a drink?"

I'm about to say yes, when I see quick movement out of the corner of my eye.

It's Riley.

He grabs the guy and tells him to get off me. The guy is coming back, ready to punch him, but Riley raises a finger in the air and bouncers collect my former dance partner and escort him off the dance floor.

It's really kinda hot.

But then he wraps me in his arms like he used to and kisses the top of my head. It's a sweet gesture.

One that makes me want to start crying.

But then he gives me a naughty smirk and puts his hands all over my ass. I do the same while pulling him into my body and grinding against his leg. I'm trying like hell to grind against his dick and make him hard like he was when we kissed earlier tonight.

He smells like expensive cologne and alcohol.

And this reminds me of nights spent dancing after curfew.

WE DANCE THE night away. Although, I'm not sure this should be categorized as dancing.

It's more like foreplay set to music.

I'm all worked up, barely able to control how much I want him.

This so wasn't my plan.

I was going to talk to him first.

See if we could become friends again.

Then, maybe, we could be something more.

When he squeezes my ass, I care less about my plan.

I just want him.

I move my lips toward his and he full on attacks my mouth.

Grabs my neck and forces me to keep kissing him.

Like I'd ever try to stop.

Our kisses are ravenous, hungry. I've been starving for him all this time.

"I'm taking you home with me now," he commands.

And I don't dare say a word, for fear he might change his mind.

I just nod yes.

He grabs my friend, hands her off to Knox—as in the hot movie star, Knox freaking Daniels—and tells him to make sure she gets home safely. Then he wraps his arm around my waist and staggers out to the valet.

"Are you drunk?"

"Just a little," he says. He used to say the same thing when I'd ask him if he loved me. He'd give me that handsome smile and say, *Just a little* even though he meant a lot.

"I'm driving then."

"Whatever, as long as we get there," he says, as a sleek black luxury sedan pulls in front of us.

He tips the valet a hundred and tells him I'm driving.

"Yes, sir, Mr. Johnson. Good to see you again."

Riley slides in the passenger seat, presses the home button on the GPS, and says, "She'll tell you where to go. I'll be too busy."

"Too busy doing what?" I ask as I pull out of the parking lot.

"This," he says, sliding his hand between my legs.

I know I should stop him. I know that this is cheating on my husband. And I'm not a cheater. I've never cheated on anyone. But I can't for the life of me bring myself to stop him. Not when

I've wanted and dreamed about this for so long.

He kisses my neck, which makes it difficult for me to concentrate on the road.

And it becomes even harder when he slides my thong over and roughly shoves his finger inside of me.

"Oh!" I say, startled by the suddenness of it.

"Do you want me to stop?"

"No," I moan. His long fingers have always felt like they were made just for me.

And they have become even more masterful. I'm groaning with pleasure and am close to orgasm when the navigation tells me we've reached our destination.

A valet opens my door.

Riley is already next to me, his arm wrapped around me, his lips on my neck, leading me through a pair of massive glass doors.

"Looks like it's going to be a good evening, Mr. Johnson," the doorman says.

Riley ignores him, pulling me down a hall, and then sliding a key into an elevator set off to the side.

He pulls me inside, kissing me and shoving me hard against the wall.

"I can't wait to fuck you, kitty," he says, calling me by the nickname he gave me in high school.

I melt into his arms and kiss him with voracity.

"I want the same thing," I say as his tongue forces its way into my mouth.

One hand moves to cup and squeeze my breast, the other slides under my ass, and I know exactly what he wants. I jump up and wrap my legs around his torso.

"I want you right here," he says, pushing my dress up and ripping off my thong while I'm unzipping his pants.

The elevator dings.

"Don't move," he says, putting his arms under me and carrying me through the door while we're still hooked together and ravenously kissing.

He lays me down on the closest surface. A couch, I think.

I'm shoving my hand down his pants, eager to free him and have him inside me, when I hear a loud squeaky voice yell, "Riley!"

We stop and turn toward the noise.

I see a pretty blonde with huge boobs, barely held in place by a couple skimpy pieces of leather.

"Shelby, what the hell are you doing here?" Riley asks, quickly standing up. "How did you get in?"

I pull my dress down over my exposed crotch as she pouts, "I'm surprising you."

Riley narrows his eyes and stalks toward her. "I asked *how did you get in?*"

"The doorman let me up. He's seen me here, *a lot*," she stresses, looking directly at me.

"Um, I'm just gonna go," I say, defeatedly. "I'll let you two figure this out."

"Don't you go anywhere," Riley says to me in a tone that sounds a lot like Collin's.

"I don't mind," the blond coos. "She can join in our fun too."

I'm horrified by her words.

I could never share Riley.

He grabs her by the arm and escorts her to the elevator.

"I have to get my stuff!" she protests. "I can't drive home like this!"

WHEN HE TAKES her into the bedroom, I see my chance. I hit the button on the elevator and get the hell out of here.

I run out of the elevator in tears and slam into the doorman.

"Oh, my," he says. "You no like three people?"

"No, I don't," I say, pushing past him and out the front

door.

It's at that moment I realize I don't have a car.

So I take my heels off and run down the sidewalk. Far away from the boy who still holds my heart captive.

MONDAY, SEPTEMBER 29TH
RILEY'S PENTHOUSE – L.A.

Riley

I HEAR THE elevator ding, meaning Ariela left.

I hold my head in my hands wondering what the fuck just happened.

Shelby tries to make it better by kissing me. But as soon as she gets close, I back away, touching my lips. The lips Ariela's mouth was just on.

I don't say anything, just glance at the floor. I'm so pissed and so full of adrenaline, I'm worried I might accidentally kill this girl.

I'm shocked when she immediately drops to her knees and takes my cock into her eager little mouth.

And, yeah, I let her.

So what?

I'm drunk.

When she's done, I politely take her down the elevator, tip the valet when he brings her car, and as I'm closing her door, I say sternly, "Don't you ever fucking come back."

Then I march into the lobby and grab the doorman by his shirt. "Don't you EVER fucking let ANYONE in my home without my permission. I could have you fired for this and, quite frankly, I should."

"Please, no, Mr. Johnson. I see the girl with you before and she said she was going to surprise you. I was trying to help."

"Don't EVER LET ANYONE IN MY HOME AGAIN. Do you understand?"

"Yes, sir. Yes, sir."

I go back to my apartment, strip off my clothes, stagger to the shower, and try to wash off the slimy way I feel.

I LIE DOWN in my bed and consider calling Ariela.

I remember all those nights we would talk from curfew until we knew it was safe to sneak out and be in each other's arms again.

What the fuck do I have to lose?

I pull up her contact, which I may have stolen from Keatyn's phone earlier.

So sue me.

I'm surprised when she answers with a pissed off sounding, "Hello?"

"Did you get home okay?" I ask her, worried about her taking off in the middle of the night.

"Yeah, I got a cab, Riley."

"You left. Why did you leave?" I know I'm sounding drunk and whiny, but I don't care. I have to know. Not about tonight, but me back then.

"Because there was a girl in your bed."

"She wasn't in my bed. And I don't want her."

"Never mind, Riley," she says in her pissy tone. It's sad that I still remember every pitch of her voice. "You're single and you clearly love it."

This pisses me off.

"I'm single, Ariela, because you didn't marry me. And, once

again, you just left with no fucking explanation. So why don't you go the fuck back to wherever you came from and go fuck your husband. I don't want you in my life. Do you understand me? Stay the fuck away from me and my friends."

I hang up the phone and cry in a way I haven't done since my senior graduation.

TUESDAY, SEPTEMBER 30TH
KEATYN & AIDEN'S BEACH HOUSE - MALIBU

Keatyn

I WAKE UP feeling refreshed, but notice it's still dark. A glance at the clock tells me I haven't slept for all that long. It's only three o'clock.

I snuggle my chest into Aiden's back, wrap my arms around him, and try to go back to sleep.

Except, I can't.

Because in trying to put myself back to sleep, I decide to gently rub his chest.

But rubbing his chest leads to me rubbing his abs, which draws my hand across his v-line and, well, we all know where that leads.

I tell myself that I'm just being nice. Giving him a massage. But, really, I'm only massaging one part of him.

His dick springs to life before he does.

I can't believe I'm molesting him in the middle of the night. We had sex before we went to sleep.

Although that doesn't stop me. Especially when he makes a sexy little moan.

I kiss his neck and rub my boobs against his back in further effort to wake him up.

His hand slides down over mine, which is still enjoying the instant gratification of being able to make him go from limp to "beast" mode, as he calls it, in a matter of seconds.

"Are you attacking me in my sleep?" he asks groggily, teasing me, but at the same time, pressing his hand down on mine, so I'll keep rubbing.

"I am."

He rolls over and kisses me. "Good. I need you. It's been forever."

"It's been four hours."

"It feels like forever," he says, moving his mouth down my chest.

"Ouch, that hurts. Kinda." This causes him to immediately stop sucking on my nipple and look at me. "But don't stop!"

"It hurts, but don't stop?"

"Um, yeah, I think so. My boobs are sore, but it sorta feels really good."

He puts his hand over one of my boobs and gives it a little squeeze. "They're bigger. I like."

He continues kissing me.

He's being super sweet, loving, and taking his time.

Aiden is good at foreplay.

He's kissing me, caressing me, teasing me.

Usually, I love it, but it's not what I want.

"Aiden, baby, fuck me. Now. Please."

"I love it when you say that," he says, quickly moving on top of me and doing what I asked.

And it feels so good.

Like something I just had to have at that moment.

It's perfect.

Sex with Aiden, I can honestly say, in the many years we've been doing it, is amazing, exciting, fun, spontaneous, sensual. His appetite for sex is voracious and I'm very happy about it.

Except right now, it's over.

And I'm okay with that. Because all I can think about now are waffles.

"Boots, you can wake me up like that anytime you want."

"I'm not sure I like being pregnant," I say, honestly.

He snuggles me into his arms and caresses my still flat belly. "Why's that? I'm loving it. You're super horny. Your boobs look amazing. Hell, you look amazing. I finally understand why they say pregnant women glow. You glow."

"I think it's you who's been glowing. You're quite proud of yourself for knocking me up."

I can see his smile in the dark.

He is very proud. And dying to tell the world.

"I'm thrilled to be having a baby with you."

"Does that mean you'd also be thrilled to eat waffles with me? Right now."

"You want waffles, right now?"

"Yes, and we may have to fly to St. Croix to get them. Because I don't want just any waffles. I want Inga's cinnamon waffles drizzled in her homemade pecan caramel sauce with a side of her spicy fried potatoes."

"That's going to be kind of hard to do since you have a busy day today. How about we make them ourselves?"

WE GET UP and head to the kitchen.

I make the caramel sauce while he cuts potatoes and stirs up the batter. Thank god we actually have all the ingredients, or I may have actually hopped on a plane.

"Am I being weird because I know I'm pregnant and I think I should be craving things or does being pregnant just cause me to be weird?"

"How are you being weird?"

"Aiden, I've been napping in between taping. I never do that. I'm ravenous. I'm horny."

JILLIAN DODD

He pours some batter into the waffle iron, shuts the lid, and then joins me in front of the stove, putting his chin on my shoulder and sliding his hands around my waist.

"I think napping is good for you. As is eating. And I hope you stay this horny. It's fun. I mean, don't get me wrong, we have a great sex life, but the last week has been exceptional."

I stir the potatoes and add just a little more cayenne pepper as Aiden's hand slips inside my robe, coming to rest on my stomach.

"You are obsessed with touching my stomach. People are going to know before we tell them."

"I'm dying to tell our families. They were so excited about the engagement, they'll be over the moon about a baby."

"I go to the doctor today. I'll ask him when's a good time to tell them. I mean, what if it doesn't work out?"

The waffle timer dings, so he's talking as he pops it out and starts another.

"You mean like a miscarriage?"

"Yeah, like Peyton and Damian. They were so excited they told everyone the second the line turned pink. She had planned the nursery. Then they went in for their first ultrasound and found out there wasn't even a baby. What was that called again?"

"A blighted ovum," he says. "That sucked. But they had their family to support them. You took her to Paris to help cheer her up. They've had two boys since then and she's only a few months away from having their third."

"I know. I'm just . . ."

"Scared?" He pulls me in for a hug.

"Yeah, Aiden, I'm scared." I start crying. "I really want a baby. I really am excited to be pregnant. But I don't want to disappoint you. I don't want to screw it up. I don't know how to be pregnant. What if I'm not good at it?"

He kisses me and wipes my tears. "Shh, baby. I promise, no matter what happens, you won't ever disappoint me." He kisses

70

my nose then grins at me. "If something happens, it will be my fault."

"What do you mean?"

"Faulty sperm."

I stop crying and start laughing.

"You're silly. I love you."

He kisses me one more time as the waffle machine dings. "I love you too. Let's eat."

We help ourselves to the food.

I quickly demolish mine and go back for seconds.

"Is it almost as good as Inga's?"

"Yes, it tastes amazing. So, I have a board meeting first thing this morning, then my doctor's appointment, then I'm having lunch with the girls, and then we film late tonight. It's going to be another long day."

"Don't forget, I'm taking your grandparents up to the vineyard after the board meeting. You're still meeting me this weekend, right?"

"As long as we get the scenes done. We're on a tight schedule."

"Are you sure I shouldn't go to the doctor with you?"

"Yeah, they said they'll just double check that I'm pregnant, give me prenatal vitamins, and answer any questions."

"When do we get to see it?"

"The first ultrasound is usually around twelve weeks. That's when we'll hear the heartbeat, hopefully."

"And how far along are you now?"

"I did one of those calculators online. Yesterday would have been six weeks. Speaking of that, when you asked me to marry you, when did you expect to get married?"

He stops his fork mid-stride. "How about we cancel everything and do it today? I can't wait for you to be Mrs. Arrington."

"I'm thinking Keatyn Arrington sounds like a movie star name."

"What are you saying?"

"I'm saying that I'm changing my name as soon as we're married. No maiden name. No hyphen. I can't wait to be your wife. Also, I don't want to get married with a huge baby bump. And I don't want to wait until after we have her to get married."

"Her?"

"Or him."

He places his hand gently on my belly and speaks directly to it. "So, little miss, if Mommy and Daddy get married soon, do you promise to cooperate and not make Mommy faint or throw up?"

He smiles, kisses my stomach, and says, "She says yes. And wants to know how soon we're talking."

"Three weeks. We have a ten day break in the schedule while the crew goes to set up the location. We could get married and even sneak in a honeymoon."

"So we just go away and get married?"

"Does the vineyard count as going away?"

"That's where you want to get married?"

"I can't think of a better place. And I was thinking of asking Ariela if she could coordinate it with the vineyard's event planner."

"Maggie will be thrilled. They were always so close."

"I know. I'm going to call Maggie today and make sure she's cool with it."

"No more surprising like last night?"

"Last night was a bit of a disaster."

"Yeah, no more matchmaking for you."

"Exactly. So, I asked Maggie about the vineyard's schedule yesterday and she said they're booked with weddings and events all of October. So everything we do, or most of it, will have to be at our place."

"That shouldn't be a problem. We have plenty of land. I even had your party barn built this spring."

"And we've yet to throw a party there. I feel bad," I say, covering my mouth to stifle a yawn.

He grabs my hand. "Let's finish this discussion in bed."

"But we need to clean up."

"I'll do it later," he says sweetly, pulling me toward the bedroom.

Once we're snuggled up, he says, "I get the feeling you've already been scripting out this wedding."

"A little. Mostly just trying to figure it out logistically. It's not going to be easy to plan our dream wedding in three weeks. Have you thought about it?"

"Of course, obviously, the dance floor needs to be covered in twinkle lights. And I love the idea of saying our vows in the same spot where you brought the dirt."

"Me too," I say, yawning again.

I lay my head on his shoulder and am almost asleep when Aiden says, "You know Riley and Ariela kissed last night, right?"

My eyes shoot back open. "What? When? Where?"

"When you told her to go talk to him."

"They kissed *then*?"

"Yeah, it was crazy passionate. Her leg was wrapped around him. I thought they were gonna do it up against our bar."

"Then why was he such a dick to her?"

"I think maybe when they kissed, he told her it didn't mean anything. Because they got interrupted by Marvel and when she pulled away, she said she knew it didn't mean anything. He was pretty rattled."

I smile. "He still loves her."

"She still affects him. That's different than love. It's been a long time."

"But he hasn't fallen for anyone else. And god knows it's not from lack of dating."

Aiden chuckles. "No matchmaking. He's our friend. She hasn't been our friend for ten years. And that was *her* choice. I'm not sure asking her to help with the wedding is such a good idea, honestly. We don't know if we can trust her."

"Hmm. You're right. Maybe I'll get a second opinion."

"Inviting her to lunch with Vanessa?"

"Yes."

"Good plan. Vanessa reads bullshit a mile away."

Even though it's six in the morning, I grab my phone and fire off a quick text to Ariela, asking her to meet me for lunch today.

Then I lay my head back on Aiden's shoulder and close my eyes.

CAPTIVE FILMS – SANTA MONICA

Riley

I'M SITTING AT my desk waiting for Keatyn. We always meet an hour before every board meeting. It's our routine. Something that originally helped smooth out our nerves when we started working at the company and helping to guide its future. The company was already successful when she took it over. It had done well buying movie futures and investing in classic film rights. Grandpa Douglas always says *Don't fix what ain't broken*, and we listened. With his guidance and business expertise, we kept the best of the past and followed our own vision to give it a bright future. I'll never forget how much fun we had making our first film. What a summer.

I'm lost in memories—memories of that exciting summer with Ariela, doing what I loved and being with who I loved— when Keatyn steps into my office.

"Hey," she says, a little frown gracing her face.

"Hey," I say back.

"I'm sorry about last night."

"It's okay. Believe it or not, it got worse."

"You look a little hungover. Did you go out?"

"Yeah. Called Knox. Went to a club."

"Where you were surrounded by beautiful women?"

"Until Ariela showed up."

Keatyn's eyes get big with shock. "She showed up at the club? Was she following you?"

"She said it was a complete coincidence. That when she got home her friend wanted to go out. Her friend chose the club. They waited an hour to get in."

"Maybe you should ask her out on a date."

"I have no desire to go on a date with her ever again." I run my hands through my hair, hoping my hangover will go away quickly. I don't know what I was thinking. I never go out the night before a board meeting. I hit a button on my phone and demand, "Tyler, bring us some coffee." Maybe that will help. "Shit, Keats. Why did she have to come back and ruin my life?"

"Speaking of that, I kinda hired someone without telling you."

"What? You hired Ariela? What the fuck? Work is my sacred place. You told me that I couldn't hire the girls I date. That I couldn't mix business with pleasure."

She tilts her head at me, giving me an amused smile. "You just said you have no desire to date her, so if I hired her, it shouldn't be a problem, right?"

Tyler, my assistant, walks through the door with dark roast coffees. Best hangover cure ever. And it smells amazing.

He hands one to Keatyn, comments on how lovely her new Chanel bag is, and then sets mine on the desk in front of me. "Rough night, boss?"

I wave him away and he prances back through the door. Yes, I hired a gay assistant the day I started working here full time.

Although, I originally hired him because I knew I wouldn't have to worry about sleeping with him, I hit the jackpot. He's been my assistant for the last five years. I keep giving him big raises because, quite frankly, I don't know what I'd do without him. He's my right hand man. Incredibly organized, meticulous, never gossips, picks out most of my wardrobe, and works as hard as I do.

"Thanks, Tyler!" I yell.

A few moments after he leaves, Keatyn says, "Oh, shit."

Then she rushes over to my trash can and throws up.

Actually, she doesn't throw up.

She dry heaves into it. Nothing comes out.

She's just gagging.

And it makes me gag.

I grab the trashcan from her and puke into it.

"Oh, god," she says, covering her nose and turning white. She leans over and presses the button on my phone. "Tyler! Get in here!"

Tyler rushes back in, looking confused. Then he covers his nose too.

"Riley threw up. Can you please get this trash can and that coffee out of here? And maybe bring him some crackers and a Sprite instead?"

"I'd recommend a nice reviving green tea smoothie. Shall I go fetch one?"

"No," both Keatyn and I say.

"You do realize you both have to speak at the board meeting in exactly forty-two minutes, right?" Tyler chastises.

"We know," Keatyn says, dry heaving again.

Tyler turns up his nose at us and quickly removes the offending items.

"We'll be in my office," Keatyn tells him, as she grabs my jacket sleeve and pulls me across the hall.

She plops down on the couch and pulls me down with her.

"Whew," she says. "What were we talking about again?"

"Ariela. You hired her?"

"No, I didn't hire her to work here. Although, I invited her to lunch with the girls today. And if she passes Vanessa's bullshit meter, I will probably ask her to help with my wedding."

"Bullshit meter?"

"Aiden isn't convinced we should trust her."

"And what do you think?"

"Honestly, I think she made a big mistake ten years ago and has been paying for it ever since."

"She destroyed me."

"I know. But this could be a good thing, Riley. You never got closure. Maybe, now, you will."

Tyler brings in a tray of assorted crackers then backs out of the room saying, "Excuse me, while I go bathe in hand sanitizer."

"He's funny," Keatyn says with a laugh as she shoves two crackers into her mouth.

"So, are you ready for the board meeting?" I ask, changing the subject. I don't want to talk about Ariela anymore. I can't.

"Of course, I love board days. I get to see my grandpa."

"We've come a long way from the Eastbrooke kids full of dreams. Captive Films has done well. Very well."

"That's because we always choose projects we're passionate about."

"I was looking at the reports before you got here. The board will be quite pleased. *The Keatyn Chronicles*, part three, is doing insanely well." Her ring catches my eye. "It's really cool he got you a sunset for your finger. I always thought I'd get Ariela . . ."

I stop.

Shit.

Why does she keep invading my thoughts?

Why can't I get the fucking kiss or the elevator out of my mind?

Or the way she shoved her hands down my pants like it was

her right.

Or the look on her face when she saw Shelby.

"A big pink diamond," Keatyn says, finishing my sentence and four more crackers.

"Yeah."

"Did you notice she was wearing the Hello Kitty ring you gave her?"

"Yeah, bitch move."

"She told me last night she wore it to give her strength. She came to California for you, Riley."

"I don't want to talk about it. So if not Ariela, who the hell did you hire without asking me?"

"Don't get mad, but . . ." There's a knock on the door. "Grandpa!" she says, jumping off the couch and ending our conversation.

AFTER THE BOARD meeting, Grandpa says to Keatyn, "I better see you this weekend."

"I'll be there," she replies.

"You're going up to the vineyard this weekend?" Dallas asks Keatyn.

"Yeah, hopefully I'll get there Saturday. But I'll be there, for sure, on Sunday. Aiden's flying up today with my grandparents."

"RiAnne's mother is in town to help her shop for the nursery. How would you feel about having me and a mess of kids join you?" Dallas asks Grandpa.

"Sounds like heaven," Grandpa says.

"Sounds like hell," I mutter, even though I love his kids.

Grandpa hears me and slaps me on the back. "Hollywood, you need to start thinking about settling down yourself. Money can't buy you love."

"No, but it can buy you a whole lotta sex. Right, Riley?" Dallas quips.

Grandpa laughs at Dallas' joke, but is serious when he speaks to me. "I hear your old flame is back in town."

"Where'd you hear that?"

Dallas raises his hand. "Guilty."

"Not that it matters but I've moved on."

"You need to kiss her, son."

"Why?"

"Because a kiss will tell you just how moved on you really are."

Keatyn starts to open her mouth, but I glare at her, stopping her from announcing to the world that I already kissed Ariela.

And that we both know I haven't really moved on.

I've never moved on.

RODEO DRIVE - BEVERLY HILLS
Vanessa

"WHAT'S YOUR SCHEDULE like today? Can you meet at Harry Winston's before lunch?" I ask Keatyn, when she answers her cell. "I just got the final check in my divorce settlement. I need to buy myself a reminder of why no one should ever get married."

"Aiden and I got engaged in Paris last week," she says, laughing.

"If you tell me it was at the top of the Eiffel Tower at sunset, I'm going to puke."

"Ha! It was! It was beautiful and perfect. And wait until you see my ring!"

"I can't believe you're just now telling me? And how the hell did the press not get wind of it?"

"We've really only told our families."

"Hmm. Not to talk shop, but we'll make a big announcement of it. Come of think of it, it's a great movie tie in. It will be good for you and Captive Films."

"Oh, I never thought of it that way, but I guess it does sort of show fans our big happy ending, right?"

"Exactly. And I should rephrase my original statement. I'm buying myself something fabulous to remind myself why *I* should never get married again. You should absolutely marry Aiden. How was the board meeting?"

"Short and sweet. Riley and Dallas did their presentations and told them how well we're doing. I gave them an update on new projects. Everyone left happy. I just finished an appointment and was going to kill some time shopping before lunch. So, as usual, you have impeccable timing. I'd love to meet you there."

"See you—Bitch, get out of my way!—oh, sorry, old woman in the road. See you in a few."

HEADS TURN WHEN Keatyn walks into the store.

Which makes me smile.

As the owner of the boutique public relations firm that handles her publicity, I know that it's mostly my doing. Sure, she has talent for days, but I help keep her on the front pages of magazines and in the spotlight. And since I've taken over a teeny chunk of Captive Film's PR, Riley and Keatyn are being touted on the latest Majority magazine, where Riley is looking completely delicious. If it weren't for the fact that I've been trying to get him to outsource their movie publicity for years, I'd have already slept with him.

But in the last two years, I've sworn off men.

A very good looking man, who I know on a very personal level, says, "Vanessa, darling. It's been too long."

I let him air kiss my cheeks but quickly leave to go greet Keatyn.

"I'm not buying anything from him," I tell her. "He was awkward and annoying in bed. He also didn't understand the concept of no strings."

Okay, so I haven't sworn off men completely. I just use them for sex and never allow my heart to get involved.

Keatyn giggles when she looks behind me. "Ohmigawd, is that the guy who fucked like a rabbit?"

"Shush. Yes. When did he start working here?"

"He doesn't work here, silly. He's shopping, see?"

I turn around and see him looking at engagement rings. Poor girl.

Keatyn continues. "So, I called Tristan on the way here. We'll be having a private showing. He's been loaning me jewels since my first walk on the red carpet."

Tristan introduces himself, kisses Keatyn, and whisks us off the showroom floor.

"What do you have in mind, Ms. Flanning?"

"Call me Vanessa, please," I coo, not sure why Keatyn never introduced us before. Probably because I pictured him as a little old French man, not the handsome, sophisticated one kissing my hand.

"Absolutely, *Vanessa*," he says, his French accent making me crave both a glass of Bordeaux and him in my bed.

"We're celebrating her divorce being final," Keatyn tells him. "She needs something obnoxiously large—nothing red, her ex was into red. Red cars, red rubies . . ."

"Don't forget redheads," I add sarcastically.

"I see," Tristan says. "I will be back with some baubles for you to peruse."

The minute he walks out the door, I say, "Why didn't you tell me Tristan is *hot*?"

"You were married, maybe? Then you swore off men. He's cute, right?"

"Yeah, he's cute. And just his accent has my panties wet."

Keatyn laughs out loud. "You crack me up. Are you sure you're doing okay today?"

"I'm fine. Glad it's finally over. I mean, Bam and I haven't been together for almost two years. Who knew a divorce could take so long? All I know is I'm damn glad we were married and lived in California. God bless California's community property laws."

"I have a quick favor to ask you. I invited Ariela to lunch with us. She's in California. Do you remember her from the summer when we filmed *A Day at the Lake 2?*"

"She was Riley's girlfriend, right? They were adorable to-gether. What ever happened to her?"

"Her dad forbade her to follow Riley here for college. Threatened to cut her off. Riley told her that they'd figure something out, even asked her to marry him, but she chose not to go. I don't think he's ever gotten over it."

"Is that why he always dates blonde bimbos?"

"I think so. She's getting a divorce."

"As in she hasn't gotten one yet?"

"She hasn't even filed."

"Sounds like trouble."

"Something else I need to tell you," she says, lowering her voice. "Aiden and I are getting married in three weeks. I was hoping you would stand up with me."

"You want me, your friend who hates the institution of marriage, to stand up for you at your wedding?"

She gives me her blazing smile. The one that sells all those magazines. "Yes."

I hug her, trying not to cry. "I'd be honored."

"I'm also pregnant," she whispers in my ear. "You're the only person who knows, besides Aiden. And, well, Doctor K. That was my appointment today. I don't want the press to know. And I don't want the press to know about the wedding."

Tristan comes back in with velvet trays full of jewelry, before

I can reply. I reach down and give her hand a little squeeze.

"I brought numerous jewels for you to look at, but I have one, which I think will cause you to look no further. It's a statement piece that has a philosophical meaning." He holds out a stunning ring. "The Diamond Lotus Ring. Platinum setting featuring twelve pair-shaped diamonds, two hundred and forty-eight round brilliant diamonds, and weighing 4.62 carats."

"Lotus means rebirth," Keatyn offers.

"Yes, exactly," Tristan confirms.

I hold up my left ring finger, so he can slide it on, but he says, "Oh, no, no. This goes here."

Then he slides it on my middle finger.

"I love it on the middle finger," Keatyn says, laughing. "It's like a big fuck you to marriage."

"Says the girl who is finally engaged, I see," Tristan says. "Aiden and I worked for months on your perfect ring."

"It *is* perfect," she gushes. "He told you about our sunsets?"

"And the green flash."

"Enough about engagements," I interrupt. "We are here celebrating my rebirth. What do you think, Keatyn? Should I keep looking?" I hold my hand out in front of her.

"You tell us," she sasses back. "You were always the girl who knew exactly what she wanted."

Tears start to fill my eyes as I look sincerely into hers. "I lost that girl for a while, didn't I?"

"Yeah. You've had a rough couple of years, but now you are back. Your business is prospering. You look fantastic." She squeezes my hand back and says sincerely, "And you have good friends who love you."

"You were the only client who didn't leave me when I was going through everything. I never thanked you."

"That's because you didn't need to thank me. We're friends. It's what friends do. So what do you think?"

I turn to Tristan, feeling stronger than I have in, well, a

while. "I'll take it."

As we're leaving, Keatyn wraps her arm in the crook of my elbow. "That felt good, didn't it?"

"Yeah," I say, holding up the ring so we can admire it some more. "I can't believe it didn't even need to be sized."

"It was made for you."

"You started to tell me about Ariela."

"Oh, yeah. She's an event planner and has a blog of her weddings. They're beautiful."

"And you're thinking of having her do yours? Seriously, Keatyn, how are you going to pull off a wedding in three weeks? Is it going to be small?"

She bends her head down and looks over her sunglasses at me.

I laugh. "Sorry. Of course, *you* are not going to do anything small. Let me rephrase my question. How are you going to pull off a big wedding in three weeks?"

"We're going to have it at our house at the vineyard. Probably do the reception in the new barn. That solves the location aspect. I've got to talk to Kym about a dress."

"Did you get engaged because you're pregnant?"

"No, he didn't know. I did the pregnancy test the morning he proposed. Crazy timing. But I want to be married before the baby is born and I don't want to look pregnant in the pictures."

"Understandable."

"Oh, and don't yell at me, but I'm changing my name to Keatyn Arrington."

"Well, of course, legally."

"No, for movies too."

"Keatyn, I know you love Aiden, but don't give up your name. Not professionally. What if it doesn't work out? I know right now it's all rainbows and roses, but it might not always be that way. Trust me, I know."

"Vanessa, did you think Bam was your true love?"

"I loved him. He was charming and . . ."

"That's not what I asked. We can fall in love with different people throughout our lives but, sometimes, you find *the one*. That special one. The big deal. The dream."

"The moon wish?" I say teasingly.

"Exactly."

"It's easy to say now that he wasn't but my dad had reservations about him. His family wasn't exactly loving toward me. Maybe I was just too young to see past the way he impressed me with his lifestyle. Maybe it was my fault too. Maybe I loved the lifestyle more than I did him."

"Or maybe you had to go through it all to find the person you're really supposed to be with. Maybe he's not rich and famous and you needed the lesson?"

"I know you're talking from experience on all that. I know that's how you feel about the whole stalker thing. That he pushed you to learn important lessons about life, love, and family."

"It certainly made me realize what's important. It made me grow up. And that includes listening to Aiden even when I don't agree with him."

"You don't agree on something?"

"Yes, he's worried about Ariela being back in our life. Says we don't know her and I shouldn't be so quick to trust her. What if I ask her to plan my wedding and she tells everyone when it is? We figured we'd tell everyone, like the vendors, that it's a fundraiser for Moon Wish . . ."

"If the press finds out, it will be a nightmare with helicopters flying overhead and all that."

"Exactly what I don't want."

"Let's put out a statement about your engagement. Then I'll spread word that you're thinking of a spring wedding in Paris."

"That sounds good. And you'll give me your opinion on Ariela after lunch?"

"Absolutely."

KEATYN AND I are the first to arrive at the restaurant. We're in the process of being seated when RiAnne waddles her way through the tables, looking like if she coughed too hard she would burst. Ariela and Peyton follow closely behind her.

Ariela looks exactly the way I remember her. Tall, pretty, great eyes, and a sincere smile. She walks right up to me and gives me a hug like I'm her long lost best friend. "Vanessa! It's so good to see you. You look amazing!"

"Thank you. I understand you're getting a divorce?" I say, cutting to the chase as we sit down. I think we need to find out what this girl is up to.

The waiter takes our drink orders and as soon as he's stepped away from the table, she replies, "Have you ever had one of those moments where you knew you had to change your life?"

I nod, because I know exactly what she means, but the rest of the girls are squinting their eyes.

"I'm sure you all want to know why I'm here. I'd want to know too. I thought it was dumb luck I ran into Keatyn at the store the other day, but it feels more like it's exactly what was supposed to happen. I came here to see Riley. I made a mistake. I shouldn't have listened to my dad. I shouldn't have gotten married. I knew it even before I found out he was cheating."

"I'm sorry you got cheated on," I say to her. "I know how that feels. What triggered your decision? When you found out about his cheating?"

"No, I had known that for a while. Two things made me snap, I guess you could say."

"What?" Peyton asks, as Keatyn pats her growing baby bump.

"I told my mom he was having an affair and she told me that successful men often have liaisons, but they can still be wonderful, loving husbands and good fathers."

"Bullshit," RiAnne coughs.

Peyton, RiAnne, and Keatyn, who have relationships to envy, laugh.

I don't.

I understand. Bam's mother said something similar to me when I told her why we were getting a divorce.

"Then, I went to a coffee shop and saw Riley—and you, Keatyn—on the cover of a magazine. I cancelled my appointments for the afternoon and went and saw the trilogy. I hadn't seen any of the movies until then."

"*The Keatyn Chronicles?*" Keatyn asks. I watch as a lot of expressions cross her face, ending teary-eyed. "So, you saw how much he loved you? How crazy he was for you? How he was afraid to even text you?"

"Did you really do it for him? Like in the movie?"

Keatyn nods. "I did. I was shocked he included the picture of you from the wrap party."

"That's what really did it. After the movie, I went home, packed a bag, and the shoebox full of memories I had hidden in the back of my closet, and hopped on a plane. I'm crashing on my friend's couch. She's married and has three young children. It's a little chaotic. Hopefully, I'll find a job out here soon. And somewhere to live."

"You can live with me," I say, surprising myself. "I have a guest house and a hot cabana boy. He's gay, but you'd never know from looking at him. He's great for your ego and he's training to be a masseuse."

"Are you sure?" both RiAnne and Ariela ask me.

"Yes, I'm sure. I have more space than I know what to do with." I decide to change the subject. "So, Peyton, how is our favorite rock star doing?"

"Damian's good. He's on tour. We decided it was just too much to try and take the kids this time. Jagger just started kindergarten and Jett's loving preschool. You know Damian was tutored most of his life. He wants our kids to have a more traditional upbringing."

"As traditional as you can get when your dad is Damian Moran," I say.

The waiter interrupts us, takes our orders, and refills our water.

"Yeah, well the kids don't really have a sense of that. They just know Daddy is on a work trip. And this tour is only four weeks. He wants to be home before the baby comes."

"Have you agreed on a name yet? Dallas and I are still fighting over this one," RiAnne says, patting the top of her belly. "We decided five was enough. I'm going to have my tubes tied."

"I'm pretty sure we decided on Cash," Peyton says.

"That's really cute. They all have little rocker names," Ariela says. "Peyton, do you work outside the home?"

"I have my own business. I design wallpaper and have a successful decorating blog. And I've always done interiors for my friends."

"Our Malibu beach house wouldn't look nearly as beautiful as it does if it weren't for Peyton," Keatyn says, smiling.

"And I have a lot of her wallpaper in my house," I tell Ariela. "The main bedroom in the guest house has a feature wall done in one of her gorgeous metallics."

"The guest house has more than one bedroom?" Ariela asks me.

"Vanessa married really, really well," RiAnne tells Ariela then she turns to me. "Speaking of that, was today the day?"

"Yes. After a long two years, my divorce is final. I'm a very free and very rich woman. And, certainly, my law degree came in handy."

"It's come in handy for me, as well, when you have to threaten to sue the tabloids," Keatyn says, looking tired all of a sudden.

I smile at her, happy she's finally going to have a baby with

Aiden. And get married. As most of her friends would say, it's about time for both. I also can't help but feel a little smug that she's told only me she's pregnant. That she trusts me.

And after what I've been through, she has no idea how much that means to me.

WHEN OUR FOOD is served, Keatyn raises her glass of water in the air. "I think we should have a toast. To new beginnings, fresh starts, and rings from Harry Winston."

"Rings from Harry Winston?" RiAnne asks, her eyes big.

"How can you not notice that new mass of diamonds on her hand?" Keatyn laughs, pointing at my purchase.

"That's *real*? I thought it was costume jewelry."

"Nope, I decided to commemorate today with a gift for myself. Keatyn helped me pick it out."

"Vanessa just sat there and drooled," Keatyn says.

"Over Tristan or the diamonds?" Peyton asks.

"The diamonds, but Tristan is a cutie. I can't believe you all knew how hot he was and never introduced me."

My phone buzzes with a text from an unknown number.

If you are ready for a new beginning, I'd love to take you to dinner – Tristan

I laugh. "He just texted and asked me to dinner!"

"You should go. Maybe he gets a discount," RiAnne laughs. "Dallas would probably appreciate that. He usually buys me a piece of jewelry after every baby."

"That's so romantic," Peyton says. "Speaking of romantic, Keatyn, tell us what Aiden said at the top of the freaking Eiffel Tower."

"It's all kind of a blur," Keatyn says, but I know her. I know she memorized everything Aiden said to her and wrote it down. "Just about how he promised me a life better than anything I ever scripted. It was romantic. Sweet. Everything that boy does makes me swoon. I'm really lucky."

"Speaking of that, I think you should enlist Ariela to help with your wedding." I say it out loud, knowing Keatyn's been waiting for my assessment of her. "Have you ever had to plan a wedding really fast?" I ask Ariela.

"Are you getting married really fast?" Ariela asks Keatyn.

Keatyn keeps her voice low and says, "I'd love to talk to you about it. We've been thinking about a spring wedding in France."

"Oh, that's not that fast."

"Why don't you come up to the vineyard this weekend? We can discuss it."

"Will Riley be there?"

"No, just Dallas and the kids, my grandparents, me and Aiden. Oh, and if you want, you could maybe see Maggie and Logan. Logan runs the day-to-day operations of Asher Vineyards and Maggie handles all the events there."

"That sounds fun. I'd love to. And I'd love to see them. I feel bad. Maggie was one of my best friends."

"So when do you want to move in?" I ask Ariela. We don't need to rehash old news.

"As soon as possible?" she asks.

"Perfect. Lunch is on me today, ladies. Ariela, would you have time now to go see your new digs?"

"That sounds amazing. Thank you. I'll go get my things and meet you there."

While she stops at the ladies room, I give everyone a hug goodbye, giving Keatyn a longer one.

"I think what you're doing for her is really nice," she says.

"I can relate to what she's going through. Who knows, maybe we'll even become friends."

"Still, it's really nice." She looks at her watch. "Shit, I've got to go. Three o'clock call time."

"Take care of yourself," I tell her.

VANESSA'S ESTATE – HOLMBY HILLS

Ariela

THE GPS SYSTEM in my car takes me to a gated palatial home. I press the call button, praying I'm at the right house and that someone doesn't see my rented Chevy and call the cops.

No one says anything through the intercom but the gates grind open, so I pull through.

My parents are well off. Riley's family and most of the friends I had at Eastbrooke came from affluent families. But I've never seen a home quite like this. It looks like something a Spanish prince would own. Terra cotta stucco sits under a tile roof. Paned arched windows set in dark mahogany open to iron Juliet balconies. There is a massive hand carved wooden door at least twice my height at the entrance.

The door opens and Vanessa says, "I'll have Chad grab your bags."

"Um, this is all I have," I say, holding up my suitcase and carry-on.

"I thought you said you moved here."

"Not completely."

Chad takes my bags as Vanessa leads me into a large living space featuring wood beamed trusses and a stone fireplace the size of a garage.

"I'm a little awestruck by this house," I say, hoping I don't sound stupid.

"It is pretty amazing. My ex, Bam, was a professional polo player from Argentina. His family holdings are vast but are mostly in oil, refineries, diamond mines, and yacht manufacturing. We were secretly married when I was nineteen. We were officially engaged after I finished law school. This house was my

91

engagement gift. Seven bedroom suites, ten bathrooms, separate catering kitchen, large screening room, incredible gym and massage room, walk-in wine cellar, and art gallery. It sits on ten acres, which feature a three-bedroom guest suite, championship tennis court, pool with grotto, and an equestrian center."

"It's amazing."

"Let's go outside and have a drink by the pool."

Once we're seated by the pool, she says, "Tell me how you moved here with just one bag."

I let out a big sigh. "When I came here, I did it on a whim. I packed quickly before I lost my nerve. My goal was to see Riley again. I wanted to tell him I was sorry and that I made a mistake. I saw in the magazine article that he was still single. So I packed up and here I am."

"Interesting."

"But then I got here and decided that I shouldn't see him until I got my life together. I wanted to find a job and a place to live first. I made the decision to stay in California before I ran into Keatyn. I realized that it wasn't just about him. It's what I wanted. I can't say it will be easy though. That's part of why I wanted to get settled before I looked him up. My family will be mad when they learn I want a divorce. They love Collin."

"It doesn't matter if your family loves him. The important question is, do you? You need to know the answer to that before you drag Riley into your mess. Haven't you put him through enough?"

I lower my head. "Yeah, I have. I don't want to hurt Riley. I never wanted to hurt him."

"I'm not saying you shouldn't go through with it. I'm just saying do what you want, not what you think he'd want."

"I don't love Collin," I mutter. "My dad talked me into marrying him. He's the son of family friends. We went to the same college and I tried to love him. I really did. We dated, he was cute, my parents approved. Getting engaged and married was expected. I told my dad on my wedding day that I didn't think I could go through with it. I knew I shouldn't, but he told me cold feet were normal, that he was the man for me, and drug me down the aisle." I keep rambling. Other than the kid from the coffee shop, I've haven't told anyone how I've been feeling. "Status and conspicuous consumption turn him on. He wants me to quit my job and have kids because it makes him look stable and successful—not because he really wants them. Who knows, maybe I had some kind of breakdown."

"Or maybe you'd just had enough. Hit your breaking point," Vanessa offers. "What did you tell him?"

"Originally, I just left a note that said I came here because a friend needed me. But when I spoke to him the other day, I told him I wanted a divorce."

"How did he take it?"

"He started begging. Told me he'd give up the secretary. That she was a mistake. That I was the only girl he ever loved. Whatever. I have a call with Annie Johnson tomorrow. Hopefully, the fact that's she's Riley's sister-in-law won't keep her from helping me."

"I can help you find a good attorney, if need be." She looks at her watch.

"So, I have a party to attend tonight. Why don't I show you where you'll be staying and then you can freshen up. We'll leave at seven-thirty."

"You want me to come with you?"

"Yes. It will be a little boring, but it's always fun to get dressed up."

"I didn't bring anything formal."

She studies me. "I'll have Chad bring you a selection of dresses to try on."

"Thank you," I say.

As she drops me off at the guest house, she says, "One thing I wanted to tell you. You better not jerk my friends around.

They graciously, and maybe a little too quickly, accepted you back into their lives. You owe them some respect."

"I know. And I'm very grateful to you for letting me stay here."

She smiles at me. "We have a lot in common. But we'll save that conversation for another day."

HOTEL BALLROOM – BEVERLY HILLS

SOMETIMES HOLLYWOOD PARTIES get old with the same boring food and same boring people. But it's been more fun since Knox broke up with his girlfriend. I have someone I can party with and who can actually pay his own way. He can get into places even I can't just because of his famous face.

Just to be clear, I'm talking about establishments and VIP areas that money can't buy. Not girls' panties; I have him beat in that department. Girls want him but only the bold will approach him.

He sets two drinks in front of us. "Did you see that chick in the yellow dress? I can honestly say I've never seen boobs that big up close. And they look real. Did you see them? Did they look real to you?"

"Harder to tell nowadays. But, yes, they sag a little in a way that fake ones don't. I think she's blessed."

"I want to bless her with my dick."

"Keatyn said she had to work late tonight. Why aren't you?"

"We've been doing some green screen stuff. Tonight they are working on shots where she's alone. But starting tomorrow, we'll be doing sex scenes. Tough job lying in bed all day kissing

Keatyn Douglas." He laughs. "I remember the first time we did a sex scene. I told her in advance that I was sorry if I got hard and I was also sorry if I didn't."

"Ha. I suppose it's a double-edged sword. Damned if you do and damned if you don't."

"Exactly. If you don't get hard, they get pissed and think you're not attracted to them. If you do get hard, they get pissed because you are. And depending on what's going on off camera with the actress you are with, that can get a little dicey. Part of why I need to get laid tonight. Don't want to go there all horny. Sex scenes are tough."

"Yeah, yeah, you all say that. But you're the one rolling around almost naked with a hot chick."

"The worst thing ever is to have to do a sex scene with someone you're not attracted to. It's grueling."

"But with Keatyn?"

He smiles. "I've never minded it. And after all these years, it's natural between us. Easy, I guess. And when I'm basically naked in front of the crew, even though it's always a closed set, I usually don't get hard. But when we're clothed, sometimes I do. Obviously, I would not be a good fit for the porn industry. Aiden has been there for some of them. That's awkward."

"I'm sure. I remember when we shot the love scenes with her and Jake. I made him leave. Jake kept sneaking peeks in Aiden's direction. It threw the whole thing off. As the director, you'd think it would be hot. But most the time the actresses' contract is running through your head, like we can show breast but no nipple or side of the buttock only. So you're trying to do the shots in ways where you're not wasting camera time."

"In one of the scenes we're filming tomorrow, Keatyn's character attacks me in the shower. We will have strategically placed soap, cock socks and pasties, and nude colored underwear. All that fun stuff. I'll be told how to hold her, where to move my face."

"It is all camera angles and body positioning."

"And damn good acting," he adds, as he raises his glass up to toast the girl in the yellow dress. She smiles back at him.

If you ask me, she looks like a really big bird. Her hair is even short in that style where it stands up in the back. Um, no, thank you.

He clinks my glass. "I'm gonna go make my move."

"Have fun," I say, looking around to see who else I should talk to tonight.

I'M MAKING MY way back to the bar, chatting with an older woman about Captive Films' movie futures program, when I see her.

"What the fuck is she doing here?"

"Who, darling?" the woman asks, causing me to realize I just spoke out loud.

"I'm sorry for cursing, Mrs. Taylor. Someone I know just walked in."

"Old flame?" she asks, turning toward Ariela. "Is it that woman in the lavender dress? She's very striking. You would make a handsome couple."

"Excuse me, please," I say to Mrs. Taylor. I walk straight up to Ariela and grab her arm. "What are you doing here? How did you get in?"

"She was invited," Vanessa says from behind me. "And we have dates so, excuse us."

Vanessa hooks arms with Ariela and leads her over to two men in suits. Handsome men, I might add.

Oh, this is bad.

Vanessa is a man eater.

At least she has been since she broke up with Bam.

And why the hell is Ariela with her? My mind is racing trying to figure out how they even know each other.

Keatyn.

Knowing she's on set tonight, I decide to call Aiden.

"Dude, Keatyn is trying to ruin my life."

"How so?" he asks me.

"Did she introduce Vanessa and Ariela?"

"Oh, yeah, today at lunch. That was my idea."

"Your idea? What the fuck? We want Ariela to go the fuck back home, not make new friends."

"You may want Ariela to go back home, but Keatyn wants her to plan our wedding."

"When is it?"

"Don't tell anyone, obviously, but it's in three weeks."

"Three weeks and then she's gone?"

"Uh, maybe."

"Fine, I can handle three weeks. But I swear to God, if that guy doesn't get his hand off her ass . . ."

"Riley, where are you and what are you talking about?"

"Industry gala. Ariela is here with Vanessa and they have dates."

"Oh, boy." I hear Aiden talking to someone in the background.

"Who are you talking to?"

"I'm sitting on the front porch with Logan and Grandpa Douglas. Logan thinks you should steal Ariela away from her date. Grandpa thinks you should kiss her. I think you should get the hell out of there."

"I like your advice the best. I'm out."

I end the call and look around the room. It's times like these, I wish I were a smoker.

Maybe I just need some fresh air.

I walk past Ariela and step outside onto the balcony. The view is gorgeous. The lights of L.A. spread out before me. I stare at them until they blur.

Ariela and I are lying on a blanket in the center of the lacrosse field one gorgeous fall night of our senior year. We're holding hands and looking at the stars.

We couldn't see the stars like this when we were in L.A. this summer, I say.

There are stars everywhere there—Movie stars. And, at night, the city lights are so beautiful. I really loved it there, Riley. It surprised me.

Why did it surprise you?

Because I'm an East Coast girl. I've lived here my whole life. California is so different. It's so shiny and clean. I love the palm trees, the beach, and the weather. There's something special about it.

I'm going there for college. I want you to come with me.

She rolls toward me and smiles. I'd go anywhere with you, Riley.

I become aware of someone standing next to me.

Female.

Silk dress.

Smells like lilac and a summer breeze.

Bitch.

"Riley, can I talk to you for a minute?"

I turn to look at her. God, she's beautiful.

"Sixty seconds, no more," I reply harshly. Why do I turn into a complete dick every time she's around?

"I'm sorry. I'm sorry I listened to my dad. I'm sorry I left after graduation and never spoke to you again."

"Okay," I say. What the hell else do you say to someone when they try to use stupid words like *I'm sorry* that could never begin to make up for the hurt they caused?

"That's it? *Okay?*" she asks.

"It's my understanding that Keatyn wants you to help with her wedding. Because Keatyn and Aiden are my friends, I'm going to be cordial to you until then. But I want your promise that once the wedding is over, you will go back to where you came from. Get the hell out of our lives." I'm starting to get pissed. "What are you even doing here if you're married?"

"I'm not sure, Riley. You always seemed to know exactly what you wanted to do. Who you wanted to be. Are you the person you hoped you'd become?"

"You read the article. You know how successful I am. I'm living *our* dream. Without you."

"That's why I'm here, Riley. My life isn't a dream."

"Serves you right," I say with a huff and walk away.

I'M HEADED TOWARD the door when Jennifer Edwards, one of Hollywood's hottest young stars, grabs my arm.

"Riley Johnson," she says with an exuberant smile. She's barely twenty-two, blonde, down to earth, a little awkward, and has a reputation for photobombing on the red carpet. "Just the man I wanted to talk to."

"Oh, why's that?"

"I heard through the grapevine that you're getting ready to cast a project I'd like in on."

"Which one?"

"*Daddy's Angel*," she whispers.

"But it's a television series. You're a movie star."

"I know, but it sounds fun." She takes my hand and leads me to the bar. "Buy me a drink."

"Drinks are free."

"Okay, then, take me back to your place and make me a drink. We should discuss this in private." She looks at me and starts laughing loudly.

"What?"

She slaps my arm. "Ohmigawd, it totally just sounded like I was trying to pick you up!"

"Are you?" I flirt.

She rolls her eyes at herself. "I'm an idiot. I want to talk to you about the role. There are a lot of ears here, if you know what

I mean."

I look over at Ariela, who's looking straight at me, and can't help but grin.

See, Ariela? I love my life.

I place my hand on the small of Jennifer's back, lean toward her, and whisper, "I'm starving. Let's drive through In-N-Out Burger, take it back to my place, and eat it in the hot tub."

She flirts back. "Do you have tequila?"

"Tequila, huh? I like you already." And I seriously do. She's adorable, bold, and funny.

She gives me a kiss on the cheek. "Burgers. Tequila. Hot tubbing. Better watch out or I just might fall in love with you."

"That, would be an honor. Let's get the hell out of here."

Jennifer, being the goofball that she is, turns back around and yells to the crowd. "I'm leaving with this hottie! Good night, everyone. And, if you are a member of the press, I'm spending the night with him. No need to follow us covertly."

I'm laughing out loud as I lead her to my car.

"Ohmigawd!" she screams loudly. This girl is loud. I can't wait to hear what she sounds like in bed. "You have a Bentley Continental GT3-R. Do you know how rare those are?"

"Yeah, I do."

"How did you get one?"

"Tommy Stevens helped me."

"Keatyn's step dad, of course. You're lucky."

"How do you even know about a car like this?"

"I made a lot of money doing the Sector movies. Just for fun, my friends and I started making a list of the most ridiculously expensive cars. I didn't really want to buy an exotic car until I saw this one. Now, I'm obsessed. I've seen this around town. I didn't know it was yours."

I open the passenger door, letting her in. "Maybe if you're good, I'll let you drive her."

"No way!" she says, her eyes big. Then she narrows them at me. "Wait. What do I have to do?"

"Oh, I'm sure I'll think of something."

WEDNESDAY, OCTOBER 1ST
CAPTIVE FILMS - SANTA MONICA

"SOMEONE GOT LAID last night," Tyler sings, the second I come in the office smiling.

Keatyn looks up from her paperwork and yells out of her office, "Tell me it wasn't Shelby."

"It wasn't Shelby," I yell back. I go plop down on her pale grey suede sofa, pushing a pink pillow out of my way.

"Why do you always throw my pillows on the floor?"

"You sound like an old married couple," Tyler says, dropping off my usual coffee and making a quick exit.

"I have news," I say, trying to contain my grin.

"What kind of news?"

"Your little project, *Daddy's Angel*, if you could choose any actress to play the role, who would you choose?"

"Well, that's easy, Jennifer Edwards, but she's done so many movies, I doubt she would consider television."

"What if it wasn't television?"

"What do you mean?"

"I was thinking. What if it was a movie serial?"

"What's that?"

"Back in the day, movies were cheap. People went every weekend to see the newest black and white films. What if we tried something radical? Big screen weekly showings."

"Like a television mini-series, only at the movies?"

"Yeah, we could roll it over later to pay-per-view, and then maybe get a cable network to pick it up. We'd make money at each stop." I grin at her, letting it sink in.

"It's innovative. I like it. And the script, you know I love it. But to be at the movies, we couldn't use an unknown. We'd need a big star like Jennifer."

"Hey, guys," Knox says, interrupting our meeting. He drops a newspaper on Keatyn's desk and another in my lap.

I read the headline.

Jennifer Edwards' new plaything, Captive Films CEO Riley Johnson

"You dog, you," Knox says, throwing another pillow on the floor before sitting down next to me. "Jennifer Edwards. You're fucking Jennifer Edwards? Tell me about it. She's freaking hilarious. She's got to be crazy fun in bed."

Keatyn covers her face with her hand. "Tell me you didn't sleep with her."

"What's with that rule, anyway?" Knox asks. "Riley can sleep with whoever he wants. Wait? Does that mean you're going to do a movie with her? I want in on it."

"You what?" Keatyn and I say at that same time.

"She's box office gold, just like our friend here," he says, pointing toward Keatyn. "Whatever you're doing with her, I want in. I'll clear my schedule. After *Trinity*, of course."

I take the lid off my coffee to cool it down.

"Oh, Riley," Keatyn says, covering her mouth. "You've got to get that coffee out of here. The smell. It's making me sick."

She starts doing that dry heaving thing again.

"What's with you lately?"

"I think I just have a touch of the flu," she says.

"Great," Knox says, "I have to kiss you all day on set. I suppose I'll get sick too."

"Riley, please?" she begs.

"Oh, sorry. *Tyler!*"

Tyler rushes in. "What?!"

"Take this coffee out of here. It's making Keatyn sick."

"Well, I never!" Tyler grabs the coffee out of my hand and marches out, slamming the door behind him.

Knox laughs. "Never a dull moment around here. Back to the matter at hand. Jennifer Edwards."

"I have to think for a minute," Keatyn says, wrapping her nose in her sleeve then talking through it. "Knox, you're too old to play the boyfriend."

"Not necessarily," I say, disagreeing. "You just have it in your head that Daddy chooses someone young. Why couldn't he choose someone older?"

"Hmm, maybe. Do you really think that she would do it? And, Riley, *did* you sleep with her?"

"Yes, she approached me about it specifically. She's looking for a fun project. Something outside the box."

"Are you gonna be the something *inside* her box?" Knox asks under his breath.

"I didn't sleep with her, okay?" I finally admit. "She spent the night. We had a lot of fun. I like her."

Keatyn goes, "You like her, like her?"

"What are we? In seventh grade?" Knox laughs. "Riley, did you hold her hand? Feel her up?"

"Shut up," I say with a goofy grin on my face. "She makes me feel like I'm back in college. It's fun."

Keatyn squints her eyes at me and I know that means she's running all the scenarios through her head and about to make a decision. "Riley, if you can get her and Knox to both do this project, you can sleep with whoever you want. As long as it doesn't affect her relationship with Captive."

"If you haven't slept with her yet, that makes her fair game, right?" Knox asks.

"This isn't a competition. If you want to get in her pants, go for it. Our relationship is . . ."

"Is what?" Keatyn asks.

"Real."

"You have a relationship?"

"I didn't ask her to go steady, yet," I tease, "but I'm taking off early today and we're hanging out."

"Who are you going steady with?" my older brother, Dawson, asks from the doorway.

"Dawson? What the hell are you doing here?" I get up and give him a hug. I haven't seen him since this summer. And he was still a wreck over losing Whitney. Today, he's smiling and looks put together.

"That's what I was supposed to tell you the other day!" Keatyn says, rushing over to give Dawson a hug. "How are you?" she asks him.

"About to be better, I hope," he replies. "I think you're right. A new beginning is probably just the thing I need."

"New beginning?" I ask.

"I hired Dawson," Keatyn says. "He's going to commute for a while, see how things go. Then if all goes well, he'll relocate here permanently."

What Keatyn did hits me in the chest, almost bringing tears to my eyes. My brother has been through so much.

I slap my brother on the back. "I'm glad you're joining the team, bro. So what are you gonna do?"

Keatyn answers before he can. "I figured all his experience working with luxury brands would allow him to get great placement for our movies." She's biting her lip. And I know why. We have a marketing group that does placement for us. "He'll be our new, uh, Senior Vice President in charge of product placement."

Senior Vice President, a role just for him. She probably overpaid him too.

But I don't mind.

"Knox, this is my brother, Dawson. I think you've met before over the years."

"Yeah, we have," they say, shaking hands and sharing pleasantries before Knox says, "I've got to get going. Same time tomorrow morning. Bring the girl."

"Will do."

I sit down. Still a little shocked that my brother is here and going to work for me.

"Tyler!" Keatyn yells. She never calls him on the intercom, she just sweetly yells his name and he drops whatever he's doing and comes.

"You called?"

"Will you take Dawson on the grand tour of the offices?"

Tyler herds Dawson out of the room. I shut the door.

"Before you say anything . . ." she starts to say.

"I'm not going to say anything but thank you," I tell her.

"Really? I'm so relieved. I wasn't sure how you'd feel about it."

"I offered him a job a long time ago and he turned me down. Of course, that was before. . ."

"I know. It's so sad. It's been almost two years and he's still carrying the guilt around. I thought maybe coming here might help. I way overpaid him."

"I wouldn't have expected anything less. I'm touched, Keatyn. Really touched."

She gives me a beaming smile and then a hug. "Good. In case I haven't told you lately, I love that we work together."

"I love that we work together too."

When she pulls away, she's in tears.

"What's wrong?"

"I thought you were going to be mad at me. Aiden told me I needed to tell you. I went behind your back, and I feel bad. I don't want you to be mad at me."

I pat her back. "Why are you crying? Normally, when you want your way, you just tell me how it is. Or you pout until I cave."

"I don't know. I'm just really emotional right now."

"'Bout to get your period, I suppose. You want some chocolate?"

She brightens up. "Chocolate sounds yummy. Also, we had his office nicely decorated. It was expensive. And we're leasing him a house on the beach. And got him a really nice car."

"Wow. Rolling out the red carpet?"

"He only agreed to give us until after the holidays to see if this would work. I want it to."

"And he *needs* it to."

"Yeah, he does. Oh, there's Vanessa. I have a meeting with her before my call time."

I look at my watch. "And I have a meeting in five minutes."

When I get in my office, I take a moment to read the article.

Jennifer Edwards' new plaything, Captive Films CEO Riley Johnson

Jennifer Edwards is on the prowl again.

And this time the man in her sights is none other than Riley Johnson, CEO of Captive Films.

Unless you've been out of the loop, you know who Riley is. (If not, please see this month's Majority Magazine. And study it, we'll wait. P.S: Page 87. Abs. Scruff. Sunglasses. Swoon.)

You gotta give the girl credit, even though she's leaving a lot of broken hearts in her wake, (we're talking to you, Parker Hudson) she's got good taste.

According to our sources, the couple met last night at the Minds at Play event. She walked up to the CEO, intro-

duced herself, and whispered something in his ear. Moments later, she surprised the press by loudly announcing that she would be spending the night with Mr. Johnson and they didn't need to follow her.

But, follow they did.

As evidenced by these photos of the couple driving through In-N-Out Burger. And later, being whisked up to his penthouse at the swanky WestBeverly residences.

Sources close to Miss Edwards say she's looking for a new role.

Looks like that role will be Riley's new girlfriend!

P.S. Ladies, we should all try the Jennifer Edwards' method of picking up a man. I'm totally walking up to the next hot guy I see, introducing myself, and whispering in his ear. (Will report results later.)

P.P.S. Knox Daniels was also at the event sans Keatyn Douglas, although rumor has it they have been filming what sources say are THE HOTTEST Trinity sex scenes to date. (Can't wait to see the movie!)

I set the paper down, pick up my phone, and call her.

"Hey," I say. "Keatyn loved our ideas. I think that calls for a celebration."

"I like to celebrate. And I know just the way. Come to Malibu. I'm renting a cute little place on the beach."

"I have a couple meetings . . ."

"Cancel them."

"Uh . . ."

"When's the last time you just said fuck it and had some fun, Riley? Wait, don't answer that. I've heard about your reputation. And we're famous. Page six."

"I don't think I've ever been referred to as a plaything before, but I like it."

"Then cancel your meetings and come play with me."

All of our conversations have been fun and upbeat, but when she says *come play with me*, there's a sensuality to her voice. One that arouses me.

"I'll be there this afternoon."

"Perfect," she says happily.

CAPTIVE FILMS - SANTA MONICA
Vanessa

KEATYN GREETS ME with a kiss and says, "I don't have a ton of time, I'm sorry. My call time just got pushed up for today."

"That's okay. I'll read you the press release. *Keatyn Douglas and her longtime beau Aiden Arrington, owner of Asher Vineyards and Winery, the brand best known for their charitable Moon Wish wine, were engaged in Paris after the worldwide premiere of the hit trilogy,* The Keatyn Chronicles, *based on their life.*

"It's pretty simple and to the point," she says. "I do like that you threw in the part about Moon Wish. A little extra publicity is a good thing."

"Do you want me to add more details about your engagement? Usually, you're pretty private when it comes to your personal life."

"I know. I want to leave it the way your have it, but I'm so excited I'd like to shout it from the rooftops. It was so romantic and so perfect."

"Everything Aiden does is romantic, isn't it?"

She beams. "Yeah, pretty much. I'm really lucky."

"Are you feeling okay?"

"Mostly, although the smell of that strong roasted coffee Riley drinks every morning makes me want to throw up."

"Morning sickness?"

"More like morning gagging. I haven't gotten sick yet. Did you see the article about Riley and Jennifer Edwards this morning?"

"I did. I wanted to talk to you about that. Ariela and I were at the party last night. We had dates."

"And Riley saw?"

"Yeah, he told her she could help plan your wedding and that when it was over he wanted her out of your lives."

"That's harsh. But you know how guys are. They don't really like to deal with their feelings."

"That's for sure."

"But, Riley's man whore ways may have just paid off."

"How so?"

"The reason he and Jennifer left is because she wants the lead in *Daddy's Angel.*"

"Are you shitting me? That would be amazing!"

"I know, right? She was who I thought of when I was writing the script."

"That's so cool."

"I have some other news. We hired a new Senior Vice President. The two of you will be working closely together. I got Riley to okay your firm doing the publicity for *Daddy's Angel.* You have done well with Riley's PR. This is the next step. If this is a hit, you'll get all you can handle."

"Really? That's amazing. Who is the new VP?"

"He's right here," Tyler says from behind me. I stand up and turn around. "Vanessa Flanning meet—"

"Dawson Johnson," I say, finishing his sentence.

"You two know each other? Perfect. I can stop playing tour guide and get my work done. Dawson, I'm leaving you in Vanessa's capable hands."

I stare into the eyes of the boy I met at Keatyn's eighteenth birthday party. His dark brown eyes lock with mine, reaching inside my soul and grabbing something deep inside me and pulling it to the surface.

I have two simultaneous desires. I want to both comfort him and screw his brains out. And I have no idea why.

The comforting part, I mean.

It's obvious why I would want to screw this man.

Dawson leans in and gives me a sweet kiss on the cheek. "The Alpha of all Alphas. How are you? You look amazing."

Amazing doesn't begin to describe how scrumptious Dawson looks. He's matured, obviously, in all the right places. His shoulders are broader. His neck is thicker. I can't see what's under his perfectly tailored navy pinstripe suit, but based on the way his jacket tapers in at the waist, I'm guessing it's good. His dark, thick hair is cut short and he's a walking advertisement on the perfect amount of scruff. He and Riley look a lot alike, but Dawson is bulkier, his face fuller, and his shoulders even broader.

"Thank you," I finally say, tearing my eyes away from his. "Long time no see."

Oh, for god's sake, I sound like a teenager at the mall.

Maybe because that's what I feel like.

"Awww!" Keatyn says. "Everyone loved the lines you said in the movie! Vanessa, do you remember what you said to Dawson at my birthday party after I introduced you?"

"I haven't seen the movie yet," Dawson admits, "But I do remember. Keatyn said, *This is Dawson Johnson, he's headed to NYU this fall and plans to major in luxury marketing.*" He looks deeply into my eyes again. "Do you remember what you said back?"

"*We have a lot in common, then, because I plan to major in luxury spending.*"

Dawson smiles broadly and laughs. "Then you invited me to Tommy's office for a glass of scotch. That was fun."

"And here you both are now," Keatyn claps. "Working for Captive on just that. I have to get going. Vanessa, I was wondering if you might be able to spend the day with Dawson. Talk shop. Get him up to speed on your current projects and impress him with your plans for our future, especially *Daddy's Angel*."

"I'd appreciate that, Vanessa," sexy Dawson agrees. "I've already gotten the tour of the place, but Keatyn was a little vague as to what I'd be doing on a day-to-day basis."

I know what I'd like to be doing with him on a day-to-day basis.

But, somehow, I doubt that's what Keatyn had in mind.

CAPTIVE FILMS - SANTA MONICA

IT'S BE A while since I felt anything for a girl.

Make that a woman.

Vanessa may have been a girl when I met her, but now she's all woman. She still has the confidence and poise I remember, but her smile is tinged with something I see in my own.

Sadness.

When we were teenagers, everything seemed so simple. So hopeful.

You're hot. Let's hookup.

Sadly, that's still the only pick up line I know.

It's really hard to concentrate on what she's telling me. She's giving me an overview of projects Captive Films is working on. She's discussing target audiences for each. All stuff I understand well.

Except I find myself just staring at her lips.

Lips I kissed on a night that feels like it was a lifetime ago.

I've been feeling old since Whitney left but sitting here today, looking at her lips, I feel young again.

"I'm staring at your lips," I tell her.

She immediately brings her hand up to her lips, like she has something on them. "Why?"

"They're exactly as I remember them. Full. Lush. Perfect. And you still wear the same color lipstick."

She smiles. "It's funny, I just started wearing red lipstick again. I wore it back then because it made me feel confident. I guess that's why I've been wearing it lately."

"Why in the world would you need help feeling confident?"

She looks at her watch. A beautiful diamond encrusted one. The kind a man who has both money and taste would have bought her.

I look at her left hand. No wedding ring has appeared since the last time I checked ten minutes ago.

How is it that she's not married?

"It's nearly lunch," she says. "I'm going to need a martini if we're going to get personal."

"A drink sounds good to me."

CAPTIVE FILMS - SANTA MONICA
Vanessa

"DO YOU HAVE a car or would you like me to drive?" I ask him as we head outside.

"I have no idea where to go, but I'd love to drive." He points toward a gorgeous new red Ferrari.

I try not to cringe at his choice of cars. My ex, Bam, had a thing for Ferraris. He even had their prancing horse symbol tattooed on his chest. "You like Ferraris, I see," I say, trying not to choke on the word.

"Don't tell Keatyn, but it's not really me."

"It's not?"

"It's a little flashy, don't you think?"

I laugh as he opens the door for me. "Yeah, just a little."

As he joins me in the car, he's still talking. "But, I will admit, she's fun to drive. And listen to this engine purr. Maybe if I ever get one for myself, I'll get it in silver. This looks more like Riley. Have you ever seen his neon green Viper?"

"I have. And out of all the cars he has, that's still his baby. It was his 18th birthday present, right?"

"Yep. That's a tradition in the Johnson family. All the men get together and choose your first car."

"What'd you get?"

"A modified silver BMW," he says, which makes me like him even more. "So where are we going?"

"It's a gorgeous day. I think we should have lunch and drinks poolside at Chateau Marmont."

"I've heard of that place. Isn't it a hotel where lots of famous people stay?"

"Yeah, the history of the place is pretty great. And don't be alarmed when we get there, but I'll have to check us into a room."

There's an amused look on his face and I wish I knew what he was thinking. Probably that I want him.

Which, let's be honest, I do.

"A room?"

"Yes, a poolside bungalow. So that we can enjoy lunch and drinks poolside."

"Oh, I get it. You can't use the pool without a room."

"Exactly."

HE DRIVES TO the hotel and when we get there he says he'll

check us in.

Knowing what a suite costs, I balk. "Oh, I'll do it."

"Absolutely not," he says, as he takes my hand to help me out of the car.

When I stand up, we're face to face and he's staring at my mouth again.

"I changed my mind," he says. "This car matches the color of your lipstick. That alone might be reason enough to love it."

My mouth goes dry, my knees feel weak.

He totally made me swoon.

When's the last time a man made me swoon with his words and not his wallet?

I smile, I can't help it.

Plus, I don't know how to respond.

And I always have a quick comeback for everything.

ONCE WE'RE CHECKED into our suite, I open the doors to the outside.

He stands close behind me, looking out at the view.

"I have to say," he says, "I thought a lot about what my first day would be like. I never imagined this."

When I turn around to reply, my chest grazes across his suit.

Even in my heels, I have to look up at him.

Our eyes lock and we share a moment. That perfect moment right before a kiss. I tilt my chin ever so slightly upward, giving him permission.

A flash of sadness washes across his eyes and he backs away from me.

In that moment, I vow to discover the reason for his sadness.

And make it go away.

"Too bad we don't have swimsuits with us," he says. "The pool looks amazing."

"I can fix that. Let me make a quick call. Why don't you go out and order us drinks."

"Were you serious about a martini?"

"Yes, please. And, just so you know, I like it dirty."

Dawson swallows—no, he gulps—when I say I like it dirty. And I realize that may have sounded a bit suggestive.

He narrows his eyes. "You're talking about the martini, right?"

"Yes, of course," I say.

"Okay. One dirty martini coming up."

"Wait! You can't go out like that."

He looks down at himself. "Like, what?

"In your suit. May I?"

He nods, so I help him take his jacket off, fold it in half, and lay it over the back of a grey velvet lounge chair. Then I unbutton his shirtsleeves and roll them up.

"And this tie has to go." I loosen it, remove it from around his neck, and then unbutton the first two buttons of his soft cotton dress shirt. As I'm unbuttoning his shirt, I notice that he gulps again. I'm making him uncomfortable.

Which is not the reaction I'm used to.

I place my hands on his rock hard chest and playfully push him away to ease his tension. "Much better, now you can go."

He gives me a shy smile and heads out the door.

I immediately call my butler and ask him to bring me an overnight bag with a few essentials, including a new red bikini for me and swim trunks for him.

I peek outside, making sure Dawson is where I can see him, and call Captive Films.

"Tyler," I say quietly when he answers. "I need the scoop on Dawson Johnson."

"He is a fine looking man. You on the prowl for that? Meooowww."

"No, I'm not on the prowl. I'm not even interested in that," I lie. "Keatyn wants us to work closely together on some projects, and I just wanted to know his story."

"His story, why Ms. Flanning, if you're working closely with him, you should ask him yourself."

"Tyler, stop playing with me. Is he married?"

"No, he is not. And that's all I know." But then he lowers his voice. "I can tell you what was on his resume. He's had high profile positions in numerous designer companies, but he hasn't worked in the last two years. I thought that was a little strange."

"Interesting. Thanks, Tyler."

I hang up, slide out of my heels, take off my suit jacket and join Dawson at a shaded table by the pool just as our drinks arrive.

"To new beginnings," I say, carefully clinking my full martini glass with his.

"To new beginnings," he repeats. "So, back to the question that brought us here. Why does someone like you need confidence? Your confidence was one of the first things I noticed about you. You were almost cocky."

"Oh, come on, I wasn't that bad."

"I never thought it was bad. I liked it." He smiles at me again. "And your taste in scotch."

I laugh. "I did think I was the shit in high school."

"So what happened after that?"

"I graduated, went to college, then law school. I was secretly married at nineteen to a guy I had known since we were young."

"Secretly married?"

"Yeah, our parents would not have approved, but we didn't care. Bam was . . ."

"Bam? That was his name? Like on the Flintstones, Bam Bam? I can't picture you with a Bam Bam."

I laugh, picturing Bam in a loincloth during the Stone Age. No fast cars. No servants. He wouldn't have survived. If ever there was a boy who grew up with a silver spoon in his mouth, it was Bam.

"Juan Fabio Martinez is his real name. He's a professional

polo player from Argentina. His family's quite wealthy and he grew up with the best of everything. I met him when I was fifteen at a weekend party on his yacht. We hooked up for the first time that weekend and whenever he was in town. By the time I was nineteen, we were crazy in love and got married on a whim. Afterwards, he freaked out because his mother would've been crushed he didn't get married in the church. We never told anyone we were married, but we lived together while I went to college and when I graduated law school, we did it up big. Proposal in front of his family. Married in the church he grew up in. Three lavish receptions in three different countries. An amazing three week honeymoon."

"Sounds nice. What happened?"

"The short answer is he cheated on me. I'm not sure if it was often. He traveled a lot and I worked."

"Did you need to work?"

"No, but I wanted to. I didn't spend all those years getting through school just to be a polo player's wife. I suppose that should have been enough, but I wanted more. For me."

Dawson's eyes smile at me.

Yeah, I meant that. Not only does his mouth smile but his eyes too. They have such warmth and depth.

I could get lost in them.

"What about you?" I ask.

"I took it pretty hard when my wife, uh, left."

"When was that?"

"Two years ago," he says. I realize that's when he quit working. He must have taken it really hard.

Is that why Keatyn is going so overboard with him?

Does he have a drinking problem? Drugs? Is he mentally unstable?

I notice that half his drink is left, while mine is completely gone. I was sucking it down while telling him about Bam.

Probably not an alcoholic.

"How long were you married?"

"Whitney and I were married for eight years."

"Did you get married while you were still in college?"

"Yeah, we did."

"Is there anything else you want to tell me?" I ask, hoping he'll just spill the story instead of me having to pry it out of him. He's barely answering my questions.

"No, I don't think so. I'm looking forward to working with you."

Working with me? Shit. Here I am flirting with him and he wants to *work* with me.

But if he's not interested, why the comment about my lips?

Maybe his wife leaving is a touchy subject and I should stop babbling on about it.

"So what do you hope to do at Captive?"

"Mostly, make an impact. Keatyn is a good friend and I don't want to let her down."

"Just how well do you know her?"

"We dated briefly in high school. Have been friends ever since. She's a good friend."

"When I found out Bam was cheating on me, I went through a lot. My business suffered. I lost most of my clients. Keatyn stuck by me. Shit, speaking of that, I need to get her press release out. And our swimwear should be here by now. Why don't you order another round of drinks and bring them inside."

I QUICKLY SEND out the press release about Keatyn and Aiden's engagement and follow it up with a few well-placed phone calls.

My bikini has arrived along with a sinful black dress for tonight and matching slinky undergarments.

You know, just in case.

I change into my bikini and as I come out of the bathroom, he's just coming back inside with our drinks.

He stops in his track and stares at me. His gaze feels like fire as it feasts on my skin.

My insides react. I'm ready to throw this man on the bed and have my way with him. And I can't for the life of me figure out what's stopping me from doing just that.

"I have swim trunks for you to put on." I thrust them in his direction as he sets our drinks on the desk.

"Awesome. I'll go change."

While he steps into the bathroom, I take a gulp of my drink.

"Hey, Vanessa," he says, "can you help me?"

"Help you how?"

He walks out in the swim trunks, holding a knotted draw-string in his hand. "I can't get this untied. My fingers are too big."

Stop it, Vanessa. Stop thinking about what other things might be big.

You need to establish a friendly working relationship with him, so you can get a bigger chunk of Captive's publicity. That's all this is.

"I'll be glad to help." I take the drawstring in my hands and attempt to untie it. I was afraid he'd come out and be a little flabby in the middle, like many men get as their thirties approach. But, holy hell, not him. He looks like he's done nothing the last two years but prepare this body, this shrine to mankind, for me.

And here my hands are, just inches away from the one thing I want.

And I'm not talking about his heart.

I pull him toward the window where there's more light. Then I drop to my knees to get a better look at this knot.

"Uh, you know, it's probably okay," he says, shifting his weight uncomfortably. "I just won't dive. It'll stay up."

I glance up at him. "Oh, I'm sure *it* will," I reply sexily, letting go of the string and thinking how I'd love to find out just how long Dawson can *stay up*.

He takes my hand and helps me to my feet. "I'll grab our drinks," he says. "You choose the spot."

I PICK OUT two chaises with a small table set between them. It's perfect for our drinks and my need for a little separation.

This is business.

I look down at my skimpy red bikini and know that I have no intention of keeping things strictly business with Dawson Johnson.

I finish my drink as he lies back and takes his first sip. "What a gorgeous day. It's starting to get chilly enough at home to wear a jacket."

"You're still tan," I say, because how can I not notice how perfectly bronzed his skin is?

"Our family spends most of the summer in the Hamptons. Do you want to get in?"

"The water?"

"Yeah." He stands up and takes my hand. And even though I really don't want to, I get in the pool with him. Sort of. I sit on a step, being careful not to let the ends of my hair touch the water. I don't want my blowout to get frizzy.

Dawson dives in and swims the length of the pool. When he comes up out of the water, he looks just like one of my favorite men's cologne ads. The model in it is dark, his hair slicked back off his face, and his eyes are amazing. I realize now, that's why I've always been drawn to it. The model looks like Dawson.

He grabs my waist and pulls me into the water with him. "You're not one of those girls who doesn't want to get her hair wet, are you?"

"Of course not," I lie. "I love to swim."

And right now, I do love it. Dawson has walked us out to where it's too deep for me to touch. His big hands are holding my waist and I'm clinging to his muscular arms.

"Not a bad way to spend a day at work," he says, reminding me again that this is supposed to be business.

"It doesn't really feel like work." I wrap my arms around his neck and look up at him.

Our eyes meet again. He looks at my mouth and runs the pad of his thumb slowly across my bottom lip. "Do you remember our kiss?"

"Kiss?" I laugh. "I'm pretty sure we made out."

"Yeah, but do you remember it? How it felt?"

"Maybe you should remind me," I flirt.

"No, I'm asking if you remember it. Because I do. It was, hands down, the best kiss of my life."

My heart stops. My throat goes dry. "Really?"

"Really. Do you think we could top it, now that we're older?" he asks, sliding his hand under my chin to lift it toward him.

"I don't know. Yes. Maybe," I say breathlessly, waiting for his lips to close the small gap between us.

But he doesn't. He leans back a little and says, "Hmm. Well, once you decide, let me know."

Is he fucking kidding me?

Dawson is a total panty tease.

Or bikini tease, in this case.

He *is* like his brother.

No, he's not like Riley. Riley would have taken off his shirt, ordered shots, and had his choice of women. And he wouldn't get them all hot and bothered and not follow through.

"Mr. Johnson," our server says, "your lunch is served."

Dawson grins at me. "I'm starved."

I reluctantly let go of him and get out of the pool.

Because I can handle a challenge.

And my new challenge is named Dawson Johnson.

MORE TO THE STORY.

News flash, people . . .
Our favorite starlet, Keatyn Douglas is ENGAGED!
And NOT to her *Trinity* costar and long-time lover, Knox Daniels.

On one hand, we're sad they aren't going to be together. On the other hand, that delicious man is still very single, based on this photo of him sandwiched between twin pairs of boobs at one of his favorite night clubs.

Rumor has it, he and Captive Films CEO, Riley Johnson, who should definitely be in front of the camera and not behind it, have been seen partying their nights away.

Back to the matter at hand, the official statement:
Keatyn Douglas and her longtime beau Aiden Arrington, owner of Asher Vineyards and Winery, the brand best known for their charitable Moon Wish wine, were engaged in Paris after the worldwide premiere of the hit trilogy, The Keatyn Chronicles, based on their life.

Our sources tell us that, much like the movie which started a trend of top of the Eiffel Tower sunset proposals, the two were engaged at the top of the Eiffel Tower at sunset. (Yawn.)

Anywho, we're told the couple is planning a spring wedding in—you guessed it—Paris.

P.S. We're not holding our breath for this wedding to actually take place. Not when Knox is single and the two are shooting their raciest love scenes to date. Some even wonder if this "engagement" is an old friend trying to help Keatyn and Knox get back together.

P.P.S. Speaking of Riley Johnson, I'd like to get under him on a casting couch, if you know what I mean. Wink wink.

WEDNESDAY, OCTOBER 1ST
JENNIFER'S BEACH HOUSE – MALIBU
Riley

JENNIFER IS OUT of breath when she answers the door.

And she's topless.

Nice.

"You're finally here!" she says, sweeping me into a hug. "Come out back. Some friends stopped by."

Friends?

"I thought we were hanging out."

She stops, turns around on her tiptoes, and kisses me. "We're leaving. They'll probably stay for a while. Do you want to swim first? Need a drink?"

"How about both?"

I follow her to the refrigerator. She opens it and lets me grab my only option, Bud Light in a can. I honestly can't remember the last time I drank beer out of can.

I grab one, open it, and gulp down a flavor that reminds me of college.

Jennifer introduces me to three of her girlfriends, who are also sunbathing topless, and a couple guys in the corner who are smoking a fat joint. The way Jennifer is bouncing around, my

127

guess is she hasn't partaken.

She yells, "Cannonball!" and flies into the pool, splashing her sunbathing friends.

"Ahh!" they all yell when she comes up laughing.

I decide what the hell and do a cannonball too, knowing my splash will totally drench them.

When I come up, Jennifer is right next to me, laughing at her screaming friends, who have run into the house.

"That was AWESOME!" She pushes me against the side of the pool and kisses me hard, murmuring, "And one way to get rid of them."

I wrap my arms around her, enjoying the excitement of kissing someone new, particularly someone new and half naked. Jennifer and I didn't do much last night. We just made out.

It was refreshing.

And I realize I miss the companionship. Just being able to hang out with someone without worrying I'm giving them the wrong impression.

Like Shelby. She called me on the way here and wanted to know why I hadn't called. I told her I didn't want to see her anymore. She asked if the article she saw about me and Jennifer was true then had a little meltdown.

Actually, meltdown is a bit of an understatement.

She called me every name in the book. A few I've never been called before.

Then, thankfully, she hung up on me.

One less thing to worry about.

Especially now when Jennifer's lips are on mine.

I float us out to the middle of the pool, wrapping her legs around me, still kissing her.

"Dude, they're totally going to do it," I hear from behind us.

Jennifer must have heard them too, because she stops kissing me. "We *aren't* going to do it. Grow up. We're just kissing. And I changed my mind. Get the hell out of my house."

She gets out of the pool as they grab their things. She locks the door behind them then sits on the edge of the pool, dangling her long legs in the water. I'm ready to pull her back in with me and kiss her boobs. They are on the smaller side. Most girls would want bigger ones, but she'd be a fool. They are cute and perky.

And her nipples are the prettiest pale pink color.

I want one in my mouth.

Now.

"So, sexy, I have some plans for us today."

"What kind of plans. Besides us *not* doing it?"

She laughs loudly. "Oh gosh, did I crush that monumentally big ego of yours?"

"I think you heard the gossip wrong. They were talking about my monumentally big dick."

She giggles and blushes. Although she curses like a sailor, I realize I've never heard her use words like that referring to sex.

"You're funny. I like it," she says.

This girl is going to need the hard sell. And by hard, for once, I'm not talking about my dick.

I hop out of the pool, immediately choosing to follow her lead. "I haven't had lunch yet. Is it included in your plans?"

"Yes, I'm starving! Let's go across the street. Have you ever had their Mahi tacos?"

"I have. They also have the best martinis in town."

She grabs a string bikini top off a chaise and holds it up in front of her chest. "Will you tie this for me?"

"Sure." I glide my hand across her soft, bronzed shoulder. "You're beautiful," I whisper.

"Are you putting the moves on me? You're the big shot movie producer, shouldn't I be trying to sleep with you?"

"You slept with me last night," I tease as I slowly touch her back, while tying the bottom string. "This too tight?"

"No, it's perfect. Riley, I don't date people I work with. And

I'd never have sex with someone to get a role."

"Hold your hair up," I tell her, as I tie the string around her neck. Then I turn her around to face me. "I don't date anyone I work with either. And, although I may have a well-deserved reputation for sleeping around, I've never hired someone I've slept with."

She smooshes up her nose. "Really?"

"Really," I state, kissing it.

"You're too cute," she says, causing my frozen heart to melt a little. She grabs my hand and leads me out the door. The lust I wish she felt for me fills her eyes when she sees my car again. She pretends to pet it although, thankfully, her hand never touches the paint.

"Oh, baby, I've missed you," she says to my car.

I lean her against the side of the car, wanting nothing more right now than to forget about the paint and do her on the hood. This girl has my blood running hot. Probably, because she acts like she's not interested.

The last time I wasn't sure a girl wasn't interested in me was . . .

Shit.

I shake my head. I'm not thinking about Ariela today.

I give Jennifer a rough kiss. She grabs my neck and shoves her tongue in my mouth like Ariela did at Keatyn's.

Fuck!

Stop. Fucking. Thinking. About. Her!

I kiss Jennifer back, using my skillful tongue, but trying to play it cool. I even stop the kiss before she's ready for it to end. When I pull my lips away, it takes her a few moments to open her eyes and look at me.

"Damn," she says. "You might cause me to rethink my rules."

"I've already been rethinking mine. In fact, if you sign a contract to do *Daddy's Angel*, I'll let you drive my car. No girl has ever driven her."

"Oh, now you're just fucking with me," she laughs, grabs my hand, and leads me toward the restaurant.

AFTER THE SHORT walk there, we make ourselves comfortable in the bar and order drinks and lunch.

She crosses her arms and narrows her eyes at me. "Are you serious?"

"About which part?"

"The car part, silly."

"You mean, you really don't want to sleep with me?"

"I haven't decided yet. Look, I know I'm kinda crazy. A little wild. But I love life. I'm having a blast. I'm making amazing money doing something I love. But that doesn't mean I sleep around."

"You kissed every man standing at the last Academy Awards afterparty."

"Yeah, because I fucking won. I still can't fucking believe that. I was drunk, happy, and high on life. I'm affectionate. I kissed some girls too, by the way."

"Do you remember kissing me?"

"I kissed you?"

"Yep. Right in front of my mother. Tongue and everything."

She covers her face with her hand. "Oh shit. I'm so embarrassed."

I smirk, but try to hide it by taking a drink.

"Aww, you're fucking with me again." She shakes a finger at me. "Riley Johnson, what am I going to do with you? Tell me the truth. Did I kiss you?"

"Yes."

"Was your mother there?"

"No."

"You're bad. Good thing. I wouldn't want to have to be embarrassed when I meet her."

"You're planning to meet my mother?"

"Sure, I'll drive your car there."

"My parents live in the Hamptons."

"Shit! That's awesome. That'd be so fun. Let's do it!"

"Wait. Do what?"

"Drive your car there. Road trip!"

"It'd kill the car's value if I put too many miles on it."

"Oh, come on, Riley. It will be fun. That's how we'll celebrate. We'll go tomorrow morning to talk to Keatyn about the role. You can bring your attorneys or whatever and I'll sign. My agent will kill me because I won't ask for enough money, but if the show does well, you'll promise to pay me more for the next season."

"If only all contracts were that easy," I laugh, knowing how Dallas goes over every minute detail to protect us.

"It can be for this. Seriously, Riley, when's the last time you had a vacation?"

"I visited my family this summer."

She looks up at the ceiling and bites her lip, trying to come up with a different excuse to talk me into it.

"I'll tell you what," I say. "If we have a done deal by Friday, we'll go somewhere to celebrate."

She gives me a broad smile, leans across the table, grabs my shirt, and kisses me.

BAR MARMONT – HOLLYWOOD

WE SWAM, DRANK, freshened up, and now we're finishing dinner. Vanessa is wearing what might be the sexiest dress I have ever seen. It has a halter neck, barely covers the sides of her breasts, and is backless. The skirt flows around her curves.

She obviously isn't wearing a bra and I have to purposely not look down, so I don't look like a middle school boy who's hoping to get a peek of her boob.

I shouldn't be thinking any of this.

I came here for a new beginning. A new job. The last thing I need to do is drag down a smart, beautiful woman like her. I overheard my aunt tell someone that it would be hard for me to find someone new to love. That I have *too much baggage*.

And she's probably right.

Two little girls, who are staying with my parents so they can keep going to their school, while I figure out if this will work. If I should move them to California and take them away from everyone they know.

On the plus side, it will mean not having to deal with Whitney's family.

They never treated her well when she was here. It kills me when they pretend to miss her now that she's gone.

And I don't want them to influence my daughters.

I haven't had an inkling of a desire to date anyone or sleep with anyone since it happened.

My oldest brother, Camden, even resorted to taking me to Atlantic City and trying to buy me a couple hookers.

A fresh start in California means working with Keatyn and Riley, sunshine all the time, and getting away from all the reminders of Whitney.

Never once in the last month, while I contemplated Keatyn's offer, did I think I would come out here and want to be with a woman again.

Especially not on my first day.

But I do.

And I feel both incredibly relieved and incredibly guilty.

Vanessa sets her champagne down and licks her bottom lip.

And I'm jealous of her tongue.

I try not to stare, but I can't help it.

We've been flirting all night.

Yes, I've been flirting with her.

Although, she probably thinks I'm bipolar. I know I'm giving off all sorts of mixed messages.

Camden drove me to the airport, slapped me on the back, handed me a bag full of condoms and told me to use them.

I threw them in the first trashcan I walked by.

That wasn't even on my radar.

But, now, my radar is being jammed by a gorgeous, stealth temptress in a shimmering black dress, whose red lips I'm dying to kiss.

She leans in closer, resting her chin on her palm, and purrs, "It's getting noisy in here. Why don't we take our champagne back to our room so we can discuss your ideas further?"

"Sounds great," I say, wondering what the hell I've been saying. Oh yeah, something about the all-American designer I used to work for who I think would make a great marketing sponsor for *Daddy's Angel*.

I PUT MY hand across the small of her back, guiding her out of the room, and based on the male eyes following us, I'm hoping I don't have to get in a fight to do it.

A fight.

Would I fight to go back to the room with her?

Hell yeah.

Maybe it's because we just met and have a million things to talk about but I don't think we'll ever run out of things to say. She's stimulating both my mind and my cock in ways I haven't felt since . . .

Since that night we met. We talked for hours. Danced for hours. Made out for hours.

Then, I went home.

I thought about her a lot my freshman year in college.

Jake Worth, my roommate at NYU, and I certainly fucked our fair share of coeds.

But none of them wanted to talk. They were just horny. And that was fine, for a while.

I realize now, looking back, that Whitney and I weren't well suited. My brothers urged me not to marry her when she got pregnant. We weren't dating seriously at the time.

It was an accident.

And I wouldn't change it for anything. My daughter, Ava, is the light of my life and we went on to have another beautiful baby girl, Harlow, a few years later.

I haven't told Vanessa about my *baggage*. I haven't told her that my wife hated life so much that she killed herself.

It's not really something you want to blurt out when fate hands you a gift.

I'M STILL TRYING to figure out if I should make a move as we enter the room. The bed is turned back, soft music is playing, and the lights from the pool are shimmering outside.

Vanessa sets the champagne bottle down, saunters toward me, and grabs my tie, pulling me closer.

"The answer is yes," she says softly. "I think we could top it. I think if we kiss now, it will be better than our first kiss."

That's all the encouragement I need. I wrap one arm around her waist and slide the other behind her neck. Just like I did more than ten years ago. Our lips touch.

And then it's not about *seeing* if it's good.

It's about need.

She parts her lips and my tongue darts inside, exploring and intertwining with hers.

She's pulling my tie off and unbuttoning my shirt while I kiss down her neck.

I push away slightly as I untie the strings holding up the

front of her dress then watch as the top slides down exposing her beautiful breasts. I immediately strike, taking one nipple into my mouth, kissing it and circling it with my tongue, while caressing the other with my fingers.

And I'm harder than a fucking rock.

When she makes a little moan, I move us to the bed, supporting my weight above her, while still kissing her and sliding the dress down further.

Her hands are in my hair, my name on her breath, she's unzipping my pants, and sliding her hand inside.

God, it feels so good.

Her soft hand is running down my shaft.

I push her dress up, strip off her panties, and remember I don't have a condom.

All I want in this moment is to get inside her, but I stop.

And stand up.

Wondering what the hell I'm doing.

Fucking someone I have to work with on my first day?

Fucking someone, I think I could care about, because I'm horny as shit and it's been so long?

"Uh, um, we better stop," I say, kicking myself the second the words leave my lips.

But the damage is done.

BEACH - MALIBU

AFTER A LONG late lunch with lots of drinks, Jennifer and I walk to the beach. It's starting to get dark and we're both a bit tipsy.

She leads me in the opposite direction of her house and

toward the pier.

She runs through the water, under the pier, swinging around the supports. She's laughing and splashing water at me.

It takes me back to a clear, warm summer night with Ariela.

Jennifer waves her hand in front of my face.

"What are you thinking about?"

"Nothing," I lie.

She leans in to kiss me and I back away slightly. "Am I too young?"

"What? No. You know I like you. I've been kissing you all day."

"Then what are you thinking about? Some girl break your heart?"

I sigh and nod my head.

"Ahh, now we're getting somewhere."

She sits down in the sand cross-legged in front of me. "Tell me what happened."

"We dated for two years in high school and were supposed to attend USC together. Her dad talked her out of it. She told me after our graduation ceremony. Then she left. That's the last I had heard from her until this week."

"What happened this week?"

"She came to dinner at Keatyn's house."

"How old are you?"

"Almost twenty nine."

"So that all happened more than a decade ago? A third of your life ago?"

"Yeah, I guess."

"That's a long time to be sad, Riley. Have you had any relationships since then?"

"I recently had four dates with a girl before I cut her loose. And that was three dates too many."

"Wow, she must have done a number on you. You still love her?"

I shake my head. "I don't think I could ever forgive her."

"Stand up. Hold my hand. Run with me, Riley. Be free."

She pulls my hand, but I pull back. "You remind me of Keatyn."

She smiles at me. "That's a big compliment. She's kinda my idol. I've only met her once briefly at an awards show. I asked her to take a selfie with me. I'm so uncool. What made you say I remind you of her?"

"She's positive, free spirited, creative. And she believes in luck, fate, and endless possibilities."

"And you?"

"I stopped believing in those things a long time ago."

Jennifer holds my hand as we both stare out into the darkness over the water.

"She came to L.A. with me the summer before our senior year." I mutter.

"When you filmed *A Day at the Lake 2*? How fun was it making a movie with a bunch of your friends?"

"It was a lot of fun. I learned a ton. We used to walk on this beach at night. She ran under the piers and would make me find her."

"And when you did?"

"She'd give me a kiss. We even had sex up against one of those piers late one night."

"Oh, that sounds fun. And probably illegal. We need to get your ass off this beach. Too many memories. I heard you bought a new plane. Wanna go to Vegas tonight?"

"Seriously?"

"Yeah, seriously. Why the fuck not?"

"I have to work tomorrow. I have meetings. *You* have a meeting with Keatyn."

"Shit, that's right," she says. "Let's go back to my house, get high, and play video games."

I smile at her and take off running. Then I tell her, "You

might just be the best date I've ever had."

VANESSA'S ESTATE – HOLMBY HILLS
Vanessa

DAWSON DRIVES ME home, gives me an awkward goodbye, then pulls off in that fucking red Ferrari.

What is it with a red Ferrari that makes a man . . .

No, bad example.

What the hell?

I mean what the fucking hell?

Why did he stop?

I STOMP IN the house, feeling like crap. I ate too much, drank too much, almost had sex with my new co-worker and got stone cold shut down. Now, I'm horny and alone.

Thank god for vibrators.

My butler, Bernard, is waiting for me. "Ms. Flanning, may I get you anything before you retire?"

"No, thank you. Actually, do you know if Ariela is still awake?"

"She had a rough day. I just took her down a pint of ice cream."

"I think I'll have one of those too. I'm going to change."

"Yes, ma'am."

I THROW ON a cashmere loungewear set, grab my ice cream, and walk down to the guest house.

Ariela answers with spoon in hand.

"Rough day, I heard?"

"Yeah, dealing with my ex. I'm emotionally drained."

"What happened?"

"We talked on the phone tonight. I told him I'm filing for a divorce. He freaked out and hung up. Then he called me back, crying. Making promises he won't keep. Begging me not to tell my parents. That we'll work it out. That I just need to come home. Hung up again, then called back. That happened about ten times."

"Typical," I say. "Wait, why is he so worried about your parents?"

"He's about to become a partner in my dad's firm." She tilts her head at me. "Do you think that's the real reason why he's so upset? He's more worried about the partnership than our relationship?"

"I don't know him," I say, carefully. "What do you think?"

"I think . . ." She takes a bite of ice cream, lets it melt in her mouth, and then says. "I think he might be."

"There's one way to find out," I tell her.

"How?"

"Has he been seeing the secretary while you've been gone?"

She sits up straighter. "He said he'd never see her again. But . . . I bet you anything he still is."

"I happen to know a private detective. He's very good at getting photos of asshole husbands and their mistresses. Those photos are often quite helpful in divorce proceedings."

"So everyone can see them?"

"Well, depending on the man, sometimes that isn't necessary. Sometimes it just helps them realize that you're on to their bullshit game and aren't going to stand for it. And, for a man, particularly one who is married to the boss's daughter, I would think that would mean you would have him by the balls."

"I just want out."

"I'll call first thing in the morning and put the two of you in touch. He'll need a lot of information. Where he works, the girl's name, things like that."

"Okay. Thanks, I appreciate it."

"Anything happening on the Riley front?"

"No. There was an article in the paper about him and that actress from the party. Apparently, they're an item."

"Don't believe everything you read, Ariela. This town is built on gossip and rumors."

"Just up your alley. How was work? Are you just getting home?"

I roll my eyes. "Yes. Keatyn hired Riley's brother to work for the company and asked me to help him get acquainted with their projects."

"Ohhh, which brother?"

"Dawson."

"I have to admit, I had a bit of a crush on Dawson when I was younger. All the girls at Eastbrooke crushed on the Johnson brothers."

"How many are there?"

"Four. Camden is the oldest. He was a senior when I was a sophomore. He had partying down to an art form and a body that girls swooned over. Dawson was next. He was a junior. Riley, who's a year younger than Dawson, got kicked out of school his Freshman year, got sent to military school, and came back our junior year looking like a man. That's when we started dating. And their younger brother, Braxton, is three years younger than Riley."

"Tell me more about Dawson."

"Well, he dated a girl named Whitney for most of high school. They broke up the end of their junior year. He looked even hotter when he came back for his senior year. Had spent the summer doing what Johnson boys do."

"And what's that?"

"Partying in the Hamptons. Working out. Screwing every girl in sight."

"He looks like he still works out. That Whitney girl from high school. That's who he was married to."

"*Was* married to?"

"She left him two years ago."

"She tried to commit suicide during her senior year, which really shocked all of us. She was the school's Queen B, The Alpha, Mean Girl, whatever you want to call her. Things changed when Keatyn came. Keatyn didn't give a shit what Whitney thought. I feel bad saying this, but I was glad Whitney went to some sort of counseling facility instead of coming back to school. I was a cheerleader and kind of popular, but it didn't matter. She could belittle you and make you feel like shit with one sentence. I kinda felt like whatever bad she got in life, she deserved."

"Well, he must have loved her. He hasn't worked for two years."

"Dawson is, or was, really sweet. He and Keatyn dated for a while, before she and Aiden got together."

"They dated? Why didn't she tell me?"

"I don't know. Because it was a long time ago?"

"Or she's trying to play matchmaker! Oh, my gosh. Do you think that's why she told me to spend the day with him? Was she hoping I'd sleep with him? I mean, I would have, but just when things started to get hot and heavy in the hotel room . . ."

"Wait! You were in a hotel room with him?"

I wave my hand at her. "It's a long story." I hold up my phone. "I know it's late but I'm calling her."

"Hey, Vanessa," Keatyn answers in a really chipper voice. "How did your meeting with Dawson go?"

"Did you set me up with him? Are you trying to play matchmaker?"

"What? No! . . . Ohmigawd! Did you sleep with him? I told you to have a meeting with him, not sleep with him. Although, it wouldn't be a bad thing, Dawson is hot and you like hot guys."

"Is that why you leased him a red Ferrari? Because you thought I'd like it?"

"A what?! No! Is that what he got? I told Tyler to pick out an exotic car that wasn't too flashy."

"Well, compared to Riley, that probably isn't flashy," I mutter.

"Shit, Vanessa, I'm sorry. I didn't know. Really. Are you just now getting home?"

"Yes."

"From meeting with Dawson?"

"Yes."

"That was a very *long* business meeting."

"Fine. He complimented my lipstick, asked about my life, and next thing I knew we were getting a poolside suite so we could have lunch."

"That was twelve hours ago."

"Yes, I know *exactly* how long ago it was. We talked. I flirted with him. He sorta flirted back. What's his deal anyway? Why hasn't he worked for the last two years? And why was he living at home? And why did he bail when he had me naked and hornier than hell?"

"Oh . . . So, thing's did happen."

"Fuck. I knew it. You knew I'd like him."

"No, I didn't. I mean, I sorta maybe hoped. But I didn't think it'd happen that fast. Dawson's charm is more subtle."

"His charm? What did this Whitney do to him? Did he love her so much that it broke him when she left?"

"Yeah, Vanessa. And you of all people should understand that. Give him some time. Dawson's one of the nicest people I've ever met."

"If it weren't for the fact he and Riley look alike, I wouldn't believe they were related. He doesn't ooze sex appeal like Riley. Except, sometimes it slips out, I don't think he can help it."

"All the Johnson brothers ooze sex appeal. It's in their genes.

Dawson is just more thoughtful and sweet. He's the kind of guy who sneaks up on you."

"Why didn't you tell me you dated him?"

"It was for like a month, in high school."

"And? Did you sleep with him?"

"Yeah."

"Was it good?"

"I used to describe his kisses as molten lava hot and neither one of us were very experienced at that point."

"His kisses were hotter than that," I mutter.

"See, that's what happens when you grow up. You get better at everything. Obviously, if he had you naked. Wait, did you put the room on your credit card?"

"No, he said he would take care of it."

"Shit. He doesn't have a corporate card yet. It's supposed to be here tomorrow."

"Maybe he put it on a personal one."

"But he, uh, never mind, I'll call and take care of it."

"Keatyn, what the hell aren't you telling me?"

She sighs. "Look, Vanessa, this isn't my story to tell. Suffice it to say that Whitney did a number on him, and he's had a rough two years. Be nice to him. He doesn't need drama in his life. That's part of why I wanted him to come here."

"Fine," I say, hanging up the phone, more confused than I was when I started.

DAWSON'S BEACH HOUSE - MALIBU

MY PHONE RINGS, just as I'm drying off from taking a cold

shower.

"Hey, I know it's late," Keatyn says. "But I just wondered how your first day went. Sorry I didn't have more time to spend with you."

"My first day—" How do I even describe it? "—was interesting."

"Is everything okay? Do you like the house? I heard Tyler leased you a red Ferrari. I know that's not your style. I should've been more specific when I said low key. Compared to your brother . . ."

"It is low key," I laugh. "It's hard being here without the girls."

"They're coming out this weekend, right? Would you want to bring them to the vineyard? Dallas is bringing his four kids, the girls would have a blast, and if you move them here, they will already have friends. You could relax a little too. Drink some wine."

"That sounds really nice. I'm a little worried about them flying by themselves, but Ava is ten going on twenty and she told me she can handle it. Thank you for getting them set up with a charter flight."

"You're welcome. Why don't we change it and send them into Sonoma? You can fly up with me Friday afternoon and we'll meet them there."

"That would be great. Thanks, Keatyn."

"You're welcome, Dawson."

"And thanks for not telling Riley you hired me. I realize now that probably wasn't easy for you. Was he mad?"

"He was thrilled. I mean, how many times has he tried to hire you over the years?"

"Yeah, I guess you're right."

"I heard that you liked Vanessa's lipstick."

I chuckle, a little embarrassed. "I take it you talked to her."

"Yeah."

"Is she mad?"

"Frustrated might be a better word."

"I haven't slept with anyone . . . since . . ."

"I know, Dawson. You came here for a fresh start. I'm not saying it needs to be Vanessa, but you probably need to, you know, again."

"I've never forgotten her."

"Vanessa?"

"Yeah, we kissed at your birthday party. It may have been the best kiss of my life."

"Really?"

"Yeah. And that scares me a little. She's smart. Bold. Why the hell isn't she married?"

"Well, she was."

"Guy was an idiot if you ask me."

"I agree, but there's more to her story, just like there is to yours. Don't be quick to assume you have her figured out."

"Now, I'm intrigued."

"I think you were intrigued before, when you had her naked."

"Shit. She did tell you everything."

"Not everything, just that you left her hot and horny. Just a warning, when she's that way, she's hard to resist."

"I feel guilty. I just can't get over the guilt."

"You have to let it go, Dawson."

"I know. Keatyn?"

"What?"

"Tell Aiden I said thanks. He and my mom are really the ones who talked me into all this."

"You can tell him yourself this weekend."

"I will. Night."

THURSDAY, OCTOBER 2ND
CAPTIVE FILMS - SANTA MONICA
Riley

I WAKE UP to the sun streaming in the windows.

Holy shit what time is it?

I lift my face up off Jennifer's couch and find her passed out next to me.

When was the last time I spent the night at a girl's house who wasn't a relative or Keatyn?

College! Now I rarely go to a girl's place. I've heard too many stories about getting robbed or beat up. I always take them to my place. An environment I can control. I can also bring them downstairs, put them in a cab, thank them for a nice night and say goodbye. Sure, sometimes they try to come back, but other than a recent lapse in judgement regarding Shelby, the doormen never let them get past their post.

I push Jen with my finger. "Hey, we need to get up. I'm usually in the office by now."

"Last night was fun," she states.

"Yeah, it was. Although, are you ever going to let me do more than kiss you?"

"I don't know, we'll see how things go. I like you, Riley."

"I like you too."

WE GET TO the office and I introduce Keatyn to Jennifer and say, "I'm gonna let you girls talk."

"Okay," they both say back in happy unison.

I go to my office, look over my calendar for today, and start to prepare for my first meeting when Dallas strolls into my office. He makes himself at home on my couch, putting his feet up on the glass coffee table as Tyler follows him in with coffees.

"Get your feet off the glass," Tyler says to Dallas, holding up his cup. "Or no coffee for you."

Dallas begrudgingly moves his feet, causing Tyler to reward him with a cup of what is probably the best coffee in California.

As soon as Tyler leaves, Dallas says, "I heard you and Miss Contract rode here together this morning."

"Yeah, I spent the night at her house."

"Oh, do tell," Dallas says, blowing on his coffee before taking a sip.

"It's not like that."

"So, what's it like?"

Knox lets himself in and interrupts. "Is it true she's here and Keatyn is signing her? Like now?"

I look pointedly across the hall at the two of them talking.

"As you can see," Dallas states, "they're talking. If it goes well, Keatyn will call me in and I'll take over."

"What about me?" Knox asks, looking perplexed.

"What about you?" Dallas replies coolly.

I've got to give it to him. Dallas is a master at negotiating contracts and making the talent think they need us more than we need them, whether it's true or not.

"Do you have a contract for *me*?" Knox whines.

"Not yet. Keatyn said if Jennifer signs that we'd put you two together and see if you have chemistry."

"Chemistry?! Hell, that girl is so hot, I'll blow up your fucking chemistry set, Dallas." He turns to me. "Speaking of that, Riley, did you bang her yet?"

"I was just asking the same question," Dallas says.

"Inquiring minds want to know," Knox adds.

"No, not yet. But I'm letting her drive my car this weekend," I say, knowing that will get them going.

Both their mouths drop open in shock.

"The *new* car?" Dallas asks. "Have you *ever* let a girl drive *any* of your cars?"

"Shut up. And, yes, on occasion, I have."

Knox holds up his hand. "Wait, I'm confused. You aren't banging her, but you're letting her drive it? You won't let me drive it! And I'm your friend!"

"You're a bad driver. You totaled your DB9."

"Yeah, well that wasn't my fault."

"Light post jumped out at him," Dallas quips.

"Whatever," Knox says, waving at Dallas. "Although, thanks for getting the ticket taken care of."

"No problem," Dallas replies.

Knox turns back to me and says, "So where is she driving it? Are you taking her out to the middle of nowhere where she can't hurt anything?"

"She wanted us to road trip to my parents' place in the Hamptons . . ."

"You can't put that many miles on it!" Knox exclaims.

"I know. I know. Calm down. I figure we'll go up north, maybe Sonoma. Hit a couple wineries or something."

"Come to Aiden's," Dallas says. "I'll be up there this weekend with the kids."

"We'll see." I don't want to commit to anything just yet. Hopefully, we'll be busy banging somewhere."

"I'm just saying," Knox says. "If you haven't banged her, she's fair game. Wait until I put the old Knox charm on her."

"Old, is right," I say, teasing him.

"Oh, low fucking blow," he says, picking up his coffee and looking across the hall to Keatyn's office. "I'm making my move."

CAPTIVE FILMS - SANTA MONICA
Keatyn

"ARE YOU SURE this is right for you?" I ask Jennifer. I've told her about the project, the time it will entail, and how it's risky. And the fact that we want to pay her based on the gross of project rather than a standard upfront fee.

"You're excited about it and so is Riley," she states. "Tell me this, if the tables were turned, would you do it?"

"Well, yeah, but I'm . . ."

"A risk taker?" she says, finishing my sentence.

"In some ways. Doing the *Trinity* series hasn't exactly been risky. And that's paid for . . ." I stop. "I get what you're saying. You made more than enough money to live off of from doing the *Sector*. You followed it up with two box office hits and an Academy Award. You can do whatever the hell you'd like."

"Exactly! And I want to."

"Awesome. I'll have Dallas go over the contract with you. I know you are excited and so are we, but I want you to have your people read over the contract. Make sure they're good with it."

"I already told you I'm good with it and I trust you. Don't make me regret it," she says boldly.

"I don't think you will."

"Good!" She gets more comfortable on the couch, pulling her legs up and crossing them like a pretzel. "Now, we can gossip."

"What do you want to gossip about?"

"Who do you picture playing Nathan, the guy my dad sets me up with? And what about the town bad boy, Jackson?"

"We have someone who's really interested in the project." I glance toward Knox sitting across the hall in Riley's office. They're having an animated discussion. More than likely it's about sex, not work.

Jennifer follows my eyes and turns around. Then she starts bouncing on the couch. "Holy fucking shit, dude! Knox Daniels? Are you fucking kidding me? Please, please, let him play Nathan. Wait, which one do I sleep with?"

"You sleep with pretty much everyone."

"Shit, that's right. I'll be emailing you my fantasy cast later today. I'm gonna have to sit on the deck, have a few beers, and dream a little. This is like the best role ever. I mean, I know sex scenes are awkward and shit, but still."

I can't help but laugh at her. She's hilarious. "Knox is very interested in playing Nathan."

"No shit?! That's fucking nuts!" She uses her hands to muss up her hair. "Riley and I literally rolled off the couch, I brushed my teeth, and came here. So unprofessional of me. I shoulda got all done up. Am I going to meet him? Now? Today? Is that why he's here?"

"When he heard you were interested, he told me he wanted in. He hasn't even read the script yet. My first thought was that he's too old, but then I realized it would be easy to change the script to accommodate his age. And he can play younger."

Jennifer sits up straight, crosses her legs, and puts her hands in her lap, getting into the Angel character. "I think my daddy would be impressed by an older man that could provide for me, as long as he's a churchgoing man."

I laugh. "That's exactly my thought. And I think people are going to love the bad boy, Jackson. It will make for an interesting love triangle."

"Because I fall for the guy my daddy chose even though I think I want to marry the bad boy?"

"Exactly, and when the audience finds out that Nathan isn't all that good—"

"Why isn't he good?"

"He was in a juvenile detention facility during his teens. He was from the wrong side of the tracks. Got into trouble. Found religion in jail, mostly because he thought he would get out faster. All of that was wiped from his record when he turned eighteen. So her daddy has no idea. Nathan and Jackson really aren't that different at the core. And Nathan has an ulterior motive. Daddy is rich. He bought some land outside of town for the church to use as a camp. Underneath it is loads of oil. Nathan wants to swindle Daddy out of the land by marrying his daughter. But he has to act like he can resist you."

"This just keeps getting better. What a messed up story. I love it. Am I gonna tempt Nathan? Make him be bad?"

"Actually, he thinks he's making you bad. He thinks if you sleep with him, you'll fall in love with him. Remember, he thinks you are a good girl. Because that's what your daddy told him."

"Oh, that's awesome. Who do I end up with?"

"Who do you think you should end up with?"

She smacks her hands together in mock prayer, thinking. "I think audiences will want the bad boy, Jackson. They tend to cheer for the underdog, but I'm assuming that in this story, the good boy is the underdog. And what a twist it will be that she actually falls for the guy her dad chose. I say she finds out he's a fraud, he makes the right choice in the end, and then she chooses him."

"She does."

"Knox for the win!" she yells, holding her arms up in the air, as Knox opens the door.

Her eyes get big and she quickly pulls her arms down.

Knox gives Jennifer his bad boy smirk. "I'm all about the

win, sugar."

I fake pout. "And here I thought I was the only one you called sugar."

"Don't worry, Keatyn, you know what we'll be doing tonight. I'm looking forward to it." He winks at me.

"What are you doing tonight?" Jennifer asks, her eyes still big.

"Jennifer, Knox," I say, ignoring his reference to the sex scenes we're filming later today. "Have you two ever met?"

"Not formally," Knox says. "Although she did give me a hot kiss after she won the Oscar."

She covers her face with her hand. "Note to self: Don't do shots at the Oscars. Ever. Again."

"Unless, you win," I add, causing her to uncover her face and laugh.

"That's right," Knox says, sitting on the couch next to her. "Unless you win."

She holds out her hand. "It's nice to meet you."

He takes her hand in his, stroking it gently. "I liked our first meeting better. We should have a repeat."

Jennifer laughs. If there's one thing Knox knows how to do, it's how to put a coworker at ease.

Although, he's probably serious.

"Knox, Jennifer needs to meet with Dallas to go over the contract. I'd love for the two of you to do a scene together soon."

"I'll do a scene for you right now. Jennifer, follow my lead."

He leans closer to her and starts reciting lines from the *Daddy's Angel* script. Obviously, he talked Riley into giving him a copy because he sure as hell didn't get it from me.

He glides his hand slowly across her shoulder, the sexual intent very clear. "Angel, in this case, I don't think your daddy knows best. Your body is yours to give to any man you deem worthy."

Jennifer, who hasn't seen the script, heaves her chest toward him, giving a full shot of cleavage, and licks her lips. "Are you worthy, Nathan?"

Knox pushes her hair behind her ear and softly kisses her neck. "I'm kissing your neck."

A little gasp escapes from Jennifer's mouth. I can't tell if it's her real reaction or brilliant acting but, either way, it's perfect.

"Now, I'm kissing your lips," Knox says, putting his lips against Jennifer's. She's sitting with her hands to her side. Like she's in shock.

And I'm thinking she is, until she says, "You shouldn't be," wraps her arms around his neck, and deepens their kiss.

They are now totally making out.

I see a shadow cross over them, look up, and see Riley standing outside the glass, pointing down.

He mouths, *What the fuck?*

"Now, I'm going to kiss your breasts," I hear Knox say.

"Knox!" I yell. "Cut!"

Jennifer smacks him on the arm in a cute way, then narrows her eyes at him. "Is that even a line?"

Knox stays close to her, seriously flirting and holding her gaze. "No, but it should be."

Riley bursts through my door, dragging Dallas along with him.

He takes Jennifer's hand and pulls her up off the couch. "Jennifer, Dallas will see you now. And, Knox, you're fired."

Jennifer is still swooning, and stumbles as she follows Dallas out the door because her eyes are locked with Knox's.

As soon as the door shuts, Riley says to Knox, "What the fuck was that?"

"We were reading lines. Keatyn wanted to see if we had chemistry."

"I stopped him before he felt her up." I laugh. "By the way, Knox, I'm jealous. You don't look at me like that anymore."

"Just wait until tonight. Guess who's soft little lips I'm going to be thinking about?"

Riley holds up his hands. "No. Just no. It won't work."

"They do have chemistry, Riley. I felt like I was intruding on something private."

"Shit," Riley says, pushing his hands through his hair and marching back into his office.

Knox grins at me. "It was good, right?"

"Yeah, Knox. It was really good. You're in."

"Fucking aye! You want a ride to the set?"

"Yeah, but can we stop and get something to eat on the way? I'm so hungry I feel sick."

"What's with you and this flu thing?"

"I don't know," I lie. "At least you haven't gotten it."

"No, but I plan on getting *something,* pretty damn soon."

"Knox, I don't know what boy code you and Riley follow, but unless Riley stops hanging out with Jennifer, she's off limits to you."

"What?! No. That's not how it works."

"It's how it's gonna work if you want the part."

"That's blackmail. And I thought you wanted him back with the chick who stomped on his heart?"

"I just want him happy, Knox. He took the afternoon off yesterday to hang out with her. He never does that."

"He's letting her drive his car," he says, defeated.

"Then that ought to tell you something."

CAPTIVE FILMS - SANTA MONICA

I KNOCK ON my brother's office door. I can see through the glass that he already looks stressed. He's running his hands through his hair and pacing.

He looks up and motions for me to come in.

"You got a minute?" I ask.

"Sure."

"I just wanted you to know that it's my fault Keatyn didn't tell you I was coming. I asked her not to tell you."

"But why? I've offered you jobs over the years. You knew I'd want you to come."

"I wasn't sure if I could leave the girls. Leave home. I didn't want you to know if I couldn't do it. It was embarrassing enough to tell her."

"Dawson, I know I was probably a little rough on you this summer, but it's for your own good. You can't let—"

I hold my hands up and interrupt him. I know what he's going to say. It's what everyone has said for the last two years. "I know. And you're right."

He sits down behind his desk. "So, Keatyn and Aiden talked you into it, but I couldn't?"

I take a seat in a chair across from him. "They helped, but it was actually Mom who tipped the scale. She told me that Harlow came home in tears after visiting Whitney's mother."

"Why?"

"Because she hurt her feelings. Told her she didn't know how to behave like a lady. You know how spunky she is. She stood up for herself and said, 'that's because I'm a girl'."

"Ooh. What did she say to that?"

"That she had just proved her point. That a lady would also never speak to her elder in that tone. And then something about how I wasn't teaching her manners and she'd grow up to be a social misfit."

"I bet that pissed Mom off."

"It did. She told me that although she'd miss the girls terribly, she loves California and would visit often. She doesn't want them around that kind of influence."

"I don't know why you didn't tell Whitney's mom to fuck off a long time ago."

"Because she threatened to sue me for custody, Riley. And I was scared to death that she'd win."

"How could she win?"

"Because I was a *deadbeat dad*. No job, no home."

"And you don't have a home because of goddamned Whitney," Riley says, getting pissed.

I hold up my hand. "Don't, please."

"I'm sorry. So, is that what made you come?"

"It was a big part of it. I don't want my girls to grow up like Whitney did."

Riley leans back in his chair and grins. "I might be a little biased because they have me wrapped around their little fingers, but they *are* my favorite nieces. Also, you know what's mine is yours. I told you so many times I'd help you financially."

"I guess I just wasn't ready for help. And you're helping now. Keatyn offered me a ridiculous salary, not to mention the perks. That's not what I wanted to talk to you about, though. Do you think it's too soon for me to, like, maybe go on a date?"

"You don't need a date, bro. What you need is to get laid."

"I haven't been with anyone since Whitney left."

"Dawson, stop saying that Whitney left. She fucking *killed herself*, made you feel guilty about it, and left you broke to raise the girls alone! It was selfish of her, and a chicken shit way out of the mess she'd made."

I run my hand through my hair, much like the way my brother did earlier.

"Yesterday, Vanessa and I were at this hotel. And . . ."

"And?" he asks, a smirk on his face.

"And, it was hot. She was naked. I was going to. But then I stopped. Felt guilty."

"You know, if you don't use your dick, it will turn to stone and fall clean off your body."

I start cracking up and so does Riley.

"I remember when Camden told us that when we caught him beating off in his room."

Riley says with a laugh, "I know I sure as hell never risked finding out if he was right."

"Mine hasn't turned to stone. Well, except for yesterday. I was as hard as granite. Vanessa's beautiful. Smart. And those god damned red lips. I know you have a rule about not having sex with coworkers."

"That's Keatyn's rule for me. You should totally fuck Vanessa. And, as your boss, I'd highly recommend it."

I squint my eyes, the thought of my brother having been with her bothers me way more than it should. "You recommend it because the two of you have . . . ?"

"What? No. I've never been with her. I'm just saying you should."

"What do you know about her ex?"

"He couldn't keep his dick in his pants. But I think it was more than that. He destroyed her. She almost lost her business. I suppose the two of you have a lot in common. You both got fucked over. You need to get back in the saddle again. And Vanessa has a fucking equestrian center. She's got lots of saddles. So go for a ride, bro. Hook up with her this weekend."

"I won't be here this weekend. Keatyn's flying the girls to Sonoma. We're meeting them there and spending the weekend at the vineyard. Dallas is going with his kids too."

"So, then, you better get on her *today*," Riley says as I head out.

I SEE KEATYN'S still at her desk. She waves me in.

"You and Riley okay?"

"Yeah, we're good. You know all my brothers are encouraging me to, uh, get back in the saddle again."

"Dawson, you'll know when the time is right. Actually, it sounds like the time was almost right yesterday."

"How long do you think a widow should wait before he starts dating again?"

"My mom started dating about a year after my dad died."

"How old were you?"

"Almost ten."

"And what did you think?"

"I was kind of a little shit about it, until she met Tommy. Are you thinking about asking Vanessa on a date?"

"Maybe. Does Captive have a rule about that?"

Keatyn grins. "That rule is only for your brother. And, technically, Vanessa isn't an employee. So you like her, huh?"

"Yeah, I think I do."

"Good, we have a meeting with her in your office in ten minutes."

"We do?"

"Yep. I want to get you both up to speed on *Daddy's Angel*. I'll see you in a few."

AS I WALK out of Keatyn's office, Tyler joins me. "I have all sorts of stuff for you in your office. So do you like the decor?" he asks me.

"Yeah, it's great," I reply, taking it all in again. The walls are dark teal and there is a coffee table made from a tree trunk sitting in front of a comfortable brown leather couch. I have an industrial looking desk with a lush suede chair to match.

"Keatyn worried about the color."

"She has good taste."

"That she does," he says. "Have a seat. On the desk, you have your new cell phone, business credit card, business cards, swipe key to access anywhere in the building, and laptop." He hands me a piece of paper. "After your meeting with Vanessa and Keatyn, you have an appointment with Human Resources to get

159

your benefits set up, and then a meeting with the marketing staff. From there, you're having lunch and playing golf with Riley and Dallas."

"Golf? I'm not really dressed for that."

Tyler turns and presses his palm into the wood-sheathed wall behind him. A door pops open revealing a large closet stocked with clothing ranging from golf attire to formal wear.

"Behind here," Tyler says, opening another door, "is your full private lavatory. There are many times when you will go directly from work to another event, so all the executive suites are set up in similar fashion."

"Wow," I say. "This is great."

"And there's Vanessa," Tyler says. "I'll leave you now. I'm interviewing assistants for you today. Do you have any special requirements?"

"Can you clone yourself?" I joke.

"I'll see what I can do," he says, exiting, and leaving me face to face with Vanessa.

"Good morning," I say politely.

"Good morning," she replies brusquely, setting her briefcase on the coffee table. She's wearing a tailored black skirt that reveals long bare legs and leopard print high heels, but all I'm seeing is her lying on the bed last night, naked.

I feel myself start to harden.

And it drives me toward her.

"I'm sorry about last night," I tell her, sweeping her into my arms and lowering my lips to hers.

At first, her body feels stiff against mine.

But as our lips touch and our tongues collide, her stance softens.

She returns my kiss with passion.

I hear Keatyn say, "Oh, um, I'll just be in my office whenever you two are finished with your, uh, meeting."

Vanessa untangles herself from my arms and looks up at me

through long dark, lashes. Then she laughs. "You have a little—"
Her thumb glides across my bottom lip. "—lipstick on you."

"I love your red lipstick, but I probably shouldn't wear it to a
meeting," I laugh. "We better go."

Vanessa walks to my door, but then leans her back against it,
facing me. "In case you couldn't tell, I'm forgiving you for last
night. But for the record, if you're ever lucky enough to get me
naked again, I expect you to follow through."

I lean my body into hers, pressing her against the door, and
kiss the hell out of her again.

AFTER OUR MEETING, I follow her back to my office.

"Keatyn didn't say anything about us kissing. I thought she
would."

Vanessa doesn't respond. When my office door shuts, she
locks it and takes off her jacket. And the way she's eyeing my
new desk makes me very thankful that my office doesn't have
glass walls like my brother's.

I know exactly what's going to happen next.

I pick her up and set her on my desk as she undoes my belt. I
don't have time to think about if I should or if I shouldn't.

She unzips my pants and untucks my shirt, kissing me hard
as her nails scratch down my back.

I roughly push her back on the desk, causing her skirt to ride
up around her waist, and allowing me to push aside the thin strip
of lace separating her from my dick.

My fingers slip into her. Fuck, she's wet. Thank god, I
jerked off in the shower last night, or just feeling her would have
me blowing my load.

Her arms are wrapped tightly around my neck, and we're
kissing deeply. Ravenously. Her tongue sucks on mine like she
owns it. I've never been kissed like this before. I've also never felt
such pure, raw desire.

I push my boxers down, pulling my dick out, and push into

her. Harder than I planned, but I can't help it. She moans into my mouth, setting me in motion. I grab her ass and pull her toward me, thrusting deeper. She spreads her legs wider by wrapping them around my waist. I can feel a spiked heel raking across my back with every thrust.

She grabs my tie, pulling it tightly, as her breathing gets more ragged. When she tightens against me, I know she's on the verge of orgasm. I take her hips tightly into my hands, moving her quickly with me, as I plunge into her, quickly pull out, then thrust in again.

"Oh, fuck," she says, moving her lips from my mouth to my neck. She sucks my skin into her mouth, but the harder I thrust, the more she uses her teeth, biting me. I go faster, harder, rocking her against my desk, and finally lose control.

I pull her into a hug while trying to catch my breath.

"We better get cleaned up before someone comes looking for us," she says, the blood returning to her brain much faster than mine. I was just thinking that as soon as I could breathe again, I'd move her to the leather couch and start round two.

"Oh, yeah, probably," I reply.

She starts to push away from me, but I hold tight, putting my lips on her neck and slowly kissing up to her ear. "Now, I'm really sorry about last night."

She throws her head back and laughs. "That's fucking right. You should be. Now, let me go clean up."

"I have a bathroom," I say, trying to pull out without making a mess and realizing I didn't use a condom.

She runs to the bathroom. I grab a couple napkins off the bar and clean myself. I'm buckling my belt when she returns.

Her hair is mussed, her cheeks are flushed, and the red lipstick is gone.

God, she's beautiful.

I have to taste her lips once more.

"I like your office," she says, coolly. "That was fun, but we both have meetings to get to."

"Uh, okay," I say, a little shocked at how business-like she is acting all of a sudden.

How can she be so together when I feel like I was just taken completely apart?

She unlocks my door and grabs her jacket. "You might want to take a quick look in the mirror."

I WATCH HER ass until the door shuts behind it.

I straighten my tie, tuck my shirt in better, and then go look in the mirror.

There are red lipstick stains on my cheeks, neck, and lips, not to mention on my shirt collar. My hair is a mess and there's a bite mark on my neck.

I quickly take off my shirt and tie, throwing it into the bag designated for dry cleaning. A little soap, water, and some scrubbing have the lipstick off my face. Not much I can do about the bite mark. I reach around and feel my lower back, then turn to examine it in the mirror. Nail marks show where she scratched my back and there's a chaffed spot from her heel.

I should be freaked out by the fact that I just fucked a co-worker on my second day.

That I smell like sex and her perfume.

That I didn't use a condom.

But I'm not.

I feel fucking amazing.

I throw the closet doors open and choose a black shirt with a wide spread collar, thread a Hermes belt through the loops, and decide not to wear a jacket.

There are a few different brands of cologne on a shelf but I forgo it and head to my meeting.

As I walk by Riley's office, Vanessa steps out. "I understand you're golfing this afternoon."

"Uh, huh."

"I'm told you will be done in time to accompany me to an event tonight. I'll be at your house at eight."

"Uh, okay," I say, stumbling on my words.

"And your brother would like to see you before your meeting."

I WALK INTO my little brother's office, forcing myself to be cool. "What's up, Riley?"

"I asked Vanessa to accompany you to an event tonight," he says with a grin that implies I'll get laid.

"What kind of event?"

"Some sort of fundraiser for the Arts. Captive bought a table."

"Will you be there?"

"Nah, after golf, I'm taking Jennifer to Vegas. We're celebrating."

"She signed the contract?"

"Yes, sir," he says proudly. "Now, we'll work on a more personal contract." He studies me. "You look different. Did you change?"

"Tyler told me I should be more casual."

Riley moves closer to me, studying me and narrowing his eyes. I tilt my neck slightly to the side, hoping to hide the mark. "You look happy."

I smile. "I really think I'm going to like working at Captive Films."

VANESSA'S ESTATE - HOLMBY HILLS
Vanessa

"ARIELA, IS THIS crazy?" I ask, carefully sliding on another black stocking.

"Are you kidding? He's going to love it."

"But I lied to him. I told him we were going to the event when I have no intention of doing so."

She laughs. "I don't think he'll mind."

"So, tell me what Keatyn said when you talked to her," I say.

"Well, she told me they want to get married in less than three weeks. On October the eighteenth."

"Can you do it?"

"She says the vineyard works regularly with an event company, so it shouldn't be a problem getting flowers, tables, linens, things like that. I'm worried about a cake."

"I'm sure any cake company would fit it in, just so they could brag about the wedding."

"If we could do that, it would be easy. But she doesn't want anyone to know it's a wedding."

"Right," I say, knowing that, but trying to decide if I should do what I'm about to do is consuming my brain. "Which shoe do you like? No, I take that back. Which shoe will Dawson think is sexier?"

"That one," she says, pointing to a black caged bootie with silver straps that have a bit of a dominatrix look. "And if I had to worry about a venue, I'd say it couldn't be done, but it sounds like she's got that covered. I just need to see it."

"The vineyard is gorgeous. Acres and acres of grapes set on rolling hills. Their house is built on the highest point and from the back you can see the ocean."

"She said something about a barn? I just can't picture Keatyn getting married in a barn."

"Oh, this isn't just any barn. This is the barn Aiden built just for her parties. It's gorgeous. All wood and beams. If it weren't for the fact it's in the shape of a barn, has barn doors, and is wood, you wouldn't even call it a barn."

"Oh, now you're getting me excited!" Ariela says, her eyes wide and a big grin on her face. "Did I tell you I'm going there this weekend?"

"You did. But lie to me. Tell me it's my outfit that has you excited and not the barn," I joke, throwing on the fur coat. "Okay, here's the full effect."

"You look amazing. I should hug you before you leave, because I don't think Dawson will let you out of bed all weekend."

I laugh, hoping she's right. "So were you able to get ahold of the investigator today?"

"Yeah," she says with a sigh.

"Did he find out something, already?"

"Yeah. He got someone to follow Collin today. Guess where he went for lunch?"

"To her place?"

"Yep. I even have pictures."

I sit on the bed and take her hand in mine. "I'm sorry."

"I knew it was happening, you know," she sniffles. "But seeing the proof. Seeing them kiss. There are other photos too. They didn't bother to close the blinds. You could see their passion. It just reinforces what an idiot I was to have married him. He never, ever kissed me like that. They barely made it in the house. Did it on her couch."

"And here I am going on about seducing Dawson. I'm sorry, really."

"It's okay."

"You shouldn't be alone tonight. I can do this a different night."

"Are you kidding? Don't you dare. Besides, I have a baby shower to go to." She gives me a hug. "Now, get your sexy ass over to Dawson's."

MY DRIVER TAKES me to Malibu. I'm nervous, anxious, excited, and horny.

Mostly, horny.

Dawson told me our kiss was the best of his life.

And I have to admit, today, on his desk, was the hottest sex of my life.

Bam and I had a good sex life. But it's weird how age and perspective can change what you thought. I loved Bam. I did. But I'm starting to wonder if Keatyn might be right about the whole true love thing.

But if I think that way, it would mean Dawson could be that guy. And that's something I'm not ready to even consider.

I'm just trying to figure out what made it so good.

It's not like it's the first time I've done it in a guy's office before. So it's not that. And in the two years since Bam and I broke up, I've been having a whole lot of revenge sex. Angry sex. One night stands.

So it's not like I'm just in need of sex.

Today, just felt like more.

And it scares me a little.

I stand on his front porch trying to decide if I should ring the doorbell or run like hell in the other direction.

When my driver pulls away, my choice becomes easier. I can't go running around Malibu in nothing but a fur coat.

I take a deep breath, stand up straight, and push the button.

Dawson answers wearing a black tuxedo complete with bow tie.

"You look nice," I say. *Nice* being a severe understatement.

"Come in," he says, leading me into a comfortable, shabby chic decorated home. "There was champagne in the fridge," he points to a bottle on the kitchen island. "Would you like some?"

"Of course."

He heads toward the champagne then turns back around. "I'm sorry. Where are my manners? May I take your coat?"

"I thought you'd never ask." I slip out of my coat and lay it over his outstretched arm. But he doesn't seem to notice the fur.

His eyes are glued to what I'm wearing.

Or, not wearing, as the case would be.

"Wow. This is straight out of one of my fantasies." He gives me a naughty smirk, tosses my coat over a chair, and trails the back of his hand across my shoulder. "I should have come to L.A. sooner. Will all the women be dressed like this for the benefit?"

"Probably not," I say as his lips follow his hand, leaving kisses in their wake. Goosebumps form on my skin from the cool ocean breeze blowing through the deck door, but on the inside I feel hot, like I'm burning up from within.

He touches the lace on my bra, the lace on my thong, and the tops of my garters.

"I have a new fantasy," he says, grabbing my coat and putting it back on me.

"What's that?" I whisper.

"Would you mind going back outside and ringing the doorbell again?"

"Uh, um, sure," I say, wondering why he wants me to, but if he has a fantasy about me, I'm all for exploring it.

A few seconds later, he shuts the door in my face.

My insides are throbbing, my panties are wet, and he's yet to kiss me on the lips.

I hit the doorbell.

He answers, looking like I caught him in the middle of getting dressed. His pants are on, but his jacket, tie, and shoes are gone. His shirt is on, but not buttoned.

And, my god, is it a sight.

His chest is so well formed. His muscles taut and hard.

His abs so perfectly sculpted they almost don't look real.

"I've been waiting for you," he says, exposing my shoulder and giving it a kiss. "Well, well. What do we have here?" He slides his hand inside my coat, running it from my neck to my thong. He hooks a finger around the lace, quickly stripping it off me. Then his tongue retraces his hand's path. He grabs my ass as he slides his tongue down the side of my neck, across my collar bone, and down through my cleavage. I push my fingers through his thick hair, not sure what's going to happen next, but eagerly anticipating it.

His tongue grazes across the swell of my breast then he lowers himself to his knees and kisses my stomach.

Although his kisses are hard and hungry, there's something different about the way he kisses my stomach. It's sweet, almost loving.

His tongue works its way lower, until it's nearly between my legs.

He surprises me when he stands, effortlessly picks me up, and lays me on the closest surface, the dining room table.

The silk lining of my coat feels even more sensual than usual. I reach out and guide his face toward me, eagerly kissing him.

"Hold that thought," he says, moving to the end of the table and sinking his head between my legs.

His hands slip between the silk and my ass, bringing me closer to his mouth. While his tongue is smooth, the slight scruff from his five o'clock shadow is rough. The combination of that and the back and forth motions of his tongue send me over the edge.

I grab his hair with one hand, and my fur with the other, my pelvis taking over the motions, causing his tongue to move exactly how I want it.

"Oh, oh, oh, god, that feels good."

He moves his tongue in a circular motion and slides two fingers inside me.

It's abrupt. Hard. And I immediately have another, deeper orgasm. This one, racking through my entire body. I moan his name until I can't speak.

Then he picks me up and carries me into the living room.

Somewhere along the way, he removed his pants, because when he sits on the rug in front of the blazing fire, he pulls me down directly on top of his massive hard on. My insides are still contracting and I want to ride him.

Hard.

I may have even said something to that effect, I can't even remember.

But he says, "Slow down, baby. We're doing this my way." His hands are wrapped around my hips, slowing my motion. He pushes the fur off and kisses my shoulder. Then, while still slowly moving himself inside me, he takes my hand and kisses it.

I melt.

I'm not sure if it's because of the fire on a hot day or him.

But I'm a fucking puddle.

And Vanessa Flanning is never a puddle.

We kiss, slowly at first, my hips moving in rhythm with his. His hold on me tightens.

Our kissing becomes deeper.

Our rhythm becomes faster.

I glance down, noticing how my hips seem to fit perfectly in his big hands.

He moves me up and down on top of him, faster and harder, giving me a frenzied burst of thrusting that causes my insides to tighten.

We're both vocalizing our pleasure, when he shudders and gets suddenly still, leaning his head into my chest.

As he exhales, I caress his back, run my fingers through his hair, and kiss his temple.

Tears spring to my eyes as emotions run through me.

And I have no idea why.

This was supposed to be a hot fantasy fuck.

"Are those tears?" he asks. "Why?"

"Because no one has made me feel this way for a long time." I say, admitting the truth and suddenly feeling very naked.

"No one has made me feel this way for a long time either," he says.

"I liked your fantasy," I tell him with a smile, trying to lighten things up. "Do you have any more?"

"You were the object of almost every fantasy I've had since the day I met you," he says, which tugs at my heartstrings even more.

"I should have looked you up when I was in New York," I say, suddenly wondering why I didn't and wondering how different my life might have been if I had.

"Yeah, you should have. Let's have some champagne, eat something, and if you're good, I'll show you some more of them. I'm assuming we're not going to the event."

I shake my head. "Nah."

"Is there even an event?" he laughs.

"Yes, there is, but I gave away our tickets."

"So you planned this?" he teases, handing me his white shirt to put on.

I can't help but smile. "Well, I planned to show up like I did, but I didn't know if you'd be interested."

He wraps his arm around my waist and pulls me close. "I'd be a fool not to be interested. Tell me about the coat."

"The coat?" I ask.

"Yeah, why the fur and not a trench coat? It's hot out."

"It's soft?" I say, tentatively.

"And—?"

"Fine, it's possible that I hate this coat. But it's so incredibly beautiful. And I wanted to look nice for you tonight."

"Vanessa, I love that you wanted to impress me, but I'm already impressed. I think you're beautiful. Why do you hate the coat?"

"My ex bought it for me after he cheated on me."

"He was trying to win you back?"

"Yes."

He gives me a sweet kiss and touches the fur. "It's my new mission to make this your favorite thing."

"How are you going to do that?"

"We're not done with the fur," he says in a way that sounds almost like a threat to both my fur and my ex.

HE LEADS ME to the kitchen, where he grabs a tray of fruit, cheese, and nuts out of the fridge and opens the champagne.

"Are you expecting company?"

He laughs. "No, it's a welcome gift. Keatyn thinks of everything."

"Actually, Tyler thinks of everything."

"Well, I'll be sure to thank him then." He hands me a flute and says, "To luxury spending."

"And to fur," I say with a laugh and take a sip. The bubbles go straight to my nose and cause me to sneeze.

"Bless you," he says.

"Thanks."

He picks a grape off the tray and feeds it to me.

I'm shocked by how natural it feels. How it doesn't feel like I'm submitting, but rather he's taking care of me.

And for a woman who's trying hard to hold everything together, it's really, really nice.

"So, um," he says, "we've done it twice now without a condom. I keep meaning to ask, and I know it's not very responsible of me, but . . ."

"I can't get pregnant," I admit.

"Why not?"

"Well, after I lost my baby—"

"Wait, what? When did that happen?"

"A few years ago. I was pregnant and miscarried at about four months."

He moves quickly around the island and wraps me in his arms. "That must have been horrible for you."

"It was. And I don't know what all went wrong, but they told me I wouldn't be able to get pregnant again."

"I'm sorry. Your husband must have been crushed."

"Uh, not exactly."

"Didn't he want children?"

I take a gulp of champagne. Why the hell am I talking about this? I don't talk about it to anyone.

Not even Keatyn knows the details of how it all went down.

"I, um, it's not something I want to discuss."

He nods, while studying my eyes. "I understand. But, Vanessa, just so you know, you can tell me anything."

"Does that go for you too?"

"What do you mean?"

"Why haven't you worked for the last two years?"

"My wife left." He pauses for a moment, seeming to reconsider his words. "Actually, that's not exactly right. My wife, um, she died."

My eyes get huge and I feel horrible for prying, especially when I see tears shining in his eyes. "I'm sorry. That must have been horrible for you."

"It was. That's why I stopped last night. It's not because I didn't want you. I just, well, you're the first woman since . . ." His voice trails off.

And I'm thinking no fucking way. He hasn't been with anyone since she died? Two years ago? Oh, god, no. Please tell me he went out and got laid like I did after Bam. I just wanted to be fucked.

But I don't want that with Dawson, because I want . . . I want . . . Ohmigawd. I want him to love me. I don't want to be the girl he fucks to get over his dead wife.

"Since, uh, when?" *Please say since you've been in California.*

"Since she died."

Shit. I'm so fucked.

THURSDAY, OCTOBER 2ND
FOUR SEASONS HOTEL – LAS VEGAS

"RILEY, YOU'RE DRUNK. I don't think this is a good idea," Jennifer says, trying to get away from me.

I give her my sexy grin and pull her back onto my lap. "You were grinding on me all night and gave me a lap dance in the club. Got me hot."

"I'm sorry. I was just dancing."

"On my dick."

She rolls her eyes. "Fine, I was a little drunk and dancing in a totally fun but inappropriate way."

I slide my hands up her shirt. "I like inappropriate."

She pushes my hands down. "Riley, you're drunk."

"So?"

"I don't want to have sex with you when you're drunk. We're going to be working together. I don't want to mess up our business relationship."

"Fine, you're fired."

"You can't fire me. I have a contract."

"Dallas always gives me a way out."

She frowns, gets up, and walks toward the huge bank of

windows overlooking the strip.

I follow her. My horny thoughts conjuring up visions of fucking her from behind while we both look out at the lights. That would be a beautiful shot in a movie, actually.

I wrap my arms around her, pulling her ass against my hardness. "I was just thinking. . ."

"Just stop it, Riley," she cries.

And it hits me that she's actually crying.

This sobers me up.

"What's wrong? Are you crying?"

"Yes, you jerk, I'm crying. I like you. And you're ruining it. If sex is all you want—if you aren't interested in me, or in being friends—then just get the fuck out of here, call Dallas, and get me fired."

I start to feel nauseous.

"Uh, excuse me," I say, but I only get as far as the ice bucket before throwing up.

"Gross," she says, coming to help me. "I'll call down for some coffee."

I throw up again and then shake my head. "Make it a nice greasy cheeseburger, fries, and a Coke."

"That sounds good," she says, taking the ice bucket away from me and handing me a larger version, one that held the magnum of champagne we drank to pre-party.

I hear her ordering room service and slide to the floor with the bucket, praying I didn't just screw everything up.

DAWSON'S BEACH HOUSE - MALIBU

MY HEART GOES out to Vanessa for not only having a miscarriage, but also for not being able to get pregnant again. I can tell it's something that hurts her deeply, and I'm pretty sure, based on the little she said, that her husband wasn't supportive.

Whether or not I was a supportive husband is a question that has gone through my head a million times over the last two years. *Was I a good husband? Is it my fault Whitney's dead? Did she know I wouldn't stand by her?*

It's weird how you can look back on your life and so clearly see all the mistakes you made. If you knew then what you know now, how would your life be different? Or would it be? For example, would I have used the condoms Whitney gave me when we had sex or used my own?

I was going to tell Vanessa about my daughters tonight. But, after her admission, I'm thinking now's not the right time.

Plus, she's wearing nothing but my shirt.

I glance at the fur coat she showed up in. I need to come up with a few more ways to make her love that coat. To make her think of me every time she sees it. Because for the first time in a very long time, I feel like maybe things are turning around for me. That everything I've been through, from Whitney getting pregnant to the aftermath of her death, is over. My brothers were right. It's time for me to put the past behind me and start living again.

It's dark outside and although I'm more than ready to fuck her again, I don't want it to be just sex with us.

"Do you want me to open another bottle of champagne or would you prefer something else?"

"You got any good scotch?" she says to me with a grin.

I grab two lowballs from a cabinet, drop a couple ice cubes in, and pour us each a drink.

"Would you mind carrying these?" I ask, handing them to her while I grab the fur.

"Where are we going?"

I don't answer, just give her a directional nod.

"Is that the way to the bedroom?" she asks.

"Sorta," I say, leading her through the master bedroom, bathroom, and then out a side door.

"Wow," she says, echoing my own thoughts when I first saw the little Zen courtyard. "This is so pretty. It must be for meditating and doing yoga."

"And relaxing," I say, turning her toward the round daybed tucked into the corner.

"I've never seen anything like that," she says, taking in the daybed which looks like something you would find at an exotic resort. It's layered with red cushions and pillows and has a pointed wicker top. There are even curtains for privacy.

I set our drinks on a wicker cocktail table next to it, lie down, and snuggle her into my chest, using the fur as a blanket.

"I feel like a genie in a bottle," she says, looking around and laughing.

"Does that mean I get to rub you and make three wishes?" I ask.

She quickly stops laughing, her breath seemingly taken away by my question. "What would you wish for?" she whispers.

"Love," I say softly.

"I want love too. Big love. Do you know what I'm talking about?"

"Like Keatyn and Aiden?"

"Yes. The kind of love that can't be torn apart. The kind of love that heals and inspires. The kind of love that lasts forever. What else would you wish for?"

"Happiness and forgiveness."

"What do you need to be forgiven for?"

"I feel responsible for things I really had no control over. I feel like I need to be forgiven. What would you wish for?"

"I wish I could have children," she says. "And I'll second your love and happiness."

I rub my hand across her naked stomach three times. "Ask me what I want, genie," I say.

She holds my hand in place. "I'm going to grant you three wishes. What would you like?"

"I want Vanessa to find big love, happiness, and children."

"That's three wishes. Don't you want to save some for yourself?"

"Nah," I say, pressing my lips against hers.

We kiss while lying naked under her fur coat, for a really long time.

FRIDAY, OCTOBER 3RD
DRIVING UP THE CALIFORNIA COAST
Ariela

I'M CRUISING UP Highway 1 when my cell rings.

"Hey, Keatyn," I say. "Hang on." I carefully pull to the side of the road and put my flashers on. "Sorry, I have the top down and couldn't hear you."

"It's okay. I was just calling to see if you wanted to fly up to Sonoma with me today."

"Oh, thanks for asking, but I decided to drive up the coast. I've never been farther north than Malibu. Vanessa said the drive is breathtaking. She even lent me one of her convertibles."

"How fun! I'm jealous. It is so beautiful. You'll love it. And there's something so freeing about hopping in a convertible and blaring your music."

"That's exactly my plan. I didn't even make reservations anywhere for tonight. I'm just going to stop wherever I feel like it."

"What time should I expect you on Saturday?"

"Is around noon okay?"

"Yes, that'd be perfect. Um, have you talked to Maggie yet?"

I sigh. "No, I'll be honest. I'm kind of chicken."

179

"Don't be. Maggie definitely speaks her mind, but she was really excited to hear you're coming. I do think you owe her a call though."

"You're right. I'll do it as soon as I hang up."

"What about your parents? Have you talked to them? Or your husband?"

"Vanessa gave me the name of a private investigator, who had Collin followed yesterday. There are pictures of him screwing his secretary. He lied when he said he would stop. Not that it matters. I'm not going back."

"Do your parents know?"

"I haven't told them. He works for my dad. They won't understand."

"I know it's been a long time since I've seen your parents, and I know you blame them for some of the past but, Ariela, you chose your path. You were eighteen when you left Eastbrooke and were in your twenties when you got married. You may have felt pressure to stay on that path, but *you* chose it. You can't blame your parents. I'm sure they thought they were doing what was best for you."

"Wow. Tough love, huh? I expected that from Maggie, not you."

Keatyn laughs. "I may be quoting Maggie. I'm also a little worried."

"About what?"

"Riley is my best friend. All I want is for him to be happy. And I'll love whoever he chooses as long as she makes him happy."

"I saw him leave with Jennifer Edwards and saw the article about them. Are they dating?"

"Yes. I know you came here on a whim, Ariela. I get it. But until you are sure about what you want, don't mess with his life."

"I understand. Thanks. I'll see you tomorrow."

I press *end* on my phone and just stare at it, Keatyn's words echoing in my head. She's right. I did come here on a whim. But at the same time, I've wanted to do it for so long.

Before I chicken out, I call my father. I was going to call Mom, give her my typical update. *I'm fine. I just need a break.* It's time I take responsibility for my life.

After getting through his assistant, my father answers with, "When are you coming back home?"

"I'm not. I've hired an attorney and am filing for a divorce."

"You're what? Why?"

"Our marriage falling apart isn't all Collin's fault, Dad. I never loved him the way I should have."

"Is that why you're really in California? Are you looking up that boy from high school?"

"The boy who you said would never amount to anything?"

"Yeah, what was his name?"

"It's Riley Johnson. And you were wrong, Dad. Riley is the CEO of a movie production company. A multi-billion dollar company. He's more successful than Collin, and even you."

"So, you want to trade up?"

"No, I'm following my heart. I wasn't strong enough to do it when I was eighteen, but I'm strong enough now."

"Collin will be devastated."

"Oh, I think he will be fine, since he's sleeping with his secretary. But you probably already knew that."

"Ariela, you have a good life here."

"No, I don't. I'm miserable. And even if Riley doesn't give me another chance, I'm staying in California. This was my dream too, not just his."

"You're a little young for a midlife crisis, darling. Your mother went through something like this in our marriage. She started seeing Dr. Vance. Maybe we should make you an appointment."

"Let me guess, that was about the time she found out you

weren't faithful, and she decided she liked her life enough to settle for part of you? Or she was fucking Dr. Vance to get back at you?"

"Ariela! How dare you?"

"Mom told me about your arrangement. I think it sucks, and I don't respect it. Call me a fool, but I believe in true love. And I'm going to find it. Collin will be getting the divorce papers next week. Goodbye, Dad."

I'M SHAKING AND crying when I hang up. I look over at the ocean. I didn't realize when I pulled over that there's a beach right here. I get out of the car, grab a mat out of the trunk, and go sit in the sand.

As I sit down, I decide to call the one person who always understood what my parents were like, my best friend from high school, Maggie.

"Maggie?" I say when she answers.

"Ariela?" she asks. "Are you crying?"

I say yes and tell her everything that happened after high school. What my dad had said. How he told me going to California would be the biggest mistake of my life. How I got back together with Collin, the boy I had dated from home. How I married him. How unhappy I've been. What made me decide to come to California. What's happened with Riley. What my dad just said. And, finally, how I've missed her.

I figured she would chew me out, but she says, "I missed you too. I heard you're coming up here."

"I am."

"It'll be okay, Ariela."

"Do you really think so?"

"I don't know if Riley will forgive you, and I don't know if you will end up together. But that really isn't the point. You have to be happy with yourself, first and foremost."

"You're right, as usual. I thought you were going to chew me out."

"Oh, I still might," she says. "But I can't do it when you've been crying."

"Thanks. See you tomorrow."

TRINITY MOVIE SET – STUDIO CITY

Keatyn

KNOX KISSES MY neck and then my lips.

We're both shirtless. Nude pasties cover my nipples and we're both wearing underwear for this scene since a sheet is strategically covering Knox's ass. My legs are both outside the sheet, one bent on the bed, the other wrapped around him.

"Slowly arch your back into him," the director whispers. "This is the night you're going to conceive your love child. Good. Now, Knox, gently wrap your arm around her buttocks and pull her even closer. Good. Can we get that?" he says to the camera man. "Close in right there, their chests coming together."

"*Coming together*," Knox whispers in my ear.

I try not to laugh, but I can't help it. It bursts out of me.

"Cut!" the director yells. "Come on, guys. Stop screwing around."

"But we're supposed to be screwing around," Knox says innocently, which makes me bite my lip to keep from laughing even harder.

"Start over," he says. "Let's do it again."

"*Yes, let's*," Knox whispers to me.

"Stop it," I say out of the corner of my mouth. "The sooner we get this done, the sooner I can catch a plane."

"I'll be serious if you let me come with you this weekend."

"Fine."

"Action," the director says.

Knox kisses my neck and then my lips. I slowly arch my back toward him. He gently grabs my ass and pulls me closer.

"That's it, beautiful. Knox, run your hand across her cheek and look into her eyes. Now, together, tighter, you're doing it. Perfect. Okay, cut. Let's remove the sheet. You ready for this, Knox? Your ass' first film appearance?"

I laugh again. "It's about time, Knox. My naked ass has been in the last two."

"Yeah, I am."

We both take off our underwear, him leaving on the sock that covers his male parts and me with a pastie that covers mine.

Getting back in bed, Knox gets on top of me. The makeup artist spritzes his back with mineral water, so he looks like he's sweating then she works on his butt cheeks, adding body makeup so they look perfect on camera.

My makeup artist is doing the same, spritzing a little water in my cleavage, checking that the body makeup is still covering my tattoo, and adding highlights.

The whole time they're getting us ready, Knox is talking to me and asking me if I'm okay. He's always made me feel comfortable doing sex scenes, which are awkward at best.

"Action," the director says.

Knox grips my hips, pulling his chest up off mine and grinding into me.

"Hang on! Wardrobe, we forgot to take off the nipple pasties."

I roll my eyes at Knox, as he leans up so makeup can come in and fix my chest. She decides to add some shading to highlight my cleavage and then retreats.

"Action!"

Knox grips my hips and we pretend to make love. Compared to all the other sex scenes we've done together—although the papers are speculating their raciness—these scenes are more sensual. More loving. And we're definitely showing more skin. After five movies—and a whole lot of sexy times—our characters have finally let their guard down. We think the enemy is gone, and we're allowing ourselves to fall in love.

I reach up and run my hands through Knox's hair then down his muscular arms as scripted.

"I love you, Harper," he says to me.

"I love you too," I whisper as he pushes his hips into my spread legs.

Then we kiss. Lots of open mouths. The lip sucking his character is known for. We pick up the pace as per the script.

"Alright, Keatyn, we're coming in for a close-up of your face. You're in ecstasy."

I toss my head back, letting my breath become ragged. I'm pretty good at faking an orgasm. As Knox continues to grind against me, I'm instantly transported back to Aiden's dorm room, to a time before we had done it, when my insides throbbed just from the friction.

"Oh, oh," I moan, letting myself go. My insides start contracting and I moan again.

"Knox, it's your turn now, faster. Faster," the director whispers.

Knox goes faster causing more friction between my legs.

"Holy shit," I say as Knox fakes an orgasm and collapses on top of me.

"Perfect, cut."

I slide into my robe.

"Where the fuck did that come from?" Knox whispers to me. "That was the best orgasm you've ever done. Aiden would kill me if he heard me say this, but your moaning was making me hard. I was afraid the sock was gonna fly off."

"I'm sorry. I just really got into it. This was supposed to be our special night, right?" I say, trying to cover up the fact that I did have an actual orgasm. What the fuck has pregnancy done to me?

"I don't know what it will look like on camera, but it felt smoking hot. We're gonna burn up the screen on this one."

"That's what people want, right?"

"It's sad, though, don't you think?" he says somberly. "That this is our last *Trinity* movie."

"Yeah, it is. Ten years of on-screen love." Tears start to form in my eyes. I can't believe this is the last one. This set is like a second home and these people are like my family. "What are you doing?" the makeup artist asks. "Is there something in your eyes?"

"Um, no. I just need a minute," I tell her, then I run to my dressing room and cry.

Knox peeks in the door. "I didn't mean to make you cry."

"I know, Knox. It's just—it's just—I really did get turned on."

He slowly sits down, shocked by my admission. "What? Why? Are you and Aiden okay?"

He hands me some tissues.

"We're fine, but I remembered this time before we had ever done it. We were kissing and sort of dry humping and it totally got me off. But there's another reason."

"What?"

"You're going to figure it out eventually. I don't have a weird flu thing, Knox. I'm pregnant."

His mouth drops open for a few seconds then he grins and pulls me into a hug. "Congratulations!"

"Thanks. No one knows. We haven't even told our families yet. But it's doing weird things to me. I'm nauseous. Hungry. Smell everything. My boobs hurt. My emotions are everywhere. And I'm really freaking horny."

"Aiden must love that. How far along are you?"

"Almost seven weeks."

"Um, I think it's best you don't tell Aiden about this."

"But I tell him everything. And I was thinking of him."

"He'd probably understand, but he'd still want to kick my ass. I don't want it to affect our friendship."

I blow out a big breath of air. "I'm sorry."

"Don't be. I used to have to beat off before our sex scenes. Otherwise, I wouldn't have been nearly as professional."

I laugh. "Well, thank you for that."

Knox laughs too. "You ready to get back at it?"

"Yeah."

WE'RE IN THE limo heading toward the office when Knox says, "While we're alone, I want to talk to you about something."

"What's that?"

"I've been working on a script."

"Really? What's it about?"

"A guy who's immortal. Sort of."

"Is he a vampire?"

"No, he was hit by lightning. It plays out in the present, but it goes back into the past too. The guy always dies—getting hit by lightning—but instead of being dead, he wakes up in a different time. Every time he wakes up, he looks for her."

"Her?"

"His true love. He's found her in every life he's lived. You get to see pieces of his past lives as he's trying to find her in the present."

"And when he does?"

"They're speed dating."

I laugh. "Speed dating? That's kind of funny."

"It's a romantic comedy with a time traveling twist."

"So, when she meets him in the present, is it instant? She falls in love with him?"

"Well, that wouldn't be any fun. She hates him, of course. She's jaded. She's had some bad relationships and doesn't want a man. Her friend dragged her to speed dating. On the surface, it's a funny love story but, at its core, there's this epic romance that transcends time."

"Can I read it?"

"Yes. And, if you like it, I want us to do it together. It's so different from anything either one of us have done. And if Captive will take it on as a project, we could set our own schedule. Work around your life and *Daddy's Angel*."

"My mom is the queen of romantic comedies. I haven't really done anything like that."

"Your action films are all commercial successes, just like your mom's romantic comedies, but as you get older, don't you find yourself wanting a different kind of success?"

"Like an Academy Award?"

He nods. "This is the kind of project I think they would like."

"Now, you've got me excited."

He laughs. "Oh no, not again!"

I swat him on the shoulder as we pull into the Captive Films lot to pick up Dawson.

"I BET YOU can't wait to see the girls," I say to Dawson when he joins us. "How was your day?"

"It was good. I made a lot of calls, caught up with people who think I fell off the face of the earth. They're all interested in this project, so I asked the marketing team to pull together a few vendor-specific presentations."

"That's great. Everything else going well?" I want to ask about Vanessa, but I don't.

"Yep. How about you two? Good day on set?"

"I humped Keatyn all day and made her orgasm," Knox says.

"Knox!"

"I'm just joking," he says, giving me an evil grin.

"Better not say something like that in front of Aiden," Dawson warns.

"I might. Just to get him going."

"Please don't. My grandparents are in town. They fast forward our sex scenes."

"They do?"

"Yes! Thank God!"

Dawson and Knox both start laughing. And they tease me the whole way there.

REGIONAL AIRPORT - SONOMA
Dawson

MY GIRLS BARREL down the steps and into my arms, crushing me with their hugs.

"Daddy! Daddy!" they say and start talking at once.

"We had popcorn and soda on the plane, and we got to watch two whole movies!"

"And Grandma didn't make us go to school today. We made pancakes and took Mango for a walk. And I got an A on my spelling test this week!"

"That's amazing. Let's get your bags and then we'll—"

"Keatyn!" the girls scream as soon as they see her. My youngest, Harlow, is seven and obsessed with the princess movie that Keatyn did the voice for. "We watched *The Princess* on the way here! I told the lady on the plane that we knew you! A real life princess!"

"And everyone at school," my oldest, Ava, says, rolling her eyes. At ten, she's at the age where everything her little sister says and does is uncool.

"I'm not really a princess," Keatyn says, giving them both

hugs. "I just got to be her voice."

"Same thing!" Harlow says.

"I'm a movie star too," Knox tells them. "Knox Daniels."

Harlow looks up at him. "I've never heard of you."

"Pint sized critic. I'm crushed," Knox says, holding his heart.

"*I've* seen you on magazines at my friend's house," Ava says, knowingly. "Her mom says you're on her list."

"What list is that?" I ask.

"Her freebie list," she says. Keatyn glances at me with wide eyes. "You know, like she would go see all his movies even if they were free."

We both sigh with relief, but Knox grins. "We should take a picture so you can show your friend's mommy."

"Really!?" She quickly pulls out her phone and holds it up. Knox gives her his best grin, the one that shows off his dimples. "If my daddy would let me watch your movies, you'd be on my freebie list too," she says, causing me to cringe.

Keatyn covers her face to hide her laughter, while Ava posts the photo. Then she looks up at Keatyn with her puppy dog eyes.

"Do you want to take one with me too?" Keatyn asks her.

She nods happily then holds up her camera and takes a picture. She snaps it and then studies it. "My hair was blowing in my eyes. Can we try another?"

"Sure."

They pose again. *Snap.*

"Now, I just look stupid," she huffs.

Snap.

"What do you think?"

Keatyn says, "Hmmm, let's change the coloring a little, like this. What do you think?"

"You look beautiful," she says.

"No, *you* look beautiful. Look how green your eyes are."

"Alright," I say. "Let's get going!"

Keatyn picks up Harlow and puts her on her hip. "My grandma and grandpa are at the farm and Grandpa wants you to go horseback riding with him tomorrow!"

"Yay!!" Harlow screams.

KEATYN & AIDEN'S HOME - ASHER VINEYARDS

Keatyn

THE DRIVER WINDS up the long road leading to our home. The second I'm on our land, I completely relax. There's something so comforting about the rows of grapes, the rolling hills, and the big stone house.

I give Dawson and the girls a quick tour then send them and Knox down the hill to find Dallas and his kids.

I find Aiden in our party barn. The sleeves of his plaid flannel shirt are rolled up, showing off muscular forearms. His ass is highlighted by a pair of Wranglers. His dark blonde hair is windblown and his cowboy boots are dusty.

"There's my gorgeous girl," he says, jumping off a ladder and swinging me into his arms, kissing me. "I have something to show you. Close your eyes and don't peek."

I do as he asks. I can hear him closing the barn door then he comes up from behind me, kisses my neck, and whispers, "Open."

"Oh, Aiden! It's beautiful," I say, my smile probably beaming as bright as the strands of lights he's strung across the barn's ceiling joists. "It will be perfect for our reception!" I stare up at the lights for a few moments and am overcome with emotion. I turn around to face him. "You've always made my life more beautiful."

"I'm glad you like it."

"I missed you." I notice dirt on his face and try to wipe it off. "You're all dirty."

"You like it when I'm dirty," he replies, his voice deep and sexy.

"Maybe I should help you get cleaned up for dinner."

He kisses my neck again. "Where is everyone?"

"I sent them to find Dallas and the kids. Where are they?"

"Helping your grandpa feed the horses. That means we have just enough time."

"Just enough time for what?"

"This!" he says, sweeping me off my feet, carrying me in the house, and tossing me on our bed.

He unbuttons his shirt, his green eyes holding mine, then strips off his boots and jeans. When he's naked, he strips off my clothes. Sometimes, he likes to slowly undress me and kiss every part. This is not one of those times.

He stays standing and pulls me down to the end of the bed. I wrap my legs around him as he pushes inside of me.

"Oh, Boots, I think you missed me."

"Oh, god. Yes, I did," I say raggedly, pleasure rushing through me. "Do it harder, but don't come yet."

"That's easier said than done, Boots. It's been three days, and you keep grabbing my ass."

I immediately put my hands up in the air.

He pins them down above my head and pumps harder.

"Oh, that's it. That's oh. Oh . . ." I moan, my insides contracting and pulsing.

He slows down and leans in to kiss me.

"You're not done? Are you?"

He chuckles against my lips. "Just taking a little break."

He slowly pulls out of me, then slowly glides back in.

"You're so freaking hard."

I push my arms up, because I want—no, I need—him to go

faster, but he holds firm, still toying with me.

Finally, he has me exactly where he wants me, begging.

"Aiden, please."

He slams into me, lifting my body up off the bed with every thrust, faster and faster, until I'm wrapped in the throes of ecstasy and he's collapsed on top of me.

He kisses my nose. "I missed you too, in case you couldn't tell."

I give him another kiss. "We should probably go check on our guests."

"I suppose you're right, although I bet they could fend for themselves."

Aiden pops in the shower and I get in with him.

He starts soaping up my body.

"Can I have a rain check on that?" I ask. "I've got to get some food. I'm starting to feel sick."

I quickly dry off, put my clothes back on, and run into the kitchen and grab an apple off the counter. Then I run back to the bathroom because I have to pee.

When I wipe, it's pink.

"Ohmigawd! Aiden! I'm bleeding!" I say, instantly panicked.

He jumps out of the shower and I show him the toilet paper.

"Aiden, did we do it too hard? Am I having a miscarriage? What are we going to do?"

He stands naked, dripping in front of me. "Is that it?"

"Is what it?"

"Like, that's barely pink. It doesn't really look like blood."

I stay sitting on the toilet and start crying.

Aiden bends down next to me. "Baby, it's okay. Whatever happens is okay. We talked about that, right?"

I shake my head. "No, I lied. It's not okay!"

"Keatyn, you need to calm down. Why don't you wipe again and see if it's gotten better or worse. I read that a miscarriage is like getting your period. There's a lot of cramping and blood.

Are you cramping?"

"Maybe! I don't know!"

He grabs my chin. "Look at me. Do you have cramps?"

I take a deep breath. "No."

"Wipe, please."

"I'm scared to."

He hands me a wad of toilet paper. I close my eyes and wipe.

"I can't look."

"It's not pink, baby. You're not bleeding."

I open my eyes, not believing him and expecting to see a river of blood. But the paper is white.

I cover my eyes with my hands.

Aiden wraps a towel around his waist, types in his phone, and then he reads from it.

"It says that spotting after sex is normal during your first trimester. It says that your cervix—that's what the baby comes out of, right?—is sensitive. It says up to thirty percent of women have some bleeding in early pregnancy and half of them don't have miscarriages."

"So, if I'm in the thirty percent, my odds are fifty-fifty?"

"I don't think that would really qualify as bleeding. It's going to be fine, I promise."

I stand up, zip my pants, and flush.

"Aiden?"

"What, baby?" he says, sliding his hand across my face.

"It just got real."

"What do you mean?"

"I was excited to be pregnant, but other than some vague flu-like symptoms and the ability to smell a cheeseburger from two miles away, it didn't feel real. It does now, and I realize just how much I want to have our baby."

"And you will, don't worry. Speaking of that, we need to start thinking up names. I actually have an idea."

"You do?"

"Yeah. I think we should name the baby Monroe."

Tears fill my eyes again.

"My fake last name? If it weren't for me almost being kidnapped by the stalker, I never would have went to boarding school."

"Or met me."

"I'm glad I met you. And I don't know if I ever told you this, but my mom chose that name because it was my great grandma's maiden name."

"That makes it even better," he says. "Monroe Arrington. What do you think?"

"It would work for a boy or a girl." I kiss him. "I love it, Aiden. It's perfect."

IT'S LATE AND I'm sitting on the back porch drinking lemonade with Grandma, Grandpa, and Aiden. Knox is helping Dawson and Dallas put the kids to bed with a crazy bedtime story. Logan and Maggie left, since they have a busy day at the winery tomorrow.

"So, Hotshot," Grandpa says to me. "We have some news. Me and Ma are homeless."

"What?"

"We sold the ranch, dear," Grandma clarifies.

"Better than, *We bought the farm*," Grandpa says, slapping his leg with laughter.

"Grandpa, don't joke about dying. I hate that. And why did you sell the ranch? You love it there."

"I've decided, after careful consideration," he leans over and whispers to me, "and after Ma hit me over the head with a frying pan and knocked some sense into me—"

"Don't listen to him," Grandma interjects.

"—that it was time. We've been spending a lot time in California, between the board meetings at Captive and coming here. We decided to put it up for sale and see what happened. We got a good offer, fast. We weren't really expecting it to sell so quickly. When we go back home, we have to pack up forty years worth of crap."

"I've already gone through the house and downsized it," Grandma says, rolling her eyes.

"She got rid of everything that wasn't nailed down. I'm lucky she kept my chair and my bed."

"And you," Grandma says with a laugh. "Anyway, we kept what was important, and we're going to buy some new things for our new house."

"Where are you moving to?" I ask, shocked by all of this. I just can't picture Grandpa in a condo somewhere.

Aiden squeezes my hand. "We have plenty of land here for them to build a house on, and they can stay in the guest house until it's done."

Tears flood my eyes. I couldn't be happier with the thought of my grandparents being around every day to see my baby grow up.

"Really?"

"She's crying, Ma," Grandpa says. "Better not draw up the house plans yet."

I get up and hug my grandma. "I'm crying because it makes me so incredibly happy." I give Grandpa a hug next. "You and Aiden have already been talking about this, haven't you?"

"I needed to talk to him man-to-man," Grandpa says seriously. "But, yes, we've picked out a spot. I just didn't want to put the cart before the horse."

"He's going to help Logan manage the vineyard," Aiden tells me.

"That's great news." I still can't believe it.

"And it'll keep him outta my hair," Grandma teases.

"Don't worry, were gonna put her to work doing something. Woman's gotta earn her keep," Grandpa teases her back.

"Maggie asked if I would consider working a few days a week

in the store. I'd need to learn more about wine but I'm thinking that might be fun. Getting out there and talking to people. Although, Aiden says he'd rather I make him ribs and bake pies."

Aiden rubs his flat stomach. "Wouldn't that be awesome?"

"So, I hear you're planning a quickie wedding," Grandpa says, changing the subject as he takes another drink. "You knocked up?"

My heart stops beating. I can't lie to my grandpa, and Aiden's freaking grinning like a Cheshire cat.

"Wow," Grandpa says. "It suddenly got so quiet you could hear a cricket fart."

"I am," I say.

"You're what?" Grandpa asks.

"You're pregnant!?" Grandma yells out.

"Shhh! We don't want anyone to know. We haven't told anyone yet."

"Jeez, I was just joking," Grandpa admits. "Although, now I understand."

"Understand what?"

"Why old Fox over there," he says, pointing toward Aiden, "can't wipe the smile off his face. I was afraid he was going gay on us."

"Grandpa!" I chastise. "People don't *go* gay—"

"I don't mean gay as in homosexual. Gay used to mean happy before all the rainbow equality stuff. *He was a gay old lad,* meant he was really chipper. Unusually happy. And, in my experience, a man who is *too* happy usually's got something up his sleeve. You gotta watch out for gay—*as in happy*—people. And Aiden's been smiling so much, I half expected him to break out in song."

"Well, now you know why I'm over the moon," Aiden says, still grinning.

"And please don't tell anyone," I add.

"Your mother is going to be happier than a tick on a fat

dog."

"Why haven't you told your family?" Grandma asks.

"I'm only about seven weeks, and Aiden's sister had an early miscarriage. We're waiting until I'm twelve weeks and have had an ultrasound to tell everyone."

"You won't be able to wait that long," Grandma replies, shaking her head at me.

"Why not?"

"You're skinny. You'll start showing soon."

"No, I won't! You don't start showing until you're, like, three months. And you don't have to wear maternity clothes until five months."

Grandma laughs. A loud, belly laugh. "You been reading those pregnancy books already?"

"Uh, maybe."

"When I was pregnant with your daddy, I noticed my stomach at eight weeks. Couldn't button my skirt anymore."

"Seriously?"

"Yes, and based on how much you ate at dinner tonight, I reckon you'll be the same."

"You have been eating a lot," Aiden confirms.

"I can't help it that I'm hungry all the time. And nauseous."

"Morning sickness, dear?"

"A little. I haven't thrown up too many times though. Mostly, I just gag."

"You need to eat a gingersnap every morning when you first wake up. Keep them by your bed. And if you can have a cup of lemon tea with it, all the better."

"I've looked everywhere online for a cure for morning sickness. I haven't heard of that," Aiden says.

"It's something grandmothers just know," Grandma says to Aiden, matter-of-factly. Then she turns to me. "I'll bake you a mess of gingersnaps tomorrow. And, you should probably cut out the alcohol."

"I didn't put alcohol in her drink," Aiden says quickly.

"So, that's why you were so gung-ho on making them."

Dawson, Dallas, and Knox join us on the back porch.

"They're all out," Dallas says.

"Fell asleep during my stirring rendition of *The Three Little Pigs*," Knox adds, looking slightly offended.

"Fresh air makes little ones sleep," Grandma states. "They've had a long day, not to mention, Dawson, yours had a three hour time change. Aiden, would you get the boys some lemonade?"

"No offense, Grandma," Knox says, "But I had something a little stronger in mind."

"Oh, it's something stronger. It'll put you right to sleep too, young man."

Grandpa stands and grabs Grandma's hand. "Ma and I are gonna hit the hay. Let you youngins have some fun."

Aiden and I walk them in the house and give them hugs goodnight.

"Congratulations," my grandpa whispers to me. Then he hits Aiden on the shoulder and says, "You old dog, you," and walks off.

"While you make their drinks, I'm gonna look for something to snack on," I tell Aiden.

He pins me against the counter, putting his hand across my belly. "Do you think we should tell our families sooner?"

"I'm dying to, but I don't know what to do."

"My parents are watching my sister's kids this weekend. What if we got everyone together this coming week for dinner? What's your schedule looking like? Back to early morning call times?"

"Yes, we're finishing up all the indoor scenes. Sex scenes. The emotional stuff."

"Probably a good thing you're doing them now, before you start showing," he says, his hand still across my stomach. "I love you and our baby."

"We love you too."

KEATYN & AIDEN'S HOME – ASHER VINEYARDS
Dawson

KEATYN AND AIDEN bring some snacks out to the porch along with our drinks.

One sip tells me that this is seriously spiked lemonade.

"Oh, this is gooood," Knox drawls.

"Gotta love good ol' Southern hospitality," Dallas agrees, taking a big sip.

"So, Dawson," Aiden says, "I hear you and Vanessa have been hooking up."

"Oh, Van-es-sa. Why have I not hit that yet?" Knox asks.

I want to pick Knox up and pound him against the wall.

I glare at him instead.

He holds his hands up. "Jeez. If looks could kill, I'd be dead. Do you like her or are you just hooking up?"

"Dawson and Vanessa know each other from a long time ago," Keatyn interjects. "They will be working closely together."

"Really closely," Aiden teases.

Keatyn smiles at Aiden, but says to me, "Ignore him. Did the girls decide to sleep in the loft room?"

"Are you kidding? They're in heaven. It's like a big camp slumber party with all those bunk beds and sleeping bags. And Harlow, being only seven, hasn't been allowed to go on sleepovers yet, so she's thrilled."

"Ava and Fallon seemed to hit it off," Dallas says about our oldest daughters.

"They did. It's nice."

"Next time they come out, we'll have to let them tour the kid's school."

"I'm sure they would like that. I really appreciate this." I look around. "Everyone. It means a lot to me."

"You've had a rough couple of years," Aiden states.

"And we're glad to hear you're back in the saddle again," Dallas drawls. "Camden may or may not have called us and told us you needed to get laid."

"I don't really think that's any of your business," Keatyn says, chiding them. But then she turns to me. "I don't care about the sex. How are you feeling about all of this? The job? The house? The girls? About making it permanent? About Vanessa?"

Aiden starts laughing. "In a round about way, she's asking the same question I did."

"Fine," she huffs. "Do you like her?"

"I've only known her for a few days but, yes, I do." And I miss her. "I'm beat. I think I'm going to bed. I'm sure the kids will run us ragged tomorrow."

Everyone says their goodnights and I go into my room and call her.

"Hey, Vanessa."

"Hey, yourself," she says. "All tucked in out in the wilderness?"

"I am. As a matter of fact, I'm lying in a big four-poster bed all alone."

"I'm taking a bath," she says, my mind immediately conjuring up naked images of her.

"That's sexy," I say. "Are you naked?"

"Uh, yeah?"

I laugh at myself. "I'm sorry. That was about the stupidest thing I've ever said. I'm so out of practice when it comes to flirting."

"Are you trying to flirt with me, Dawson?"

"I am. I miss you, actually."

"I miss you too. If I didn't have to help my dad this weekend, I'd be lying in bed with you, instead of lying in the bathtub thinking about you."

"You're thinking about me?" I ask, feeling both shocked and happy to hear so.

"I'm thinking how I may never have sex without a fur coat again."

"Does that mean I succeeding in making you love it?"

"You did. Just thinking about it gets me all hot and bothered."

"When can I see you again?"

"When will you be back?"

"Sunday night."

"Hmmm," she says. "Okay, well, I could probably pencil you in for Thursday of next week."

"Oh, uh, okay," I say, trying not to sound as dejected as I feel.

"I'm teasing you, Dawson. Why don't you come to my house when you get back. I'll text you the address."

"I think I should take you out on a date."

"I'll have my chef make us dinner here, although it's highly doubtful I'll let you leave my bed."

SATURDAY, OCTOBER 4TH
VANESSA'S DAD'S HOUSE - BEVERLY HILLS
Vanessa

MY DAD IS downsizing. Moving from the big house I grew up in to a condo near his office. I can see why he wants to move. The upkeep on a house this size and age has been a pain for him and all he really wants to do is work and golf. Mostly, golf.

I'm helping him declutter the house to get it ready to go on the market. Apparently, a lot of the stuff he has is stuff from my youth. High school yearbooks. Prom favors. Clothes I didn't think I could live without but have been without for the past ten years. He probably has my old stuffed animals. I'd bet he even has some of my mom's stuff too.

My mom passed away when I was in kindergarten, so I don't really remember her much. Since then, my dad's always treated me like a grown up, teaching me to be self-sufficient and confident. We had a live-in housekeeper who cooked for us and picked me up from school, but he was home for dinner and to tuck me into bed almost every night.

Even though I don't really want to waste a beautiful Saturday mucking through the attic, I want to help him.

When I show up at the door, I'm shocked that he's already

accomplished a lot.

"All I have left is this pile of your stuff." He points toward the empty dining room.

"That's it? What did you do with everything else?"

"I donated a lot. And I have a few things I've been meaning to give you."

"Like what?"

He holds out a burled wood jewelry box. "This was your mother's jewelry. I was going to give it to you when you got older, but then Bam bought you such amazing jewelry . . ."

I slowly open the box. Dad takes a ring out and holds it in front of me. This was her engagement ring. Just a chip, really, but we didn't have much money back then. I always told her I'd buy her a bigger one someday." I hold up a locket. It's oval and scrolled, the silver tarnished. "That was her grandmother's. There's a picture of you inside from when you were a baby."

I open it up and see my mother's face next to my chubby baby one.

"You look a lot like her, Vanessa. She was beautiful."

"You always said that all I got from you was your brains."

Dad laughs. "Your mother was a lot prettier than I was, but she was smart as a whip too."

I pick through other small jewelry items. A class ring. A sorority pin. A small diamond pendant. A pretty ruby ringed in diamonds.

"Thanks, Dad," I say, feeling overwhelmed.

"And, now for the boxes," he says, pointing. "I have to run and drop off this paperwork, but I'll be right back. Have fun!"

I quickly go through the boxes of clothes, laughing at how fashion has changed so much in a decade. So far, there isn't anything I want to keep.

I open a box full of bikinis and shorts. I hold up a pair of cut-offs that I only wore to the beach with Keatyn. I wouldn't have been caught dead wearing something so unrefined at school.

I laugh at myself. I thought I was so cool. I slip my linen capris off and slide the shorts on. They are ratty, a little ripped, and fringed. I don't know why I decide to keep them, but I take them off and set them next to the jewelry box. Next, I go through boxes of old stuffed animals, childhood gymnastics and piano recital ribbons, and am planning on getting rid of it all.

Buried in the bottom of a box of stuffed animals, I find a plain, wooden box. One I don't recognize.

I open it and read a letter on the top.

My dearest Vanessa-
This letter is for when you get married.

I pull the rest of the papers out and open them, quickly realizing there are letters to me from my mother for all the big events in a girl's life. *For when you get your period. For when you have your first date. For when you lose your virginity. For when you graduate. For when you fall in love. For when you get married.*

The last letter has my dad's name on the front. Inside it says: *I'm sorry. Please give these to her.*

I read through them all, mesmerized by my mother's words. The first letters are sweet and have pretty good advice. Others seem very old-fashioned, particularly the one about protecting my virtue. Others seem, I can't put my finger on it but, off. The handwriting is harder to read and the words are jumbled.

But, wait. My mom died in an accident.

I look up and see my dad standing above me.

"I didn't give you those as she requested."

"Why?"

"Your mother's death was officially ruled an accidental over-dose. She mixed antidepressants with alcohol."

"But . . ."

He holds his hand up. "I know. Why the letters? I thought the same thing when I found this box in your bedside table a few weeks after she died."

"So, it wasn't an accident?"

"I don't think so. I never told anyone. I didn't want them to think differently of her. Particularly, her family."

"That must have been hard on you. Do you have any idea why she did it?" I ask, knowing there was a time in my life when even I didn't want my life to go on.

"She suffered from depression and was on medication. I thought she was doing well. We'd even considered having another baby. The note was a complete surprise." He sits down next to me, tears shining in his eyes. "Vanessa, was I a good father?"

"Yes, Dad," I say, hugging him, tears filling my own eyes.

"I worked a lot. I regret that."

"You taught me to have a good work ethic and you were always there when I needed you."

"I'm proud of you, Vanessa. You went through a lot, but you never gave up."

"Thanks, Dad." I hug him tighter. "Speaking of never giving up, do you think maybe it's time you started dating again?"

Dad smiles. "Actually—"

"Actually, what?" I say, my eyes getting big. "Are you seeing someone?"

He blushes a little. "Cora."

"Are you serious? She's been your assistant for fifteen years!"

"Yes, and apparently I'm blind because she says she's been interested for most of those years."

I give him another squeeze. "I'm so happy for you."

"I'm happy for me too. I know things went badly with Bam, but don't let that stop you from letting yourself feel again. Find a man who loves you—truly loves you—and nothing else really matters."

"Can I tell you something personal?"

"As long as it doesn't have to do with sex."

I laugh. "I'm sort of seeing someone."

"Really? Tell me about him."

"I can't believe I'm saying that I'm seeing him, because it seems too soon to say that, but I can't stop thinking about him. His name is Dawson Johnson."

"Is he related to Riley?"

"They're brothers. It's a crazy story, really, but we met at Keatyn's eighteenth birthday party. We kissed and danced all night, but didn't stay in touch. Somehow, I've never crossed paths with him again until the other day when he came to work at Captive. He's so handsome and sweet. He's a widow. His wife died a couple years ago and he took it hard. Hasn't worked in two years. But we've hung out and we've talked and kissed." I stop babbling and laugh at myself. "I sound like a teenager."

"Sounds like you should go see him," Dad says.

"He went up to the vineyard for the weekend, but he did call me last night and said he misses me."

"Maybe you should go up there and surprise him."

I nod my head. "I think you're right, Dad."

I DRIVE HOME, pack an overnight bag, and am back in the car in a flash.

As I'm heading to the airport, I call Keatyn. "Hey, I just got done at my dad's place and thought I'd head up that way. You have room for me?"

"Of course we have room."

"It's always so relaxing there."

"Oh, I'm not sure how relaxing it will be this time. Dallas is here with his four kids. Knox decided to come up. Aiden is still working on the barn and, of course, Dawson is here with his girls."

"Dawson brought *girls* with him?"

"Not girls, like dates. Girls as in, daughters. They came out for the weekend."

"He has kids?"

207

"Yes, two beautiful little girls."

"He didn't tell me. *Why* didn't he tell me? God dammit. I'll be there shortly."

"Vanessa, I can tell by the tone of your voice that you're pissed Dawson didn't tell you, but don't you dare come up here and make a scene. Not in front of them. It wouldn't be right."

"I agree not to make a scene, if you agree not to tell him I'm coming."

"We just had a picnic and now they're riding horses to the pond. I probably won't see him for a while."

THE WHOLE WAY there I'm racking my brain, wondering what it means that he didn't tell me.

KEATYN & AIDEN'S HOME - ASHER VINEYARDS

"SORRY, I'M LATE," I tell Keatyn, getting out of my car. "I stopped at the winery to see Maggie."

"How did that go?"

"Really well. She hasn't changed a bit. I love that she and Logan are still together. They were always so cute."

"They still are," she says.

"I need to thank you, Keatyn. For being so kind to me when I haven't talked to you for so long. For asking me to plan your wedding. For inviting me up here to relax. I really appreciate it."

She smiles and touches my arm. "I'm glad you're back in my life, Ariela. And I'm excited to have you help with my wedding. So, what do you want to see first?"

"Why don't you just give me the grand tour, as you picture

it in your head. Pretend I'm a wedding guest who has just arrived. Where will I park? What path will I take to the ceremony? What will I sit on? What will I see?"

"Oh, gosh, that's a lot of questions. Okay, so over here, to the south of the house is a lot of grass. We can park cars there, or we can have them park down the hill at the winery and shuttle them up. Although, there's a wedding taking place on the grounds there, so that might complicate things."

"Let's have them park here then. What else?"

"I want to do our vows right before the sun sets. I'd like the guests to feel welcome and relaxed right away. I was thinking of giving them spiked lemonade somewhere between here and the ceremony."

"Why spiked lemonade?" I ask.

"It's what I always drank at my grandparents' ranch in Texas. And, now, they have been coming up here a lot, so we sit on the porch most nights and drink it."

"I love that. Those are the kind of things that make a wedding personal. We'll be sure to put a sign on it that says it's Grandma's recipe."

"From there, they will walk—hmmm, this is all grass, and that's not great if you're in heels. I should probably have a path put in, don't you think?"

"Yes, I do. Okay, so we're walking along the side of your house to your backyard. Oh, wow," I say, seeing it for the first time. "I can see why you want to get married here. It's spectacular." And it is. There's a gorgeous rectangular pool, set in an expansive stone and brick patio. The landscaping is lush but minimal which is good. With the rolling hills surrounding us and the view of the ocean, you don't need much.

"Thank you. We love it and the land means so much to us."

"I saw in the movie how you bought it for him when you thought you weren't going to survive things with the stalker. You two have an epic love story. We want your wedding to highlight that."

"That's why I want the ceremony here. Aiden has wood left over from the barn that he wants to build an altar with. And while I think wood is pretty, I don't want the wedding to be too rustic. I want some glamour. Lots of flowers, maybe a chandelier. I was also thinking instead of just renting chairs, it would be cool to bring in furniture. Like you raided your grandma's attic, only classy."

"Sort of a rustic, shabby chic vibe?"

"Yes, but not too shabby," she says with a laugh. "And not too rustic."

"So, rustic, elegant, shabby chic?"

"Yes! That's exactly what I want."

"I have a photo of an altar that is so gorgeous and I've been saving it for the right setting. It's draped with silk, held in place with flowers, and has a huge chandelier hanging in the center. It's elegant, but soft. I have a picture of it on my phone. Hang on. Let me find it."

I scroll through my photos, find it, and show it to her.

"Oh, Ariela," she screeches. "It's perfect! I love it! And those flowers are the pale pastel colors I want to use. Maybe just add some feathers?"

"We can definitely add feathers. And here's a photo of mismatched pastel furniture. Is that close to what you're thinking?"

"Yes. It's like you've been saving all these pictures just for me," she says. She stops and looks at me. "Maybe you have been. It's weird, isn't it? It's been so long but, in some ways, it's like nothing has changed. I don't know what will happen with you and Riley, but don't disappear from my life again, okay?"

Tears prickle my eyes. "I won't," I say as she keeps going.

"We'd also like twinkle lights, pretty much everywhere. And ribbons hanging from all the trees. So, I guess cocktail hour would be up next. I was thinking maybe around the pool and in the attached courtyard. Do you think that would work?"

"When you built all this, were you planning to hold your wedding here?" I laugh, taking it all in. "This brick courtyard is an amazing space."

"The thought may have crossed my mind," she giggles. "But we also wanted to have big parties and fundraisers here. Since the vineyard's grounds are booked for so many events, we wanted a place to have our own. And, we keep adding on. It's sort of our own private oasis."

"I want to see what's in here," I say, going over to a pavilion. "Oh, this is cool."

"We sit out here a lot. With the fireplace, we can use it pretty much year round."

"This looks like it would be a great place to raise a family."

"We think so too."

"Would you be opposed to moving the furniture out of the pavilion and setting up some of the cocktail tables in here? We could run the silk fabric from the ceiling similar to the altar. And it's on the way to the barn, so it makes sense for the flow of traffic."

"I love that idea."

"Me too," Aiden says, coming up from behind Keatyn and wrapping his arms around her waist. "How's the planning going?"

"Good," she says, giving him a sweet kiss.

"So, I have some special requests," Aiden says.

"You do?" Keatyn and I ask in unison. "A lot of men prefer to just show up."

"That wouldn't be my style," he says. "But I'd like to speak to you in private when you're finished, Ariela. I may have a surprise or two for my bride."

Keatyn looks at him and practically swoons.

And, so do I.

"So, I'll let you two keep going. If you need me, I'll be down in the barn," he says.

"Ariela," Keatyn says, "let's run in the house quick, grab a snack and something to drink, and I need to pee."

"Okay," I say, following her into their massive kitchen. "This kitchen is great. Can the caterers use it?"

"They could if they needed to, but we have a full catering kitchen in the barn. Pour yourself a glass of wine. I'll be right back."

I pour myself a glass of wine. When in Sonoma . . . drink wine, right?"

Keatyn comes out of the bathroom and grabs a bottle of water.

"You're not having wine?"

"I think I'll stick with this," she says. "Let's head to the barn. I thought the dinner could be inside. And I suppose if it were to rain, we'd have to do everything inside, right?"

"We'll definitely have a rain plan. Let me worry about that though."

"Okay," she says, leading me down a brick path to a massive redwood barn. She stops and points out an old tree with their initials carved in the center. "Aiden carved our initials in this tree when I showed him the land. That was something we didn't put in the movie. We planned the house and everything around the tree. I don't know how old it is, but we couldn't tear it down."

"That's a gorgeous barn. Your house hides it though. I didn't even see it when I pulled up."

"It's sits a little lower than the house, so it's kind of hidden. I like that it's sort of a surprise."

She throws open the doors.

"This is spectacular. Vaulted ceiling, exposed beams, old brick on the pillars."

"Aiden, will you close the door and show Ariela your latest project?" Keatyn says to the empty space.

I hear Aiden's voice reply from somewhere to my right. "Sure."

The doors shut, darkening the space. Then, with a flick of a switch, hundreds of bulbs attached to the beams light up the ceiling.

"Isn't it pretty?" Keatyn swoons. "Could we use the silk fabric and chandeliers to dress this up a little too? And lots of flowers. And I'd like those really long tables and the food to be served family style. Then we can dance in the middle."

"And wine," Aiden says. "There will be lots and lots of wine."

Keatyn shows me the catering kitchen, the ample amount of restrooms, and built in bars and buffets.

"Aiden," I say, "if you have a minute, let's talk food. Do you have a caterer in mind? Style of food?"

"Our personal chef, Marvel, designed the catering kitchen, trained in France, and worked at many acclaimed restaurants before we hired him. He's been planning our menu since we got engaged. You can talk to him this afternoon if you'd like."

"That sounds perfect. What about a cake?"

"I'd like something tall, lots of layers, pastels, starting with white then ending up in pink, kind of an ombre effect," Keatyn says. "Maggie already called our local cake designer and she said she'd do it for us. You'll just need to get with her on the design, size, delivery."

"Sounds easy enough. How about cocktails? Or do you just want wine?"

"A full bar," Aiden says. "Good scotch. Top shelf liquor. Champagne. An assortment of cigars. I'll supply all the wine. I have a special vintage I've been saving for this event."

"I think that covers most of the basics. Aiden, did you want to talk to me now?"

Keatyn whispers something in Aiden's ear that makes him smile.

"I told you it would be okay," he whispers, giving her a kiss.

"Alright, you two have fun. I'm going down to see what the

kids are up to," she says.

"They're at the ball field," Aiden tells her.

"You have a ball field too?" I ask.

"Soccer pitch, really, but it works for other sports too. Logan and I like to relive our glory days and keep in shape." He tosses Keatyn some keys. "Take the Gator."

As soon as she leaves, Aiden leads me out of the barn and onto a flat grassy area.

"Our first kiss was on a Ferris wheel at Eastbrooke's Back-To-School Carnival, so I want to have a Ferris wheel at the wedding. Right here."

"A Ferris wheel?" I say, a little shocked. "Um, that's a request I've never had before. I'm not sure if I can find one in a couple weeks, but I'll see what I can do."

"Oh, you don't have to find it," he says. "I bought a vintage one and had it restored back to its original pale pastel colors. I just need you to help me decide where to put it. I was thinking here next to the barn. It will be all lit up and the guests can ride it. I thought it would be a fun surprise for her."

"It's an amazing surprise, Aiden. And I think here would be perfect. We can make a pathway and string lights on poles above it to light the way."

"That works for me."

"Do you have any other requests?"

"Yes. Pink cotton candy and feathers incorporated somehow. I'm going to have the crew light up the rows of grapes on both sides of the drive up here. If we do the wedding at sunset, guests won't see it when they arrive, but it will pretty when they leave." He pulls a phone out of his pocket and shows me a photo of a cute sign. "I was thinking of changing it to read, *Once in a while, in the middle of a chaotic life, love gives us a fairytale.* And we have to have four-leaf clovers incorporated somewhere."

"I saw that your vineyard's label has a clover design in the background. What if we incorporated something like that into the invitations?"

"Could we send an actual four-leaf clover in every invitation?"

"Sure," I say, adding it to my list. "What about invitations? Keatyn said something about wanting to keep it quiet."

"We'd like invitations hand delivered the first of the week for a fundraiser here. When the guests arrive, we'll hand out the wedding programs."

"That sounds like a plan," I say, wondering how I'm going to have invitations for six hundred people designed, printed, addressed, and hand delivered in a few days.

"You look a little freaked out," Aiden tells me. "Maggie will help you with all the vendor connections. We do a lot of events here. They will squeeze us in."

"Okay, and I'm glad I have Maggie to lean on. I have a vision of what she wants, but I'll need help executing it."

KEATYN & AIDEN'S HOME - ASHER VINEYARDS

"RUN, HARLOW!" I yell, cheering her on as she dribbles the soccer ball down the field and scores. She comes running up to me and leaps into my arms.

"I scored, Daddy! I scored!"

"You did so good, sweetie," I say, giving her a kiss on the cheek.

"Against boys, too," she whispers. "Carder is almost my age, but I'm taller than him. He told me that it didn't matter because boys are tougher."

"Do you think that's true?"

She shakes her head. "I think boys are dumb." Then she looks at me. "Well, not boy daddies. Daddies are smart."

"Thank you," I say with a laugh. "Are you having fun here?"

"I'm having the best time ever. Did you see me feed that pony? He loves apples."

"He did. And you did a good job riding the pony."

"I especially liked our picnic by the pond. Will we get to come back here?"

"If we all move to California, we could come back whenever you want."

"I like California. It's sunny and warm on my face."

"Next time you come, you can see the house. It's right on the ocean."

"Like Grandma's?"

"Kinda like that, but a different ocean."

"The Pacific Ocean," Ava says, chiming in. "It's on the West coast. Grandma's is on the East coast."

"Very good, Ava. Your sister seems to like it here, what do you think?" Harlow wriggles out of my arms and takes off running. Ava plops down on the bleachers next to me.

"I think Knox is funny. He makes us all laugh. And so does Fallon's daddy. He talks funny."

"He's originally from the South, so he has an accent."

"Fallon is nice," she says about Dallas' oldest. "She said if we moved to California that we could go to school together."

"What would you think of that?"

"I think I'd miss my friends and Grandma and Grandpa and Uncle Cam and Aunt Annie and Uncle Brax and my cousins."

"We'd still visit them a lot. I would let you fly back whenever you wanted."

"That's what Grandma told me. I told her that I missed you the most though."

I get choked up. "I missed you, too, Ava."

"I know it was only for a few days but Grandma doesn't put

smiley faces on our pancakes. Do you like your new job?"

"I do. But the three of us have to decide together if it's right for us to move. We all need to be happy."

"I heard Grandma tell Uncle Cam that *you* need to be happy. Have you not been happy?"

"Of course, I have been. I've been with you and Harlow."

"Grandma said you haven't been the same since Mommy died. And Uncle Cam said you needed to get back in the saddle again. Is that why we came here? So you could ride horses?"

"Ava, you need to stop eavesdropping. It's not polite. What Uncle Cam meant is that I needed to get back to work." I lie. "Next weekend, you can see our house. See if you like it."

"I loved the pictures, Daddy. Hey, who is that? She's pretty."

I look up and see Vanessa.

And she looks pissed. Hand on her hip. Lips pursed. And even though she has sunglasses on, I can feel the daggers coming from her eyes.

"Why don't you go play some more. I need to go talk to her."

"Okay, Daddy!" she yells, running off.

KEATYN & AIDEN'S HOME – ASHER VINEYARDS
Vanessa

I WATCH DAWSON cheer on an adorable little dark haired girl, who kicks a soccer ball into a goal. She runs straight to him and leaps into his arms. He gives her a kiss on the cheek and they have an animated conversation.

Soon, another beautiful girl, taller and older, sits down next to him. They seem to be having a more serious conversation, and

I'm mesmerized by the way he looks.

You can feel his love for his daughters all the way across the soccer field.

I've been pissed the entire trip here, but seeing him with the girls—who look just like him—softens me. I can tell he's a good father.

He gets up and walks toward me.

"Can we go somewhere and talk?" he asks. "Please."

"I suppose," I say, irritated that he wants me away from his kids.

He takes my hand and leads me to a Gator. I sit down and he drives us up the hill. If I weren't so pissed, I'd be enjoying the scenery.

As soon as he stops, I tear into him.

"Why didn't you tell me you have children? After all that we've shared these past few days. I opened up and told you things I haven't told anyone else! Is that why you didn't invite me to come with you?"

"Vanessa, calm down," he says.

Which I hate.

I don't fucking want to be calm right now. I can't be calm right now.

"I was going to tell you the other night," he says, softly. "But then you told me about your miscarriage and how you can't have children. I could tell how devastating that was for you. It just seemed like a really bad time to tell you about my girls. Like I was throwing it in your face."

"You had plenty of other chances."

"I wasn't keeping it from you. It's just . . ."

"It's just what?!"

"Well, first of all, you told me you had plans with your dad all weekend."

"And what else?"

He runs his hand through his hair and sighs. "I've been

nothing but a dad for the last two years. The last few days, you've made me feel like a man. And, honestly, I was afraid to tell you."

"Why?"

"I overheard my aunt telling my mom that I'd probably never find someone because of my—and I quote—*baggage*. I know you want children. We haven't been together long enough to talk about if you only wanted yours, or if you could open up your heart to someone else's. I'm a package deal, Vanessa. And I don't even know if you are interested in *me* long-term, let alone the rest of the package."

"Why wouldn't I be interested in you?"

"Riley told me that since Bam, you haven't wanted a relationship. I don't know if I'm just a notch in your belt or if there could be more, and I've been in California for all of five days."

My heart sinks.

And I hate the feeling.

I feel desperate. I know it's only been a few days, but I want more. I want everything with him. My heart wants it all, but my head thinks I must be crazy.

"Do you want more?" I say quietly, half hoping he won't hear me.

"I want to get to know you better. It's important I do. I need to be careful about who I bring into my children's lives." He stops and looks into my eyes. "And I know it sounds crazy because, on one hand, it feels so fast, but the answer is yes, because, on the other hand, it feels like it's been a long time coming."

Tears flood my eyes.

I don't want to cry, but I do.

"Why are you crying?"

"Because it feels like it's been a long time coming for me too."

He wraps an arm around my waist, pulls me close, and gives

me an epic kiss. A kiss so full of emotion, it sends the tears streaming down my face.

He looks at me and chuckles. "That kiss was way too good for you to be crying."

"I'm just happy," I say, turning into a pile of mush around him.

"I have to admit, the other night when I wished that you would find big love, happiness, and children, I was hoping you'd find those things with me. Because if you got all your wishes, I'd get mine too."

His admission takes my breath away.

And I can't stop crying.

What is with all the crying?

"Would you like to meet my girls? Can you stay for dinner? Stay the night?" he asks.

Stay for the rest of my life is what I wish he'd say.

I give him another kiss because he's so damn sweet.

"I'd love to meet them. And I most definitely can stay."

DRIVING TO SONOMA

I APOLOGIZED TO Jennifer for being an ass in Vegas.

I try not to be a jerk, but on the rare occasion I am, I usually make it up to the girl with sex. But since I'm stranded on second base with Jennifer, that wasn't really an option.

I try not to think about the last time I felt stranded on second base, way back in high school when I was dating Ariela.

Jennifer makes me feel like I'm an awkward teen, who isn't completely sure what to do. But she makes me feel alive in ways I haven't felt in a long time.

And that makes it worth it.

I've fucked a lot of women, but none of them made me feel anything in my heart.

When Jennifer cried in Vegas, I felt it in my heart.

I hurt her.

And it didn't feel good.

I knew how I could make it up to her. Instead of flowers and an apology, I showed up at her house unannounced, handed her my keys, and told her she could drive my car. I said the Hamptons were a little far, but we could go up to Keatyn and Aiden's house in Sonoma County. Dallas had mentioned that I should join them earlier this week. And if we timed it right, we'd be there for one of Marvel's wonderful dinners.

Jennifer jumped into the air, threw her arms around my neck, and kissed me.

Making things feel right again.

"SHIT," SHE YELLS, hitting the brake as the radar detector goes off and we fly by a highway patrol car.

"How fast were you going?" I ask her.

"A hundred and thirty. Shit. Shit. Shit. Look behind us. Is he coming after us?"

"We're almost to their house. Speed up."

She turns and looks at me. "Are you freaking nuts?"

"It's not like he can catch you if you speed up."

"No, but he can call ahead to all his patrolman friends. Then I'm fucked."

"It's about two miles. He can't get any one here that fast. And he sure as shit can't catch you."

She beams at me as she drops the pedal. "If you're wrong, you're bailing me out of jail."

"Deal," I say.

"Shit! One fifty! This is nuts!"

221

"The road splits up ahead, get ready. You're gonna go to the right. Nice easy curve. Slow it down. You're doing awesome. Only about another half mile."

She slows down to ninety.

"Okay, see that street light up ahead? Turn left there."

She brakes hard and makes the corner.

"Okay, now I need you to go really slow. Dallas' kids are here and they may be running around playing Ghost in the Graveyard."

"Oh, I used to play that with my friends! Was Keatyn excited we are coming?"

"I didn't tell her. She loves surprises."

After we park in the driveway, Jennifer pulls me into a kiss.

A good kiss with lots of tongue.

"That was so much fun, Riley! And, for the record, I forgive you."

"I was going to bring you flowers, but I thought you'd like this better."

"You already know me so well. Will we have a place to stay?"

"Yeah, but we'll probably have to share a bedroom."

She gives me a wicked smile. "I'd like to share more than that tonight, Riley."

"Really? Hell, I should have let you drive my car sooner."

"You're bad, Riley Johnson," she says, playfully slapping my arm.

Knowing it's going down tonight, I flirt, "You have no idea just how bad I can be."

SATURDAY, OCTOBER 4TH
KEATYN & AIDEN'S HOME - ASHER VINEYARDS

Keatyn

THE FRONT DOOR bursts open and Riley and Jennifer bound into the dining room, causing all of us to stop our conversation.

"What's up?" Riley says. "We were in the neighborhood. Thought we'd stop by."

"Riley let me drive his car up here and, ohmigawd, I was freaking out," Jennifer says animatedly. "I cruised by this cop doing well over a hundred. Riley's radar detector blared and I hit the brakes. I figured he was turning around and coming after me. But Riley told me to go faster! That there was no freaking way he could catch us! And I did! And he didn't! And, yay! We're here!"

I stand up, being polite, wondering how in the hell this is going to work out. I purposely didn't invite Riley because Ariela would be here. "That sounds like quite the exciting trip," I say to Jennifer, giving her a quick hug. "We're so glad you joined us. Let me introduce you to everyone." I turn back toward the table. "Everyone, I'm sure you all recognize Jennifer Edwards. She and Knox are going to be working together in a Captive Films project."

Jennifer sees Knox and waves excitedly at him.

223

"Jennifer," I continue, pointing around the table. "This is my fiancé, Aiden Arrington. This is Logan and Maggie Pedersen, they're our friends from school and run the vineyard. These are my grandparents, Grandma and Grandpa Douglas."

"You're on the Captive Films board of directors, aren't you?" Jennifer asks Grandpa.

"Well, yes, I am," Grandpa says, standing up to shake her hand.

"I did some research on the company," Jennifer says with a grin.

"And this is Dawson Johnson, Riley's brother and Captive's newest executive. He'll be working closely with the lovely lady to his right, Vanessa Flanning, on the campaigns for *Daddy's Angel.* And you already know Dallas McMahon."

"I was probably your easiest actress," Jennifer says, then covers her mouth. "Whoops, sorry, that didn't sound right. I mean, I was a breeze to negotiate with."

"Yes, you were," Dallas replies. "It's good to see you again."

"And this is Ariela Ross. She's, um, planning our upcoming wedding." Jennifer's look falters when she hears Ariela's name, making me wonder if she knows about her.

Knowing that Jennifer doesn't have a filter, I quickly follow the introduction with, "And, of course, you know Knox."

"So, did we miss dinner or time it just right?" Riley asks without skipping a beat and completely ignoring the fact that Ariela is here.

"You are just in time," Marvel says, bringing two more chairs to the table. "I will set more places."

"Jennifer," I say. "Would you do me a big favor? All the kids are in the kitchen, and I know they'd love to meet you."

"Of course," she says, but when we get into the kitchen, she grabs my arm. "Holy shit, is that *the* Ariela? The girl who broke Riley's heart like a decade ago?"

"Uh, yeah," I say.

"Well, like that's not awkward with a capital A. I'm sorry we just showed up."

"It's fine, Jennifer. You're always welcome. I'm sure she and Riley will be cordial. Besides, he's here with you."

The kids chatter with her excitedly and when we go back in the dining room, Riley is standing and staring at the table. I'm trying to determine why when I realize that Marvel has set the two additional place settings on opposite sides of the table. And the placement is awkward. Riley has his choice of sitting by Ariela or seating Jennifer next to her.

Marvel is ready to serve us, and he is not a patient man. "Miss," he says to Jennifer, pulling out the chair next to Knox and beckoning her to sit. "Please have a seat, Mr. Johnson."

Riley doesn't move. He just stares at Ariela like she's a live grenade about to go off.

"Um," Riley says to Marvel.

Oh, if he says he doesn't want to sit next to Ariela, I am going to kill him. I give Aiden the eye, begging him to step in and do something.

But Knox quickly jumps into the fray. "Oh, Marvel, we mustn't separate the love birds. Ariela, dear, why don't you sit by me?"

Ariela gives Knox a grateful nod and switches chairs. I notice that Jennifer looks disappointed.

When everyone gets settled, Marvel serves our first course.

Riley's got one arm around Jennifer, trying to pull her closer.

He's messing with her hair, kissing her hand, and saying flirty stuff about later tonight.

I keep trying to get everyone to talk about something to drown it out, but I think we all feel like we're watching a train wreck about to happen.

Ariela looks sad, and I feel bad for her. It's obvious that Riley is purposefully trying to make Ariela jealous, because he keeps glancing up to see if she's watching.

THEY SAY IN acting that timing is everything.

And Knox is a damn good actor.

I knew when he called Jennifer and Riley *the lovebirds* that he was up to something.

He has waited until just the right time to start flirting with Ariela. He's spent the first two courses letting the tension build. Letting it appear like the more he gets to know her, the more interested he is.

And his subtlety is much more believable than Riley's obvious show.

Knox leans a little closer to Ariela and speaks softly, holding her eyes and hanging on every word she says.

If I didn't know that Knox is crushing on Jennifer, I'd think he was totally mesmerized by Ariela.

And the more mesmerized Knox seems, the more Riley stops talking to Jennifer.

Now, he's shoving food into his mouth like he's mad at it.

"What you do must be *so* interesting," Knox says to Ariela. "Planning weddings that bring a couple's love to life."

"I've never thought of it that way, but that is what we do. Showcase a couple's love by finding elements from their past to share in a fun way. At a wedding I did a few weeks ago, they had massive amounts of candles because when he proposed he had over 200 candles in the room. Instead of numbers on each table, they had the couple's favorite songs. When they kissed after the ceremony, everyone threw pink rose petals because those were the first flowers he gave her."

"So romantic," Knox says. "I, myself, have never been married, but I'm looking forward to the day I find that special someone. What you do must be *so* fulfilling."

"It is. I like doing weddings, but I plan a lot of different events. Personal, charity, and corporate."

He leans closer to her, casually draping his arm across the back of her chair.

"Really. Well, then, maybe you could help me. I'm thinking I'd like to hold a private event."

"How many people?" Ariela asks.

"*Very* private," Knox flirts. And he is good at flirting. Ariela even blushes when he winks at her.

"That sounds fun," she says.

Aiden nudges my knee under the table, getting my attention, and then darting his eyes toward Riley.

Riley is now staring straight at Knox. He's gripping his knife and fork so hard, I'm surprised they haven't broken in half.

I give Vanessa a pleading glance.

She elbows Knox and says, "Knox, give her a break. She's off the clock."

Knox ignores her, turning his full attention back to Ariela, leaning almost directly in front of her and looking very much like he's going to kiss her.

I close my eyes tightly, hoping he doesn't take it that far.

"Oh, it will be," he says, laying his hand on top of hers and gently stroking it. "Lots of candlelight. Music. And *very intimate.*"

Riley shoves himself back from the table, anger raging in his eyes.

"Leave her the fuck alone, Knox! She's fucking married!"

"Sit down, Riley," Jennifer says, running her hand down his arm. "It's really not any of your business."

"Shut the fuck up!" he yells at Jennifer, shaking off her hand. "This isn't any of *your* business."

"It *is* my business when you bring me here on a date only to ignore me, because it's driving you crazy that Knox is flirting with your married ex-girlfriend. So, you fuck off!" she yells, pushing back from the table and running out of the room in tears.

Riley shakes his head and curls his fists into tight balls.

He leans across the table, looking at Ariela in disgust. "This is your fault. You don't get three weeks. I want you out of here now!"

"Riley, stop it!" Aiden and I say. But it's too late.

Ariela bursts out the front door in tears.

Grandpa pushes his chair back from the table and stands up with a presence. He walks around the table and grabs Riley by the scruff of the neck.

"You will not talk to *any* woman in this house with such disrespect. Not to mention with such foul language. Apologize. Now."

Riley shuts his eyes tightly, takes a deep breath, but doesn't say a word.

"If that's the way you want it," Grandpa says, dragging him out the French doors to the courtyard.

"I knew there were gonna be some fireworks when he showed up, but I didn't expect all that!" Dallas says, laughing and trying to make light of the situation.

Knox gives us all a smirk and puts his napkin on the table. "Well, if you'll all excuse me, I think I'll go console Jennifer."

"He totally did that on purpose," Vanessa says, squinting her eyes in realization.

"It's easy to prey on a desperate man," Grandma states.

KEATYN & AIDEN'S HOME - ASHER VINEYARDS

Riley

I'm pissed.

No, I'm beyond pissed.

Why the hell is Knox flirting with Ariela?

And why the hell does she seem to be enjoying it.

They're talking softly.

Going on about weddings.

Like Knox gives two shits about weddings or any kind of wedding planning.

Then he puts his arm around the back of her chair.

I'm going to fucking kill him if he doesn't stop it.

I was trying to make Ariela jealous earlier by flirting with Jennifer and insinuating something was going to happen between us tonight.

But, then, Knox starts doing that thing he does.

The smile, the flirt, the dimples.

I've seen him put the moves on girls everywhere.

And the beauty is they don't even look like moves.

He asks them questions about their life and pretends to be interested in their answers. It makes him look caring and sensitive.

And I can see him doing it now.

How is Ariela falling for his bullshit?

Especially when he starts talking about having her plan an event for him. His last *event* involved four cases of tequila and a local college's dance team.

He found glitter in his house for weeks after.

Then.

He puts his hand on Ariela's.

I lose it.

I don't know what I say when I stand up. It's a blur of fury.

Until Grandpa grabs the back of my neck and drags me outside.

"What the hell was that?" Grandpa says. "You need to go back in there and apologize to everyone."

"Fine, I'll go back in there," I yell.

"You can't go off half-cocked."

"I don't even know what the fuck that means," I say, spitting out the words. As soon as the old codger lets go of me, I might just punch him.

But the man is strong. He pushes me down to my knees.

"Don't go off half-cocked means don't go off all pissed when you don't know the facts. But, in this case, it means you need to calm yourself down. I'm ashamed of you, son."

He finally releases me, by shoving my head forward toward the ground. I want to just lie down on the ground and cry.

Grandpa leans over me and says, "Get up."

I stare at him, almost daring him to touch me again.

"You're thinking about punching me, aren't you? That what you want to do? Take your anger at yourself out on an old man? I have a better idea. Go punch that tree. Go on now. Do it. I dare you."

I pound my fists into the ground madly then push myself to standing.

Punching something sounds like exactly what I need to do, starting with that bastard Knox.

I want to kill him. Fucking *intimate private affair*. Touching her hand.

I slam my fist into the tree hard, hear cracking noises, and my first thought is that I just broke the fucking tree. That's how pissed I am.

But my anger is instantly replaced with pain.

"Fuck!" I yell, grabbing my hand. I can't see it in the dark, but I can already feel it swelling. "I just broke my fucking hand," I mutter.

"Probably did," Grandpa says nonchalantly. "That's what happens when you go off half-cocked. You do something really stupid."

I plop down into a chair, cradling my hand and knowing he's right. Who in their right mind punches a massive tree?

"Now, for the most important question, Hollywood," Grandpa says, sitting down beside me. And although I know he's mad at me, the fact that he just called me Hollywood tells me he's not holding it against me.

He looks me in the eye. "Now, tell me, which hurts more? Your hand or your heart?"

Even though my hand is throbbing, it's no comparison to the way my heart feels.

"My heart," I say, feeling completely broken.

"Then go talk to your girl, Riley. Tell her how you feel. Stop holding it all inside and trying to pretend. And tread lightly so you don't muck it all up. You go with your hat in your hand—or in this case, your hand in your hand—and you apologize to that girl."

"Apologize for what? She's the one who—"

"Not for what happened in the past. For what happened at dinner. You owe a lot of people apologies for that, but I'd start with her."

I sigh.

My hand pounding.

My heart broken.

"This isn't you. I know you have a lot of chickens in the hen house, but you've always been respectful of them. You weren't respectful to that little cutie either. You need to fix it and get your shit together."

"Yes, sir," I say, getting up. I start to go toward the door, but then stop and turn around. "Thanks, Grandpa."

He gives me an acknowledging nod.

I cradle my hand against my body, go back in the house, cut through the dining room—purposely ignoring everyone there— and head out the front door to find Ariela. I close the door quietly, see that Vanessa's car is still here, and wonder where Ariela went.

I walk down the hill, instinctively, remembering the last time I hurt her feelings.

We'd been dating for a year. It was homecoming weekend and my brothers were back at Eastbrooke for it. Homecoming weekend is always one big party and it didn't help that my brothers were feeding me shots. I was a little drunk and some older chick was flirting with me. I flirted back—feeling like a big man on campus—touched her arm, used a little of the Johnson charm on her. I didn't intend for things to go any further than flirting.

Even drunk, I wouldn't have cheated on Ariela.

It was just harmless flirting. Or, so I thought. Until I realized Ariela was standing there, watching me, her eyes full of tears.

She shook her head at me and took off down the hill.

I stumbled behind her all the way to the lacrosse field, where I found her sitting on the bleachers crying.

I decided in that moment that I would never do anything to make her cry again.

And I never did.

Until she came back into my life. Now, all I want to do is hurt her.

Because having her here is killing me.

I find her sitting on a willow swing in the gazebo overlooking the winery. With my heart in my hand, I stand in front of her and say, "I'm sorry, Ariela."

"I'm sorry too, Riley."

I sit down next to her. "Just tell me how you could leave like that. I need to understand how you could do that."

"My dad told me that I was young. That I was letting love cloud my judgement. That you were just some rich kid going to California on a whim. That you'd change your mind a million times about what you wanted to do. And that you'd change your mind about me. That if I went, it'd be the worst mistake of my life."

"He was wrong," I tell her. "I did exactly what I said I'd do. Even more."

"I know you did, Riley. It may not mean much coming from me, but I'm incredibly proud of all you've accomplished."

"On graduation, your dad told me that I'd never amount to much."

Ariela's eyes get huge. "He said that?!"

"Yeah, but I didn't care because I knew I'd prove him wrong. And I've been proving him wrong every day since. Not that it matters, you didn't believe in me enough to trust that I would."

"Listening to him was the biggest mistake of my life."

"So, why are you really here? Because your life sucks and you thought I'd just wait for you? It's been over ten years."

"My husband has been cheating on me. When I mentioned it to my mother, she said a lot of men do and that I should just accept it like she has. I was upset because I thought my parents were the perfect married couple. I wanted to emulate them. Everything I thought I knew was wrong. I went to a coffee shop when I was upset and sitting on the table was you. On the cover of that magazine. I read the article, cancelled my appointments, and saw the movie. It was like the perfect storm. I had to come. I don't expect you to love me again, Riley. I just need your forgiveness. And I need to start living my life for me."

"I loved you. You walked away and never looked back."

"I couldn't have looked back, or I wouldn't have had the strength to do it. I filed for divorce yesterday. I know it might seem like I did all of this on a whim, but it's been a long time coming."

"Finally taking responsibility for your actions?"

"Yes. I've been blaming my parents for the decisions I made about my life. Keatyn and Maggie both reminded me of that."

"How?"

"They said I was an adult when I left, and I was an adult when I got married. That my parents may have influenced me, but I chose my path and I need to start owning up to it."

"They're smart women," I say, completely agreeing with them.

Ariela reaches out and grabs my hand.

"Owwww! Don't touch my hand!"

She leans back, holding her hands in the air. "Why?"

"I think it's broken."

"Broken? How? It was fine a few minutes ago."

"Grandpa told me to punch a tree."

"And you listened to him? That was stupid of you. You had to know it was going to hurt."

Looking into her eyes, I say slowly, defeated, "Sounds like what happened when you listened to your dad. You had to know it was going to hurt."

"It broke my heart," she says, tears filling her eyes again.

I touch her face with my good hand.

She grabs it tightly, leaning her cheek against it. When she closes her beautiful eyes, teardrops leak out and roll down her face.

And for the first time since she came back into my life, I feel like maybe things could be okay. I'm soaking up her love. The pain in my hand going away and leaving me feeling lost in time.

"I want to tell you something," she says, her hand still firmly pressed against mine. "I'm going to live in California regardless of what happens with us. Keatyn says once people know I did her wedding, I'll get other jobs. I don't know if that's true, but . . ."

"Don't," I tell her.

"Don't what?"

"Open a business yet."

"Why?"

"Because I'm not convinced you'll stay."

"I'm staying, Riley, no matter what. Can you at least learn to tolerate my presence?"

"Maybe we should do something about that."

"Like what?"

"Eastbrooke's Homecoming is next weekend."

"I've never been back there."

"Neither have I."

"I don't know if I can do it, Riley. It would be so hard to go back. There are so many memories there."

"I know there are, but I think we both need to. Maybe if we go back to where it ended, we can figure out where it's going."

"Where do you think it's going?" she asks, barely a whisper.

"I don't know, Ariela. I don't know if I can be your friend or not but, if nothing else, maybe this will give us both some closure. Maybe we'll finally be able to put the past behind us."

"I'll have to work my ass off this week getting stuff ready for the wedding in order to go."

"I have a dinner meeting Monday. Maybe we could go get dinner Tuesday night."

"Like a date?" she asks.

"More like a meeting."

She hangs her head. "Okay. A meeting on Tuesday night, it is."

"Good. Now, if you'll excuse me, I need to go get some ice for my hand and apologize to everyone else for my behavior."

"Riley, wait!" she says, grabbing my chin and turning it toward her.

Our lips softly touch in a kiss.

A kiss that isn't like the passionate one we shared at Keatyn's the night she showed up for dinner. This is more like our first kiss, tentative and unsure.

But her lips feel exactly the same—soft, sweet perfection.

KEATYN & AIDEN'S HOME - ASHER VINEYARDS

Keatyn

RILEY COMES BACK in the house without Ariela, which can't be good.

He stops to look at the dining room table, which is still littered with remnants of the dinner party he interrupted.

He peeks in the kitchen, finding me, Aiden, Knox, and Jennifer standing around the island, chatting.

"I wanted to say I'm sorry," he says. He looks horrible. I don't know what's happened since Grandpa took him out back and since he went looking for Ariela, but I haven't seen him look this bad in years.

Not since our graduation night.

It should have been a time for celebration but, instead, we spent it consoling Riley as he went through a gamut of emotions, from pissed to disbelief to utter sadness.

And, then, later, when we arrived in Los Angeles and remembered how we had all dreamed, talked about, and planned what we would do here. As time went on, I forgot about the hurt Ariela caused all of us when she walked out of his life.

But I realize now that Riley has never forgotten.

And it's my fault for bringing her back in our lives.

"I shouldn't have yelled at you, Jennifer," he says, "I've been an ass."

"I can agree with you on that," she says.

"Thanks," he replies.

Then he turns to me. I'm ready to rush over and hug him. To let him know that no matter what, we're always on his side. I'm ready to fire Ariela as my wedding planner. I'll figure out something else.

Seeing him this way isn't worth it.

How many times has he been there for me?

"Can I have some ice?" he asks me, holding out his hand, which is crusted with blood and grossly swollen.

"Oh, Riley, that looks—" I get hot, nauseous, and feel myself sway.

"I've got her," I hear Knox say, grabbing me as my knees give out.

Next thing I know, I'm on the couch with him and he's fanning my face.

"Shit," I mutter. "Did I faint?"

"Yeah, it's okay," he whispers. "I caught you."

Aiden sits down next to me, taking my hand. "Are you okay?"

"I'm fine. His hand just made me feel a little queazy. I guess it's a good thing I didn't choose a medical profession."

"Aiden," Knox says, "why don't you deal with Riley's hand, and I'll sit here with Keatyn. If I see it again, I just might faint too."

"Pussy," Aiden says to him with a smile, getting up and getting Riley a baggie of ice and a towel.

"What's going on out here?" Dawson asks, as he, Vanessa, and Dallas wander downstairs after getting the kids to sleep.

"Let's see. Riley came in, he's sorry about dinner," Jennifer says, giving them a play-by-play. "Keatyn fainted when she saw Riley's hand. Knox about passed out when Keatyn fainted. Riley's hand appears to be broken. Ariela is still outside. And, in case anyone wants to know, Knox and I made out while you were putting the kids to bed and Riley was chasing after Ariela."

I laugh at her, loving her crazy honesty.

Riley glares at Knox, but Knox just shrugs his shoulders, like he's so irresistible he can't help it.

Jennifer says, "Sorry, Riley, you're just a little too immature and emotional for me." Which is ironic coming from a twenty-two year old.

Dawson moves the ice off Riley's hand, smiles broadly, and punches his brother's shoulder. "That is *so* broken. We need to send a pic of it to Camden. It definitely beats his."

Riley smiles.

"What'd you do?" Jennifer asks.

"I punched a tree," he says.

"Well, that was really stupid," Jennifer dead pans. "Why did you do that?"

"Grandpa told me to."

I hear Aiden on the phone with our local concierge doctor. "Yeah, we'll see you shortly."

While they continue to discuss Riley's swollen hand, I lean toward Knox.

"You were flirting with Ariela at dinner to make Riley jealous so that you could get with Jennifer."

"Who, me? I can't believe you would think I could be so devious."

"I've known you for a long time, Knox."

"Okay, fine. I could tell he was trying to rub Ariela's nose in his new thing with Jennifer. When a guy is trying that hard to make another girl jealous, he's not that interested in the girl he's with. It was going to implode eventually. I just sort of helped the process."

KEATYN & AIDEN'S HOME – ASHER VINEYARDS

Vanessa

"I'M GOING TO check on Ariela," I tell Dawson and everyone else.

"She's down the hill on the swing," Riley says. "Grab a blanket. It's chilly."

I take two rolled up cashmere blankets from the basket in the family room, wrap one around myself, and go to the swing.

"Are you okay?" I ask her, sitting down next to her and handing her the other throw.

"Yeah, I'm just sitting out here wallowing in self-loathing," she says, wrapping the blanket around her shoulders. "Wondering how my life got so off track."

"I wonder that sometimes too," I admit. "And sometimes I wonder if Keatyn's right. If it's all part of a greater plan. If the universe teaches us lessons."

"I've learned a big lesson."

"What's that?"

"I need to start trusting my feelings."

"Follow your heart, it will always lead you home?" I say, quoting a line from the last *Keatyn Chronicles* movie.

"Exactly."

"Life isn't a fairy tale. I learned that the hard way with Bam. You think once you've found your Prince Charming, it will be fairytale moments, rose petals, and dancing. But no one tells you that the prince is an egotistical asshole who can't keep his dick in his pants. And that makes you wary of every other prince."

"I was the opposite. I had the prince and let him go." She studies me. "Have you been wary of Dawson?"

"When I came up here, I was so freaking pissed at him."

"Why?"

"He hadn't told me he had kids. I thought it was because he didn't want me to meet them. I was wrong to jump to that conclusion. So what's going to happen with you and Riley? How'd you leave things?"

"He wants us to go to Eastbrooke's Homecoming next weekend."

"Everyone else goes almost every year. They always look forward to it. Keatyn was really bummed her filming schedule wouldn't allow it this year. Why does he want you to go?"

"Neither one of us have been back there since graduation. He said maybe we need to go back in order to move forward."

"Back to where it all began?"

"And where it all ended," she says sadly.

"Do you think it will help?"

"I'm not sure. I think it's going to bring back a lot of good memories, which will be painful."

"Pleasure and pain, a weird combination," I say. "It's getting chilly out here, why don't we go inside?"

"Should I say something to Jennifer? Apologize?"

"Ariela, you didn't do anything. Actually, she'll probably thank you."

"Why?"

"When Riley ran off after you, she and Knox were making out. She likes him."

"Oh, Knox, that devil. That's why he was flirting with me, wasn't it? He knew he could push Riley's buttons."

"I think so," I agree.

"Riley was very noncommittal about if we'll even be able to be friends, but . . ."

I finish her thought. "But Knox must know Riley still has feelings for you."

"Unfortunately," she sighs, "most of those feelings are hate."

"There's a fine line between love and hate," I say with a laugh. "Come on, it's cold."

"There are headlights coming up the drive. More surprise visitors?"

"That would be the doctor," I tell her as we head back toward the house. "You missed all the fun. I'll give you the short version. Riley came in the house and apologized to Jennifer and asked for ice. Keatyn fainted when she saw Riley's bloody hand. Knox about passed out when Keatyn fainted. Aiden called the doctor. Dawson was impressed with Riley's hand and is sending their older brother photos of it."

Ariela laughs. "Never a dull moment. God, I've missed my friends."

KEATYN & AIDEN'S HOME - ASHER VINEYARDS

THE DOCTOR ARRIVES with his portable x-ray machine and verifies that Riley's hand is indeed broken. He wrapped it all up and gave him something for the pain.

After telling everyone goodnight, Aiden and I retire to our room and slide into bed.

Aiden pushes my hair back off my forehead. "It scares me when you faint."

"It scares me a little too."

"I read it's normal, though. So don't worry."

"We're lucky, Aiden."

He kisses the clover tattoo on his wrist, then kisses the matching one on mine. "We've always been lucky, Boots."

"Tonight was a flipping fiasco. I think I might have to fire Ariela. I can't do this to Riley."

"Just give them a little time. He still loves her. That was pretty obvious tonight."

"Yeah, you're probably right. I just worry about him."

"I think he'll be fine. Sometimes a guy has to be at his lowest point to realize what really matters."

"Did you have a low point with me?"

"Yes. Don't you remember me dragging you down to the soccer field?"

"I do. That's when you called me dumb."

"That's because you couldn't see how crazy I was about you."

"Then you attacked me on the desk in your room later with your tongue. I was yours ever since that kiss."

He flicks his tongue across my lips. "I can't wait to marry

you. And I want to go on record and say that your grandpa is a beast. I don't think I've ever seen him move so fast. Let alone take down a guy as big as Riley."

"My grandpa is tough." I laugh. I gaze into Aiden's beautiful green eyes that always speak to my soul. "I really appreciate you letting them build a house here."

"I knew it would make you happy," he says, gently caressing my arm. "And I may have had an ulterior motive."

"What's that?"

"I'm hoping it will make you want to spend more time here."

"That's what I meant by slowing down, Aiden. I want to raise our kids here. I have a beautiful office and can work from home."

"Except when you're filming."

"You know the movie I'm supposed to start right after *Trinity*?"

"Yes."

"I'm going to have it recast once we tell our friends that I'm pregnant. I'm lucky it's a Captive project, so I don't have to deal with getting out of a contract."

Aiden beams. "That makes me really happy."

"It makes me happy too. I'm also really excited about our wedding. Can you believe in a few weeks, I'll be Mrs. Arrington?"

He kisses me and runs his hand across my tummy. "And a mom."

"Having grown up with little sisters, I'm not as worried about being a good mom as I am about being a good wife."

He slides his hand down a little lower.

"Maybe we should work on that."

KEATYN & AIDEN'S HOME - ASHER VINEYARDS

Ariela

IT WAS A little awkward when Vanessa and I came back in the house but, fortunately, everyone went to bed soon after, leaving me alone with Riley.

"You should probably get to bed too," I tell him.

"Help me to my room?" he asks, slurring slightly. The pain medication the doctor gave him is starting to kick in, and he seems a little loopy.

"Of course," I reply, helping him off the couch and escorting him to his bedroom. I turn on the lamp and turn down his covers.

"You're going to have to help me undress," he says, giving me a lopsided grin and holding up his wrapped hand.

"Maybe I should ask your brother to come help you."

He moves closer to me. "Come on, Ariela. It's not like you haven't done it before."

"That's true." Okay, I can do this. I'll help him get un-dressed and tuck him in. It's the least I can do.

I grab the bottom of his cashmere V-neck, gently pulling it up over his head, then working it off his hand. "Do you want to sleep in the T-shirt you have on underneath?"

"Have I ever slept with a shirt on?" he says, laying his hand on my hip.

"No," I laugh, loving how on the medication he seems so much more like the Riley I used to know. But when I slip off his T-shirt, I see that his body is not the same. What were long, lean muscles are now fuller and more defined. His four pack of abs has been replaced with a hard eight.

"You're staring. Like what you see?" he slurs, but his eyes

have a hungry look. It's a look I remember well from our weekend parties at Eastbrooke. We'd get a little high, a little drunk, and then sneak off somewhere to have sex.

"It's obvious you still work out," I say, noncommittally, while fighting the urge to run my fingers across his new muscles. "Let's get these pants off and get you into bed. You're slurring a bit, so the medicine must be kicking in. Why don't you sit on the bed first, so I can take your shoes off."

He does as I ask, so I slip off his shoes and socks, bring him back to standing, and remove his slacks. All that's left on him is a pair of boxer briefs that leave nothing to the imagination. And I'm trying really hard not to look.

"Okay, hop in bed." I pull back the comforter, making it easy for him. And praying that he doesn't say—

"I always sleep naked. You know that."

Yes, I do know that. And that's all I can think about.

"I think tonight it would be best to leave these underwear things on," I stutter and motion to them with my hand. "If you would need something in the middle of the night, it would be hard for you to put them back on by yourself."

"Are you afraid of what might happen if you take them off?"

"Riley, just a few hours ago, you hated me. The pain medicine is messing with you. I think you should just go to sleep now."

"We had a lot of sex," he states, his eyes playful.

"Yes. Yes, we did." I gulp. Why did I agree to help him? "Please, Riley, just get in bed."

He uses his good hand to push the boxers off his hip. Fortunately for me—or unfortunately, depending on how you look at it, he can't get the other side to cooperate and leaves them on.

"I'm tired," he says, slipping under the sheet. "Will you lie down with me?"

"I, uh, I'm not sure that's such a good—"

"Just lie down with me until I go to sleep," he says, my heart feeling like it's being squeezed.

I need to get back to my dorm, Riley.

Don't leave until I go to sleep, kitty. I don't like it when you leave.

"Okay," I say, lying next to him. He puts his good hand on top of my thigh and closes his eyes.

"I love you, kitty," he mutters.

KEATYN & AIDEN'S HOME - ASHER VINEYARDS

Dawson

"WELL, THAT WAS the most exciting dinner party I've been to in a while," Vanessa says entering my bedroom.

"It's about to get more exciting." I push her up against the door. "First, I need you. Now."

My lips crash into hers. I can barely maintain control, like that kind of fury that makes you see red.

Only this is a fury for her.

I pin her arms against the door, push up her dress, and slide my fingers roughly across her pussy.

Our lips never leave one another's as I fuck her up against the door.

A FEW MINUTES later, we collapse onto the bed.

"You're amazing," I tell her.

"You're pretty amazing yourself. The way you picked me up. It was different."

"Different how?"

"I mean, not to compare you to my ex, but he wasn't a very big guy. Only about five-nine. My height."

I grin.

"Why are you grinning at me?"

"I'm six-three," is all I say.

"If you're wondering if you're bigger, here," she reaches down, grabbing my balls. "The answer is a resounding yes. I also like how when you pick me up you feel solid. Not like I might topple you over."

"You? You barely weigh anything."

"Oh, my. You do know how to sweet talk a girl," she says, kissing my neck.

She keeps kissing my neck, so I grab her hips and pull her on top of me.

She leans down, her long hair falling across her face, and kisses me. This time, more urgently.

My body quickly responds, going from relaxed to taut, and I slide her on top of my dick.

"Do you like being on top?" I ask.

"Yes, but I was thinking there are some other things we haven't tried yet."

"Hmm, you're right. I wouldn't want you to get bored," I tease, taking one of her nipples between my teeth. Then I flip her over and pin her underneath me.

"I will admit, I used to think this position meant boring. Not with you."

"I don't think it will ever be boring with you," I tell her, truthfully. But then I flip her over and pull her up on her knees.

"Oh, Dawson," she says, as I slide two fingers into her.

I push my chest tight into her back, almost spooning her.

As I rub my fingers roughly across her wetness, she moans again.

"Now, Dawson," she says, and she doesn't have to ask twice.

LATER, WE'RE THOROUGHLY exhausted and tangled in the sheets.

"I won a sex position of the day calendar at our Christmas white elephant exchange," she says. "I've never used it."

"Are you suggesting we do?"

She giggles. "It might be fun."

"At the rate we're going, we'll blow through that thing in a month."

"You think you can do 365 positions in thirty days? That's over ten a day."

I give her ass a little slap. "Are you suggesting I couldn't? Are you challenging me?"

"Maybe," she says, raising an eyebrow.

"I accept. But if you win, you have to come home with me for Thanksgiving."

"I don't know if I can. I wouldn't want my dad to be alone."

"We could bring him too."

"Thanksgiving is well over a month away."

"Are you thinking we won't still be . . ." I say, not wanting to finish the sentence.

"Do you think we will?"

"I wouldn't be asking if I didn't. The girls loved meeting you. Ava told me you were really pretty and asked if you were a movie star too."

"Really? They're both such nice girls. Although, I think you might have to lock Harlow in her room until she's twenty. She's a natural flirt."

"I know. She already has Dallas' boys wrapped around her little finger."

"Can I ask you a personal question, Dawson?"

"Sure."

"You said something that's stuck with me."

"What's that?"

"That I was the best kiss you'd ever had."

"What's wrong with that?" I smile, while running my hand down her side.

"Isn't that kind of disrespectful to your wife? To say I'm the best?"

"Hmm." I frown. "Yeah, I suppose it is. My wife should have been the best kiss of my life or why did I marry her, right?"

"Yeah."

"I feel like I've known you forever, Vanessa. I forget that you don't know the details of my life. Whitney and I had a long history. We dated in high school until around the end of our junior year when she broke up with me. It was hard on me. I thought I loved her. Once I was out of the relationship, I started to realize that I was immature and what we had wasn't what love should be. She was manipulative, controlling, and needy all at the same time. My freshman year in college, she came back into my life. We hung out and had sex twice using condoms that she gave me. A short time later, she told me she was pregnant."

"And you married her? It sounds like she got pregnant on purpose."

"I told you she was manipulative. I wasn't going to marry her. My family told me over and over not to marry her. And I didn't until after Ava was born. Anyone who doesn't believe in insta-love hasn't held their baby in their arms. Whitney told me if I wanted to be part of the baby's life, we'd be getting married. So, we did."

"But you could have sued for custody or gotten visitation rights."

"I could have, but I didn't. I wanted to be with her every day. And, surprisingly, we got along pretty well. I was deter-mined to make the best of it and we had Harlow a few years later."

"How did she die?"

"She committed suicide."

"Oh, Dawson. I'm so sorry," she says, tears glistening in her eyes. "I just found out today that my mom committed suicide."

I pull her close and run my hand across her silky hair.

"When did that happen?"

"When I was in kindergarten."

"Harlow was in kindergarten when Whitney died."

"I feel bad for the girls for losing their mother, but I can say that my dad and I are very close because of it."

"And he just now told you it was suicide?"

"It was ruled an accidental overdose when it happened. She suffered from depression and mixed her medicine with alcohol. When I was going through the old stuff at my dad's today, I found a box full of letters she wrote to me. Like for when I got married or got my period. My dad thought it was an accident until he found them a few weeks after she died."

"But you just saw them for the first time today?"

"Yes. My dad didn't give them to me. I can see why, now. It looks like she started writing them when she took the pills because some were neat and very coherent. Others were messy and didn't really make sense."

"Still, it must have been tough to take."

She nods. "Your daughters seem so happy. It's hard to believe they lost their mom."

"The first few months were really hard on them. And me."

She brushes her fingers through my hair and kisses me. "Probably hardest on you. Is that why you wished for forgiveness? Do you feel like it was your fault?"

"Let's talk about happier things," I say, changing the subject. The last thing I want to talk about when I'm in bed with a beautiful woman is the mess Whitney left me with. "Like these," I say, trailing my finger across her nipples.

MONDAY, OCTOBER 6TH
CAPTIVE FILMS - SANTA MONICA

Riley

I WALK IN my office mid-morning on Monday to find Dawson telling Dallas about how happy he is that his girls got along so well with Vanessa this weekend.

"How's the hand?" Dallas asks me.

I hold my cast up and shrug. "Dawson, you're supposed to fuck Vanessa, not fall in love with her and introduce her to the girls. You haven't even been here a week yet. And Vanessa is a freaking man eater. She chews guys up and spits them out."

"It won't be that way with me."

"You didn't listen to us when we told you not to marry Whitney. Listen to me now."

"Riley, I did listen. I knew life with Whitney wouldn't be what I dreamed of. I knew our relationship wasn't going to be the true love, happily ever after stuff in the movies you make. But I knew I wanted to be a part of Ava's life. Once I held her in my arms, I was willing to forgo my own happiness for her. And it was the right decision, Riley. I have two amazing daughters. And I'd go through everything I went through with Whitney again, because of them. What you aren't seeing is what Vanessa does to me. How she makes me feel."

"How does she make you feel?"

"Like I'm eighteen again and the world is full of options. But, this time, I'm smart enough not to let her go."

"What do you mean, *this time?*"

"Remember Keatyn's eighteenth birthday party?"

"Yeah."

"What do you remember about it?"

"Ariela's tight red dress. Drinking. Dancing all night."

"Do you know what *I* did at the party, Riley?"

"I remember what I did." Dallas interjects. "Met, danced, and made out with RiAnne all night. Now look at us, married with four kids and another on the way."

"We know the story, Dallas," I say. Then I turn back to my brother. "I'm assuming you danced and partied too?"

"Yes, but with *who?*"

"Everyone?"

"Wrong. Vanessa. We danced and kissed all night too. It was one of the best nights of my life, and I didn't even get laid."

"I did," Dallas coughs.

Dawson laughs.

"So, Dawson, why didn't you stay in contact with her if it was *so amazing?*"

"She was still in high school here, and I was looking forward to college in New York. But, that doesn't mean I ever forgot her. Just like you've never forgotten Ariela."

"Point for Dawson," Dallas quips.

It's not that you haven't moved on," Dawson continues, "or that you haven't had other relationships. It's just that she's always been in the back of your mind."

"Keatyn would say that's true love," Dallas says.

"Yes, she would," Keatyn says from behind us. She pats Dawson's shoulder. "I didn't mean to eavesdrop, but I'm so happy for you. I had no idea about you and Vanessa. I remember you kissed at my party but neither one of you ever said much about it."

"Seeing her again wasn't even something I thought about when I took this job, but it certainly has made me want to stay."

"You want to stay? Really?" Keatyn says, happily.

"I think so. The girls seem open to it. They're coming here on Friday and we'll tour the school. When I called about it, they said there was a wait list, but Dallas thinks he can pull strings to get them in."

"I'm on the school board *and* donate a lot of money, Dawson." Dallas says. "I will get them in."

"You know you have my full support on that," Keatyn says to Dallas, implying that Captive would make a donation to make it happen if need be.

I sigh. "I'm sorry, Dawson. If Vanessa is the right girl for you, don't let her go."

"Thanks, Riley."

"I second that motion," Keatyn says, enthusiastically.

"Me three," Dallas says.

VANESSA'S ESTATE, GUEST HOUSE - HOLMBY HILLS

I'M SITTING ON the couch typing wedding plans into a detailed timeline when my phone rings.

Riley says, "My dinner meeting just ended. Wanna hang out?"

"I just put my pajamas on," I say, looking down at the T-shirt and boxers I'm wearing.

"Leave them on. I don't mind. We'll just sit and talk a little."

"Um, okay," I say, already running into the bathroom and powdering my face. "How long will you be?"

"Twenty minutes."

"Perfect," I say and hang up.

I quickly do my makeup—purposely doing it soft and subtle, so it doesn't look like I just got ready. I shave my legs, spritz on perfume, and brush my teeth in near record time.

"What am I going to wear?" I ask myself, looking into the closet and pulling out something very sexy. "I can't wear this—" I'm saying when a memory hits me, stopping me in my tracks.

Should I?

Yes.

No.

Yes.

No.

Shit.

I glance at the clock.

Not much time.

I decide to go for it.

What's the worst thing that could happen?

I mean, besides rejection.

VANESSA'S ESTATE, GUEST HOUSE – HOLMBY HILLS

WHEN SHE ANSWERS the door, I gulp, taking in the little pink nightie she's wearing. "I thought you were in your pajamas?"

"These are my pajamas. I was going to change but you told me not to," she says, like it's no big deal that's she's wearing sexy ass lingerie.

"That's because I didn't . . ." My voice fades off. I'm fucking speechless.

"Come, sit," she says walking over to the couch, sitting down, and patting the seat next to her.

I sit down feeling helpless, like a man who's been hypnotized and is made to do stupid things in front of a crowd.

I remind myself of what I said in the car on the way over. *Do not kiss her again until she is divorced.*

The pale pink silk of her gown is slightly see-through, allowing me to see the outline of her breast, the edges of her nipples.

I feel blood rushing toward my dick, causing me to grow harder every second.

How long do divorces take?

I've got to stop it. I came over here to talk to her about Homecoming, not to just stare at her gorgeous eyes. Her long brown hair is pushed over one shoulder but the other is forward and blocking my view of her other breast. I reach out and slide her hair up and over her shoulder.

She doesn't say anything, just smiles at me.

But then she shifts, leaning back a little and sliding one leg under her, getting comfortable.

But when she does it, I see a flash of skin.

"You used to wear underwear to sleep in," I say, locking my jaw.

"Not when you came over, Riley."

I bite my lip, trying to hurt myself and wishing I had another tree to punch. That kind of pain is the only thing that could make the raging boner I have stand down.

"You wanted to talk about old times, Riley, so here's what I remember. I remember you liked when I did this." She splays her hand across her chest then pushes it under the triangle of silk covering her breast. She runs a finger in a circular motion and when she removes her hand I can see her hardened nipple raising the pale pink silk.

Her eyes are half closed when slides her hand into her cleavage, down her stomach, and under the silk between her legs.

"You used to like when I did this too, Riley. Do you still like it?"

She tilts her hips towards her fingers, and I can practically feel her warm pussy against my own fingers.

She filed, right? Isn't that close enough?

"Do you remember what you used to do?" she taunts.

I can't take much more. I grab her hand and suck her wet fingers into my mouth. "I wanted to taste you."

And it's exactly as I remember, sweet perfection.

A man of principle can only handle so much temptation.

I slide my fingers between her legs, finding the moistness between the folds of her lips. She's so fucking wet, and I'm about to explode.

She leans her head back and moves her hips in unison with my fingers.

"Can you feel how much I want you, Riley?"

"You never used to say that. You were too shy. You only did this because you knew how much it turned me on."

Her lips graze my neck on the way to my ear. "I said can you feel how much I want you, Riley??

"Yes, Ariela. Fuck, yes."

She shoves her hand down my pants.

I can handle this, I tell myself. I can.

Until her lips touch mine.

There's no turning back now.

I devour her lips, reveling in the taste of her tongue, the urgency of her hips moving against mine. There's only so much I can take. I move on top of her. She quickly parts her legs, making room for me, and pushes my pants off with her feet.

Moments later, I'm inside her and out of control. Pounding into her over and over, going deeper and deeper the harder I get, fucking her like there's no tomorrow. I'm going to do this all fucking night.

"Oh, Riley. My god," she says, panting in pleasure.

And that causes me to lose it. A few more thrusts and I'm moaning myself.

I GET RID of the condom in the bathroom and walk back out, figuring it's about time to wake up from this dream. But she's lying on the floor, naked, on top of a fluffy white rug.

And she's fucking beautiful.

I take a moment to study her.

"You look beautiful," I tell her, lying on my side next to her and brushing my hand across her chest. "You look the same. You feel the same." I glide my hand across her curves from the side of her breast, down the valley to her waist, up a slender hip, and across her thigh.

I never allowed myself to think about her during the days since she left, but she often invades my dreams at night when I'm defenseless.

She doesn't bother with a condom this time, just sees that I'm hard again, pushes me into the rug, then lowers herself on top of me.

I sit up, wrapping my arms around her in a hug, kissing her · shoulder.

It's like I've never had sex before. This becomes my new ultimate. The feel of her hands running across my back, the smell of her hair, the way her hips feel in my hands, the perfect little motions, and the way she seems to be controlling my body.

But then she starts moving faster, riding me harder and throwing her head back, moaning.

That simple vision of seeing her in the heat of passion makes me lose myself. I grab her hips, forcing her up and down on top of me until I explode inside her.

I lay my head on her shoulder in exhaustion. Her mouth is at my neck, layering on sweet kisses. I kiss her shoulder and hold her tightly, still afraid I'm going to wake up to find this isn't real. This, this is why no one has ever compared. Ariela is the only girl I can truly say I've ever made love to.

"You look the same, but you're different," I observe. "More confident in yourself during sex."

"Who me?" she says surprised. "No, I don't really like sex much anymore," she blurts out, then realizing what she admitted, immediately lowers her head in embarrassment.

"You didn't like that?" I ask, shocked.

"No, god, no, Riley. That. Us. You. Was amazing. I just meant, before this."

"Nothing has ever compared to us," I state, knowing exactly what she means.

"That's what I meant."

"Hang on," I tell her. "I'm going to roll you over, but I want to stay inside you."

She looks like she's going to cry, but more out of happiness. I touch her face. "I still love you, in case you couldn't tell."

Holding her ass to keep her close to me, I roll over, so we're lying face to face.

"I still love you too, Riley. I never stopped."

I push her chin up and kiss her softly.

Just softly.

Then I back away slightly. "Do you remember how you wished me luck before the homecoming game? I found you naked in my bed."

"I wasn't completely naked," she says with a grin. "I had my pompoms." She grabs our underwear off the floor and holds them in front of her chest like she did the pompoms. "Go, Cougars!" she says, throwing her arms into the air and revealing her perfect breasts.

I bend down and circle one with my tongue, taking it in my mouth and sucking on it, while growing hard again.

"Riley, you're—"

"Getting hard inside you? That's what happens when you wear nothing but pompoms."

TUESDAY, OCTOBER 7TH
CAPTIVE FILMS - SANTA MONICA

Riley

"WHERE HAVE YOU been?" Dallas says as I enter my office and go straight to my closet. "We were supposed to have a meeting twenty minutes ago. And you know I fucking hate early morning meetings."

I grab a suit, shirt, and tie and take it into my bathroom to change.

"Wait. Are you wearing the same suit you had on yesterday?" he asks.

"Yeah, that's why I'm changing," I say from the bathroom.

"Must have been a hell of a business dinner last night. Who did you meet with?"

I walk out into my office buttoning my shirt. "Dave from Capital."

"Oh," he says, looking confused. "Then you went out?"

"I went to see Ariela. And I know I'm gonna sound like a girl when I say this but we are like magic together. She's so beautiful and I'm so ruined."

"Oh, boy," Dallas says, slowly sitting in the chair across from my desk.

"Oh boy is right. I'm so fucked if we don't end up together because, now that I've had her again, I don't want anyone else. I don't think I'll be able to fuck anyone else ever again.

"True love's fuck," Dallas says, while I'm looking in the mirror tying my tie.

"What's that?"

"You know how I was when I was single. My pecker always believed there was a greener pasture just beyond the fence. But it was different with RiAnne. I liked her a lot from the start. We had incredible chemistry and she was sweet and fun and all that other stuff, but when we fucked for the first time, I knew. She was the one. It was different than anything I'd experienced. Hot as fuck, but it had this power, these emotions layered on top of it. It was making love in the best sense of the word."

I hear a sob from behind us and turn around to see Keatyn standing behind Dallas, tears streaming down her face. "That's the most beautiful thing I've ever heard. Riley, you have to write that down and use it in a movie. Everyone in the audience will be crying."

"Uh, okay," I say, appeasing her. She's been awfully freaking moody lately. I wish she'd just get over her damn period already.

"Keatyn, get your ass over here," Dallas says, motioning for her to stand in front of him.

She leans up against my desk, sniffling.

Dallas studies Keatyn like she's going to be his next greener pasture. In fact, I'm a little shocked at how lewdly he is studying her chest and looking her up and down.

"The tabloids are saying you had a boob job. You're eating like a horse and not gaining any weight. You've had the flu, fainted, haven't been drinking. The smell of Riley's coffee makes you sick. And, now, a very male conversation about fucking has you in tears."

"Not just any fucking. True love's fuck. I'm so happy for you, Riley," she says, smiling at me.

"I just noticed your boobs too," I say. "They look huge. *Did you have surgery and not tell us?*"

"No, I've been in the middle of filming, I couldn't have—"

Dallas shakes his head. "She didn't have a boob job, Riley. Our little Keatyn's knocked up."

Keatyn's eyes widen.

"Knocked up?" I say. "Is that what the quickie wedding is all about?"

"Yes and no," she admits.

"What!? Jeez, you can't be pregnant now! We've got so much going on."

"Aiden didn't know I was pregnant when he proposed."

"Is that what he meant when he said she always surprises me?"

"Probably. I told him I was pregnant after I said yes."

Dallas gives her a hug. "I bet Aiden is happier than a coon dog on a bare leg. Your first little hoodlum. Congrats. How far along are you?"

"Just starting my eighth week, so not too far. We haven't told our families yet. We're supposed to have dinner with them this week."

"When are you due? How's that going to work with us starting *Daddy's Angel?*"

"Riley, I work remotely most of the time. That's why I need you and Dallas. And part of why I'm so glad Dawson is here. I'm hoping to give him more and more responsibility."

"And she'll be taking off all the time she needs, right, Riley?" Dallas asks me.

I'm happy for her, but it's such a shock and I'm trying to work out the timing of it all. "Uh, of course," I finally say.

"And the wedding is quick because I want to be Keatyn Arrington before the baby is born."

"And probably because you don't want to be fat when you get married," I quip.

She looks at me, her eyes getting big, her bottom lip puffing out, and tears filling her eyes again.

"Riley, don't you fucking know anything?" Dallas chastises. "Pregnant does not equal fat."

I walk over to her and wrap her in a hug. "For god's sake, how am I going to deal with you pregnant? It's worse than your pout. And Aiden would have my hide if he knew I made you cry."

"You can say that again," Dallas drawls.

She hugs me back.

"I'm happy for you, Riley," she says.

"I'm happy for you too, Keatyn."

VANESSA'S ESTATE, GUEST HOUSE – HOLMBY HILLS

Ariela

I'M CRAZY EXCITED to go out with Riley tonight. Last night— and this morning—was so amazing. I've been on cloud nine all day. I confided in Vanessa about what happened with Riley. She immediately got on the phone and started making me spa appointments. I spent most of the day being pampered.

I slide into the sexy black slip dress that Vanessa suggested I wear tonight. She said once he sees me, we probably won't make it to dinner. And I'm so excited. I can't remember the last time I truly felt desired.

Collin is a nice man, don't get me wrong. He's charming, good looking, and driven. Sex with him, even when we were dating or first married, was never like it was last night. I know he got served with divorce papers yesterday, and I'm a bit shocked I haven't heard a word from him. I'm praying that he'll want to get the marriage over as quickly as I do. Annie said if he contests it, it could drag on for months. I know I have the photos that the private investigator took, but I really hope it doesn't come to that.

There's a knock at my door, causing my heart to leap in my chest and my stomach to fill with butterflies. I run to the door with my shoes in my hand and throw it open.

"Collin!" I say, when I see him at the door instead of Riley. "Why are you here?"

"I wanted to give you these, in person," he says, handing me the divorce papers.

"Why?"

"Because I don't want a divorce, Ariela. Come back home with me. Please."

"Why would you want that? You aren't in love with me. You should want a divorce so you'll be free to sleep with whomever you want."

"I only want you."

"Bullshit. You've been screwing your secretary the whole time I've been gone. You didn't stop like you promised. I don't trust you and I don't want to be married to you."

"I'll fight it."

"If you do, I'll ruin your career. You can blame it all on me, if you want, to the people you work with. But if you contest it, you'll regret it."

He looks around. "Do you want a house like this? Is that what this is all about? You got out here and decided we weren't fancy enough?"

"What? No. We have a beautiful home. That has nothing to do with it."

He looks around some more. "What does a place like this go for?"

"Way more than we could afford."

"We could put in a pool. You always wanted a pool. Please come back. I have a big appointment with a customer and he'll only work with stable married men."

"Then you better get him signed while you're still married."

"Will you come back with me? Go to the dinner?"

"No. Just tell him I'm out of town on business. I know that's the only reason you're here. You don't care about me. It's all about your business. My dad will still make you partner. Enjoy it."

"I'll be getting a big raise and profit sharing, Ariela. I want to share my success with you."

"No. I don't want your money."

"Then what is it?"

"I don't love you, Collin. I'm sorry. I shouldn't have married you. And the fact that you're sleeping with people outside our marriage tells me that you aren't happy either. We don't have kids. We can amicably split the property."

"I'll buy you a bigger house, jewelry, whatever you want." He reaches out and touches my face. "Anything you want. Please don't do this. I flew all this way. I want to save our marriage."

CAPTIVE FILMS – SANTA MONICA

I SHOWER AT work and put on an all-black suit. Keatyn says I look vicious in all black, and I'm not only feeling vicious, but also hungry and ravenous. I never imagined when I went to talk to Ariela last night that she'd be wearing lingerie.

Or that we'd make love all night long and all morning.

I can't wait to get there, but I decide last minute to switch cars, driving to my garage space and hopping in the Viper I got on my eighteenth birthday. It's neon green with black stripes and totally badass, not to mention fast. I don't drive this car much, just enough to keep it in working order, mostly because it brings back too many memories. Memories of Ariela. Trips we took. Sliding the front seat back as far as it would go so she could sit on my lap when we went parking. Kissing for hours. Loading picnics in the trunk. It seems like the perfect car to drive tonight.

On the way, I pick up the big bouquet of pink peonies I ordered, her favorite flower. The ladies in the shop all swoon over my choice and tell me she'll love them.

I tell them I just want her to love me.

I'm on top of the freaking world.

I see another car in the long driveway, but don't think anything of it. I grab the flowers off the passenger seat and practically skip down the path to the guest house.

But when I turn the corner, I see Ariela and a man.

He's wearing a blue blazer and sliding his hands across her shoulders. Her shoes are dangling from her hand like she didn't have time to put them back on.

I hear her say something about marriage and know instinctively that man is her husband.

And I know she just slept with him.

Especially when he delicately touches her face then kisses her passionately.

My heart stops beating.
I turn around.
Drop the flowers.
Walk to my car.
Get in.

"Fuck!" I yell, hitting my non-casted fist on my steering wheel and suddenly hating this fucking car.

I look over and see a few pink petals still lying in the passenger seat.

What the hell was I thinking? This is not me. I don't need fucking flowers or fancy dinners to get laid. I just flash a label, a black card, a hundred dollar bill. Girls wait in line.

I peel out of the driveway and grab my phone.

"Dawson!" I say, when he answers. "I need you to get to the airport immediately. Captive business. You'll be gone over night. Meet me in twenty minutes."

"Twenty minutes? But I thought—"

"Don't say it," I say, using my harshest tone. "Just get there. Now."

"Shit," he says. "Okay, I'm on my way."

Next, I call Knox. "Dude, we're going to Vegas tonight. Meet me at my plane in twenty."

"Can I bring Jennifer?"

"This isn't boy scout dance night. This is go to Vegas, get buck wild, get a tattoo, close the strip club down because we paid all the girls to come back to our room—the penthouse with the pool, bowling alley, stripper pole. You remember the one—trash a hotel room, and steal a Bengal tiger kind of night."

"Hell," he says, "I barely remember half of what we did that night. Sure, why the fuck not. Hey, wait, I thought you were going on a date with—"

"Don't fucking say it and don't ask," I warn. "Are you really bringing Jennifer?"

"I'm not sure. I need to find out how she feels about strippers."

"Dude, she's anti-stripper. Every girl who isn't a stripper is anti-stripper."

"Should I call my guy? Have him hook us up?"

"Absolutely. And, hell, the good news is if we bring Jennifer, we can write the whole fucking thing off. A *Daddy's Angel* contract celebration."

"You gonna invite Keatyn?"

"No, and don't you fucking tell her. But invite Buckner and Phillips. We'll get the old crew together."

"Buckner is married and Phillips came out of the closet."

"No shit? I watched him do lines of coke off a stripper's ass. It was the best thing ever. Whatever. We'll make our own party."

"Hell yeah, we will. Are you sure you're not mad at me about Jennifer?"

"Nope. I don't need that shit. We hung out. I let her drive my fucking car. And still no action. If you wanna pretend you're in high school again, so be it. But I don't need to work that hard to get laid."

"Oh, uh, yeah, she mentioned that you two hadn't done it."

"When did she mention that—wait a minute. Did you screw her already?"

"Uh, maybe."

"Knox fucking Daniels, that's why I love you, you pussy getting dog you."

"Well, what can I say, she liked it Knox style. What happened with Ariela?"

"You are not allowed to say her name again, ever again. But when I went to pick her up, she was kissing her husband."

"That bitch!"

"Tell me about it."

"You do need to fucking party. Vegas, here we come!"

About the Author

Jillian is a *USA TODAY* bestselling author who writes fun romances with characters her readers fall in love with, from the boy next door in the *That Boy* trilogy to the daughter of a famous actress in *The Keatyn Chronicles* to a kick-ass young assassin in the *Spy Girl* series.

She lives in a small Florida beach town, is married to her college sweetheart, has two grown children, and two Labrador Retrievers named Cali and Camber. When she's not working, she likes to travel, paint, shop for shoes, watch football, and go to the beach.

Check out Jillian's website at www.jilliandodd.net for added content and to sign up for her newsletter.

CPSIA information can be obtained
at www.ICGtesting.com
Printed in the USA
LVOW13s1521201017
553173LV00012B/868/P